STARR SIGN

STARR SIGN

THE CANDACE STARR SERIES

C.S. O'CINNEIDE

DUNDURN
TORONTO

Publisher and acquiring editor: Scott Fraser | Editor: Dominic Farrell
Cover designer: Laura Boyle
Cover illustration: Sanya Anwar
Printer: Marquis Book Printing Inc.

Library and Archives Canada Cataloguing in Publication

Title: Starr sign / C.S. O'Cinneide.
Names: O'Cinneide, C. S., 1965- author.
Description: Series statement: The Candace Starr series
Identifiers: Canadiana (print) 20200363352 | Canadiana (ebook) 20200363379 | ISBN 9781459744875 (softcover) | ISBN 9781459744882 (PDF) | ISBN 9781459744899 (EPUB)
Subjects: LCGFT: Novels.
Classification: LCC PS8629.C56 S73 2021 | DDC C813/.6—dc23

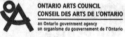

We acknowledge the support of the Canada Council for the Arts and the Ontario Arts Council for our publishing program. We also acknowledge the financial support of the Government of Ontario, through the Ontario Book Publishing Tax Credit and Ontario Creates, and the Government of Canada.

Printed and bound in Canada.

VISIT US AT

 dundurn.com | @dundurnpress | dundurnpress |  dundurnpress

Dundurn Press
1382 Queen Street East
Toronto, Ontario, Canada
M4L 1C9

For my son, because he's one of the good guys

CHAPTER I

IT IS NEVER A GOOD PLAN TO WAKE UP AND not know where you are. I know I'm not at home when I first hear the birds chirping outside the window. In the one-room apartment above the E-Zee Market where I've lived the last few years, there are only shit-disturbing pigeons to annoy you in the morning. They don't chirp, just coo and warble until you become convinced there's a Jersey girl on the roof faking her first orgasm.

But when you're a woman who has made a career out of binge drinking, waking up in places you don't expect is an occupational hazard. I open up one heavy-lidded eye and see that I am in a bedroom filled with well-placed Ikea furniture. There's a door open to an ensuite bathroom sporting sunny buttercup drapes across its frosted window. The cool of clean sheets caresses my skin, another hint that I am not on the mattress of my apartment floor where I pass out most nights after polishing off a magnum's worth of fortified box wine.

When I turn my head, I see long waves of inky-black hair flowing out onto the pillow next to me. I don't remember there being many women at the Murder Ink meeting last night, but it appears I've gone home with one. There was one broad with a tight blue-tinged perm who'd asked if I ever said a prayer over the bodies of the people I assassinated — to hasten their journey into the afterlife. I think it is safe to assume the hair on the pillow is not hers.

Murder Ink is a collection of weirdos and wannabes who spend every waking hour in online chat rooms discussing real crimes they'd never have the guts to commit. The whole business turns my stomach. But they'd invited me as a celebrity guest for a five-hundred-buck fee, along with the promise of all the premium single malt Scotch from the hotel bar I could drink. I've killed people for less. I wonder if the woman lying sleeping beside me realizes that.

I turn away from the hair on the pillow and start searching for my silver-plated hip flask amid the rumpled sheets. Instead, I find a three-by-five laminated piece of cardboard stuck to the outside of one of my naked thighs. It has a picture of me on it, taken when I was on trial for a conspiracy to commit murder charge a few years back. In it, my wild curly brown hair hangs down over my orange jumpsuit, partially obscuring the pissed-off smirk on my face. On the back, all of my stats are printed: six-foot-three, thirty-four years old, Italian/Polish extraction, number of hits, years served. The Murder Ink folks had these pictures printed, along with a few others, depicting thugs who weren't as hard up as me to accept their invitation. The little ghouls had been trading them like bubble gum baseball cards last night. Dropping my photo image to the carpeted floor, I search the bed again and find the reassuring cool metal of my silver-plated flask snuggled up at the bottom of the bed, next to a loaded gun. I grab both items with my toes and kick them up into my hands. Placing the Ruger American pistol on my taut belly, just below the silver five-pointed star tattoo, I take a swig from the flask while still horizontal, trying not to choke on the warm bourbon. My first drink of the day.

Don't get the wrong impression. I'm not an alcoholic in the traditional sense. Alcoholism is when your drinking gets in the way of your job or personal life. I don't have a job, and my personal life suits me just fine. Mostly because I am my own best company. My greatest source of entertainment. You learn to rely only on yourself when you spend the first half of your life growing up with a hitman for a father, and the other half following in his footsteps. I've been out of the game a few years now, ever since I got out of prison and my dad got whacked, but I make no excuses for the life I led before that. It paid the rent. It fed my dog when I had one. It kept me in copious bottles of Jägermeister in my twenties. But you make a number of enemies and rack up some pretty bad karma as a professional assassin. My daily drinking is just a means to an end. I'm not sure what that end is, but I intend not to be sober when I meet it. At least I don't smoke. That's a habit that'll kill you just from the sheer stupidity of it.

Both eyes open now, I am contemplating the blandness of mass-produced Scandinavian carpentry, wondering where the hell I am, when my phone lights up like a Christmas tree on the BJÖRKSNÄS nightstand. The vibration almost sends it over the edge, but I catch it in one hand before it hits the floor. My reflexes are still good. I keep myself in shape despite the booze. I answer the phone, mumbling something that resembles "hello," or possibly "fuck off."

"Candace?" my Aunt Charlotte says. "Is that you?"

I'm not sure who else she expects it to be. Charlotte gave me this phone, pays the monthly bill, and is the only one who knows my phone number. She wanted to be able to get a hold of me. She worries. She is not my aunt but has asked of recent for me to call her that, perhaps in a bid to explain our connection. Charlotte was in a long-term relationship with my Uncle Rod, who is serving time upstate for crimes I'd rather not get into. Uncle Rod is also not truly related to me. My family situation is kind of complicated, I guess. Charlotte likes to think of herself as a mother figure. My own mother having left me at the side of the road with five dollars and a map to McDonald's when I was three. Or was it at four at the mall with a Walmart greeter? I'm not sure. The story changes, depending on who you ask.

I crawl out of the bed and onto the floor, making my way to the ensuite bathroom on my hands and knees with the phone tucked into one bra cup and my gun into the other. Apparently, I'd passed out last night without most of my clothes but kept my lace push up and panties in place. I close the bathroom door softly, so as not to wake the hair on the pillow. I hate the morning after, particularly with women, who so often want to talk. I'm not a talking kind of girl. I prefer men in the aftermath of a good lay, if only for the simplicity of their lack of communication skills.

"It's me," I say quietly into the phone as I perch on the toilet. I look down between my legs and see preternaturally blue water in the bowl. The colour makes me uneasy. This place is way too domestic for me.

"I've been trying to get through to you since last night," she says. "You weren't answering your phone."

"I was on the job," I say. This used to be a family euphemism, code for stalking a guy who starts off his day without a care in the world and ends it with a carefully broken neck.

"I thought you were done with all that," Charlotte says after a pause.

"I am," I tell her. "Don't worry." But I know she does, so I elaborate. I tell her about the gig with Murder Ink. How they paid me to appear in a beige boardroom at a Delta on the outskirts of the city. A real live hitwoman to gawk at over finger food.

"You really need to get your profile taken off the dark web," she says. "Half the things they say about you on there aren't even true." She's right about that. Some asshole had posted an entry on the dark web's version of Wikipedia, outlining my supposed life story. That's where the Murder Ink people had found me.

"Since when have you been on the dark web, Charlotte?" I cannot picture my five-foot-nothing, middle-age-spread pseudo-aunt trawling through pictures of beheadings and amputee porn.

"There are a lot of things you don't know about me," Charlotte says. And I guess that's true. She moved away to Newfoundland in northeast Canada last year after a whirlwind romance with a salmon fishery owner she'd met there. This was after she dumped my Uncle Rod here in the States, and shortly before he went to prison for life. Those events being somewhat connected.

"Did you get my package?" she asks, changing the subject.

"What package?"

"My Christmas package. I sent it a week ago so you'd get it in time for the holidays." It is early December, but Charlotte is a keener. So is most of the world when it comes to the celebration of all things baby Jesus. Although, as they say, there doesn't seem to be much Christ in Christmas these days. The man with the bag has more commercial value than the baby in the manger ever did. Anyway, I'm not much for holidays. I once went searching for Easter eggs in the basement as a kid, only to find a guy tied to a chair next to the washing machine.

"I'll watch for it," I say.

There is stirring from outside the bathroom, a loud sigh bordering on a groan, a shuffling of sheets. I press my ear against the door to listen. A fluffy blue-and-white striped towel, smelling faintly of Irish Spring, rubs against my cheek. When I open the door a crack, I see a figure standing at the side of the bed with arms stretched up to the ceiling in a yawn. The amount of fur in the armpits and considerable junk swinging between the legs as he changes out of his boxer shorts tells me I'd been wrong about my bedmate's sex. A man, not a woman. I won't have to talk much after all.

"Listen, Charlotte, I've got to go," I tell her, shutting the door against possible conversation with the hairy stretcher.

"But Candace, there's a reason I was calling," Charlotte says. "It's that detective. She's been looking for you. The Asian girl."

Detective Chien-Shiung Malone. Cantonese mother. Irish father. But people always seem to focus on the visible part of minority.

"What did she want?" I ask. I've been keeping my distance from Malone lately, mostly because I've fallen off the wagon since I helped her out with a murder case last year. I anticipate rather than sense Malone's disappointment in me. Before you get the wrong impression, I don't make it a habit of making grass with the cops. Malone had offered up the identify of my old man's killer in exchange for my half-hearted assistance with her case. At first, I did it for that reason only, but somewhere along the way she became a friend. I never really had one of those, and with what I feel is good reason. Friendship, much like family, seems to come with too many attachments — like a vacuum cleaner too complicated to use. I never was good at keeping things clean.

"I'm not sure what she wants, Candace. But she said it's important. She says you need to call her. I hope you're not in any trouble, dear. I'd hate to think —"

There's a knock on the bathroom door. I drop the phone on the edge of the sink, pull the Ruger out of my bra, and train it on the heart of the blue-and-white striped hanging towel. You can never be too careful.

"Hey, I'm going to make breakfast," the man behind the towel says. He's got an accent. British, but not posh. I know the difference. I've been hooked on limey TV shows ever since I shared a cell one summer with a chick who'd embezzled from PBS. This guy sounds more *EastEnders* than *The Crown*. "You like bacon?" he asks, through the bathroom door.

I consider the offer for a moment, along with the sizable offering I saw swinging between his legs only a few moments ago. I click the safety back on and lower the gun, then pick up the phone.

"I'll call you later, Charlotte," I say.

I do, in fact, like bacon. I like bacon a whole damn lot.

With a bamboo spatula, Hardeep pokes the bacon spattering in a large cast iron frying pan. He says his friends call him Hardy, so I have decided to call him Deep to differentiate myself. He's a Sikh, thus the long hair, which most practising types would keep under a turban. But as a second-generation agnostic, Deep keeps his in a ponytail, forgoing the popular man bun, which I appreciate. I didn't think you could be both a Sikh and an agnostic, but Deep explains that it's like being Jewish — an ethnicity as well as a religion. The Sikhs are descended from a warrior race, he tells me. I already knew that, on account of watching *Wrath of Khan* with my dad once on late night TV.

These are the details he chattily provides, and I observe as he makes breakfast behind the butcher block island that separates the kitchen from the open concept living room. He's got on a pair of form-fitting bike pants that don't leave much to my vivid imagination. The dark hair on his bare chest curls like my long hair does in the rain.

"Don't you know that's dangerous?" I say from where I sit on the couch, fully dressed. I'd found my jeans and T-shirt folded neatly on a BINGSTA armchair.

"What's dangerous?"

"Frying bacon without a shirt on," I tell him. "It's like the first rule of half-nakedness."

He looks down at himself as a popping spatter of grease jumps up and hits him in the right nipple.

"Shit," he says, dropping the spatula on the counter. He rubs his palm against his chest, then smiles at me. "I reckon you're right. I'll just go get dressed."

I watch Deep's well-defined ass walk away toward the bedroom. I remember him now from last night, an unassuming tech guy in no-iron chinos, keeping himself separate from the rest of the rumpled attendees. Hired help for the Murder Ink meeting, like myself. He'd spent most of the night behind a small desk in the corner, running the AV presentation, a PowerPoint slide mash-up of the Scarpello Mob family history, my mother's people. I'd only found out she'd been a Mob brat last year. But then again, I never knew much about Angela.

The Scarpellos have a new Don, which I'd already heard. Detroit's only one state over and around the bend of Lake Erie after all. Deep had projected a black-and-white photo of the Scarpellos' new bossman attending the funeral of my mother's grandfather, the outgoing leader of the family interests. Alex Scarpello was skinnier and younger than I'd expected, but still a stud — with unruly hair like mine and dark features. We are cousins after all — once removed, or twice, I can never get that shit straight. In the picture, a well-kept, raven-haired woman stood beside him — his mother rather than a squeeze. The new Don is unattached, like me, preferring to sow wild oats instead of committed ones. "Fun fact," the morbidly obese Murder Ink president told the room after he took a hit from his inhaler, "every one of the young Don's conquests have ended up either missing or dead." This either covers up a huge disappointment between the sheets or is an extreme form of birth control in my opinion. The members of Murder Ink had grilled me for details on the Scarpello clan for the better part of the weekend but were sadly disappointed. I've never met my mother's side of the family. I'd barely met my mother.

Deep returns from the bedroom wearing the chinos that he wore last night and a pastel-pink golf shirt. I should have kept my mouth shut. I can't believe I don't remember making it with this guy last night. I don't usually have blackouts, not for the important stuff. I can hold almost any amount of liquor without getting sloppy, on account of my strong constitution and years of training.

Deep picks up the spatula and flips the bacon, a dish-towel printed with red-and-green holly draped over one well-muscled shoulder. Nobody escapes Christmas, I suppose, not even an agnostic Sikh.

When Deep sets down two plates on the round wood table by the bay window, I pull up a chair and join him there. Ask the question I've been wondering about since I first saw the contents of his living room.

"Are you a hacker?"

While the rest of the house is all clean lines and clean living, the living room is littered with disemboweled motherboards and half-cannibalized hard drives. Two long fold-out tables run end to end on the far wall, each covered with laptops, all of them connected in some way to the high definition monitor sitting at its centre. Cables and wires sprout from the back of the screen in a chaotic but carefully mastered tangle. The combined set-up looks like it has the CPU power of NASA. Nobody needs that degree of hardware, unless they're trying to get past firewalls meant to incinerate the average internet surfer on contact.

"I work for good, not evil," Deep says, popping a piece of bacon into his mouth.

"What the hell does that mean?" I ask, taking a healthy bite of my own. The bacon has a faint maple taste to it. It reminds me of the fried bologna my dad used to make. A guy whose definition of good and evil depended on who was footing the bill.

"It means I help organizations find the holes in their security. Teach them how to keep the bad guys out."

"Bad guys like me?" I ask, lifting one eyebrow. His accent is turning me on. I haven't given up on the possibility of getting this code jockey back in the saddle, so I can have an experience I'll remember this time.

But my phone on the table goes off, breaking the sexual tension with a shrieking moan that's supposed to be whale song but sounds like a strangled fart. I set up the message notification when I was hammered, and I can't seem to change it. I look over and see a text from Charlotte.

Don't forget to call Detective Malone. Smiley face emoji.

I'm about to ignore it when the whale lets another one go.

It sounded really important. Chin in hand, thoughtful smiley face.

The Humpback strikes again.

I wouldn't want you to get in trouble. Devil-horned, red-faced emoji.

She may be in another country, but Charlotte's not going to leave me alone on this one.

"I gotta call someone," I say, picking up my phone and making my way to the bedroom. I close the door and sit on the bed, which Deep has already made. Malone picks up on the first ring.

"Okay, what's so fucking important you have to track me down via Newfoundland?" I ask her in lieu of a greeting.

"I've been trying to locate you for days," she says. "Where the hell have you been? I went by the E-Zee Market and everything."

Murder Ink had put me up for the weekend at the Delta. I'd been away since Thursday, convincing the hotel concierge to add an extra day to the booking at their expense, not one to waste the full potential of free room service. It's Monday now, unless I've lost more time to the Scotch than I thought. I'm about to tell Malone that I'm not the kind of person to post an itinerary when she stops me cold in my indignant tracks.

"It's about your mother, Candace," Malone says. "We've found her."

I pause for a second, at a rare loss for words. Then I let her have it.

"I don't know whether you've noticed, Malone, but I haven't exactly been looking for my mother. I couldn't give a rat's ass where Angela is. She abandoned me, remember?"

But Malone's serious sigh on the other end of the phone has a rare hook to it. After a while, I bite.

"Where is she then?" I finally ask, still pissed off.

"She's here at the morgue, Candace," Malone says. "You better come down."

CHAPTER 2

I'VE GOT MY BACKPACK READY with all my stuff in it before Deep even has a chance to clean up the breakfast dishes. I insert my Ruger into the custom-made front holster beneath my boyfriend jeans before I grab my leather jacket off the back of the couch. When I was in the business, I never needed a weapon to get the job done. My dad taught me young how to a silence someone for good with only the use of my hands. But since I've gone civilian, I've got used to carrying a weapon for protection, like the rest of America.

"I'll drive you," Deep says, drying his hands on the holly dish towel before he drapes it over the gleaming oven handle.

"You bet your ass you will," I say. How else did he think I was going to get back downtown from this backwater suburb? Deep's place is one of those original homesteads set on a packet of land with its own woodlot, despite kissing the outskirts of the city. Some developer must be itching to get his hands on it. If this white-hat hacker owns the place, he's sitting on a goddamn goldmine.

"No need to get testy," he says, grabbing a Canada Goose parka from a hanger in the closet and a set of car keys from a hook next to the refrigerator.

"I'm not testy. I just have a lot of shit going on," I tell him. He's right, I'm being a bitch. But this news about my mother has me flustered for perhaps the first time in my cold and calculated life. I don't like being dependent on Deep for a ride, but it's because of him that I missed the hired car Murder Ink set up to take me home last night. Those little dweebs really did not spare any expense. I wonder where they get all the money. One half of them had been wearing bargain-bin sweaters covered in cat hair and the other half still lived with their parents.

Once we're in the car, Deep makes sure I have my seatbelt on before he'll even start the engine. His ride is pretty sweet — a late-model silver Toyota Celica with mag wheels. It puts to shame the shitbox hatchback that Charlotte gave me when she moved away to Newfoundland. I keep it in an alleyway out back of the E-Zee Market. You have to slam the passenger door to get the defogger to come on and the gas gauge doesn't work. It probably wouldn't have made it to the Murder Ink gig without puking up a spark plug.

"Where exactly are we going?" Deep asks as we make our way down the long gravel driveway.

"The city morgue," I say, giving him the address. He does a quick double take, then stops the car and enters the address into Google Maps on his phone. The phone is strapped on the dash by a blue rubber stick man that cradles it in bendable plastic arms. I turn up the heat control on the dash. My leather jacket isn't lined well enough for this time of year. I wish I had Deep's parka. Or even his thick-soled hiking boots. When he put them on before we left, they almost made up for the fact he's an inch or two shorter than me.

"Are you going to tell me what this is about?" he asks once we're on the main road, driving at a careful thirty-five miles per hour — the exact speed limit.

I consider not saying anything or telling him to mind his own business. But he is giving me a ride, and I don't want to piss him off and end up left on the side of the road having to thumb it. Maybe it would even help to talk about it, instead of letting what Malone told me bounce off the insides of my brain until it hurts.

"They think they've found my mother," I say, looking out the window at a car that's passing us on the right-hand side, fed up with Deep's grandpa driving.

"Angela?" he says. So, he was paying attention during the Murder Ink presentation on the Scarpellos, which makes sense since he was in charge of the PowerPoint. My mother had only been mentioned in passing in regard to the familial connection to me, their esteemed guest.

"Were you close?" Deep asks me, mistaking my silence for grief-stricken speechlessness.

"I haven't seen her since I used a sippy cup for my vodka," I tell him.

"Then I gather that would be a no."

"Yes," I tell him. "That would be a no."

The car ahead of us has forgotten to turn his indicator off. The incessant red flicker of it, coupled with our slow progress is making me antsy, even though I tell myself we're in no rush. My mother isn't going to be any less dead if we get there quicker.

"Do you think the family had anything to do with it?" Deep asks, turning on the windshield wipers. It's starting to rain, although a drop of a couple of degrees might turn it to snow.

At first, I think he means my Uncle Rod, who as discussed earlier is not really my family. But then I get who he means.

"The Scarpellos? What makes you think that?" I ask him. "I didn't say she was murdered."

"Was she murdered?"

"Shit, I don't know." Malone hadn't said, but I'd wondered about it. My mother had been persona non grata with the Scarpellos for marrying outside of the Mob. Well, for that, and for being borderline batshit crazy if the rumours were true. Angela had been known to run her mouth off from time to time. That's a serious liability for a tight-knit crime family. But you'd think they would've gotten rid of her a long time ago if she was really a threat.

"You don't think the Scarpellos are involved?" Deep asks. Much like my Aunt Charlotte, he can't let things go.

"Contrary to what those Murder Ink fuckwits might think, I don't have an 'in' with the Scarpellos," I tell him. "They cut off my mom when she got knocked up at eighteen by my Polack dad. And they never wanted anything to do with me." I try not to sound too pissy about this, but I am. My extended Scarpello family's rejection had stung almost as much as my mother's. It's not like I could have had any real power if I'd been a recognized relative. Only men get made in the Mob. But there were many times I'd wished I had access to all those Scarpello cash-cow connections. If I had, I might not be living above a convenience store frequented by meth heads.

"You're getting testy again," Deep says, his eyes still on the road.

"Listen, you lured me back to your hacker's den last night. I missed my ride. And now I have a morgue run to do. So, I'd appreciate you cutting me a little goddamn slack."

"Your nostrils are flaring," he says. "It's kind of cute."

"Just drive, tech boy."

I never was any good at conversation the morning after.

When we pull up in front of the morgue, we haven't talked since the highway. Deep had put some acid jazz on the car radio, and after a while, we'd both relaxed into the steady backbeat and left the subject of my mother and the Scarpellos alone.

"Shall I pull into the carpark?" Deep asks.

"The what?" I say, reaching for my pack on the back seat. I know what he means, but I like to mess with people.

"The carpark," he says again with that Idris Elba accent. Elba's real accent, not the American one he faked on *The Wire*.

"Do you mean the parking lot?" I ask.

"Yeah, sure. We call it a carpark in England."

"How long have you been in the States again?" I ask him.

"Since I got my scholarship to MIT."

"Wow. You'd think they'd teach you what a parking lot is at a school like that."

"It wasn't on the curriculum," Deep says, refusing to be insulted.

"Yeah, well," I say, reaching for the door handle. "Thanks for the ride."

He stops me before I can make my exit. "If you're cross because you think I took advantage of you last night, Candace. I didn't."

I'm professionally offended at the suggestion that any man could take advantage of me. Deep mustn't have gotten a good look at the stats on my trading card. But his sincerity trips me up. I stay in my seat.

"Then how come I woke up half-naked?" I counter.

"We started to, well, you know, take each other's clothes off and everything," Deep says, averting his liquid brown eyes. He fidgets with the blue rubber man holding his phone on the dash. "I couldn't sort out your bra. Too many clasps."

"A scholarship to MIT and you couldn't figure out the mechanics of a Victoria's Secret push up?"

He turns to me with a boyish grin. "Once again, not on the curriculum."

"So, why didn't you?" I ask.

"Why didn't I what?"

"Take advantage of me?" I really want to know. Maybe I need to bathe more. I resist the urge to smell at one of my pits.

"You'd had a lot to drink. It didn't seem right," Deep says, tucking a piece of hair that's escaped from his ponytail behind his ear.

I don't have much experience with gentlemen, having never been much of a lady. I admire his firm grasp of the Me Too movement, but I doubt I'll be seeing this guy again. His sweetness would be lost around a salt lick like me.

"Yeah, well, I really need to go."

"I put my number in your phone," he says as I'm getting out of the car. "Just in case you need anything."

"Sure," I say, closing the door, thinking I won't. There's not much I need from other people.

Standing on the sidewalk in front of the dull brick exterior of the city morgue, I hesitate. I can feel the wind race up the back of my leather jacket, and I resist the urge to shiver. Now that I'm here, I'm not sure whether I want to go inside. It would be so much easier to double back to my own neighbourhood, plunk myself down at The Goon Tavern across the street from the E-Zee Market and my apartment, and blow what's left of my Murder Ink money. When I go to turn around, Deep is still sitting curbside in his Celica, waiting.

I shoot him a menacing look until he drives away, keeping watch until the Celica rounds the corner. Once he's gone, I pull the hip flask out of my jacket, draining the last of the bourbon. It tastes watered down, possibly with my own backwash.

Then I march through the heavy double doors of the morgue and get ready to meet my mother.

The morgue is in a new location, moved since the time I helped Malone with her murder case. I have to stifle a sneeze from the drywall dust still left in the air from the reno. The waiting area has homey couches with dusky-rose upholstery and a neutral carpet the colour of day-old oatmeal. There are no Christmas decorations, thankfully, but the poinsettia to square foot ratio is way too high — possibly an attempt to disguise the smell. You can dress a place up like this all you want, but it still stinks of formaldehyde and lost souls.

Luckily, the woman at the receptionist desk is also new. The bitch I dealt with last time treated me too much like the white trash criminal that I am. But when I give this new woman my name, she is either too bored or too clueless to acknowledge what kind of person I am. Then again, she might just be nice. I have trouble telling the difference.

When Malone is buzzed through the locked glass doors, she walks over and gives me a hug. I try not to flinch. Like I said, she's sort of a friend.

"We should go somewhere and talk," she says. She's changed her hair since I last saw her. Grown it out, so the dark strands with a hint of Celtic red in them brush her shapely shoulders. She's got high heels on today. Italian leather, if I'm not mistaken. Not sure when she traded her black army boots in for Gucci. It must have to do with her promotion to Vice — a need to look the part. But even with the stilettos, I'm half a head taller than her.

"I'd rather just get this over with, Malone," I say, shrugging my shoulders, still recovering from the hug. "I'm not sure how you expect me to identify the body, though. I hardly knew the woman." I can't remember my mother's face, only her smell, a combination of Calvin Klein's Obsession and toast. I've seen pictures, although my dad had tried to hide them from me. I found a set of Polaroids under his collection of brass knuckles once at the back of a drawer. They were pictures a daughter should never see of her mother and father. For most of them, her ass was to the camera, anyway.

"I really think we should talk first. There's something I need to tell you —"

"I've spent the whole morning talking, Malone," I say, interrupting her. "Let's just get the show on the fucking road." I walk over to the glass doors that lead to a long hallway. Malone watches me for a few moments, raising an eyebrow over one jade-green eye without a talon of a crow's foot in sight. Maybe I should start using under-eye cream. You wouldn't think I care about stuff like that, but I do. I'm as vain as the next statuesque bombshell. Malone sighs, like I'm a bratty kid she has to humour.

"Fine, Candace. Have it your way."

With a nod from Malone, the receptionist buzzes us in.

My first thought as we stand over the corpse is that this woman is way too short. Even though the body is crouched in a fetal position, I can tell that much. I may not remember a lot about my mother, but I know that when I tried on a maxi dress of hers when I was twelve and almost six feet tall, the hem still pooled on the floor. Most people think I got to be six-foot-three from my dad's genes, and I suppose he had something to do with it. But the Scarpellos are known for their height. If the family hadn't hailed from Sicily, they might have gone into professional basketball instead of organized crime.

"What makes you think this is my mother?" I ask Malone. I assume they'd found some sort of ID on her, possibly a purse. But I'd heard Angela was a skilled pickpocket back in the day, and old habits die hard. Much like the body on the table has. The face has been peeled away and the fingers sliced off at the first joint. Somebody didn't want anyone knowing what they'd done, or to who.

"See the blood on her clothes?"

"To be honest, it's hard to tell where her clothes end and the rest of her begins," I say. The woman's skin is as dark and mottled as the dried blood on her shirt — a result of sub-zero temperatures. Freezer burn. As in, they had found her in an actual freezer. Malone said they couldn't do a proper autopsy until she thawed. That had to be done slowly apparently, in a controlled environment. They'd been working on it since Wednesday night. That's when they'd found her, in the basement of an empty warehouse after receiving an anonymous tip. The warehouse hadn't been used in years, and the cops were still trying to figure out who owned it. But Malone said there were so many shell companies listed on the lease that it was like trying to get to the inside of a Russian doll.

"What's she wearing, anyway?" I ask. The shirt is more of a smock, the pants have little ties at the ends, each done up in a double knot.

"Some sort of scrubs," Malone says. "We're trying to figure that one out, since your mom never worked in the medical field. But people wear those all the time, just as casual wear, or pyjamas. You can get them anywhere. I even have a pair."

I picture Malone lounging in front of the TV in her scrubs after a long day's work and a dinner that represents all the food groups. Our lives are so very different. It really is a wonder we get along.

"We were able to lift a blood sample off the shirt. Enough for DNA. When we ran it through the database, it was a familial match."

"To me," I say, nodding. I wish I'd paid someone in lock-up to spit on that swab for me. I hate the idea that my genetic code is sitting somewhere in the forensic databank, just waiting for my epithelial cells to rat on me.

"I'm sorry, Candace."

"Why?" I ask. "Did you kill her?"

"I mean about your mother."

I roll my eyes. Receiving condolences for a mother I hardly knew is like getting sent flowers after a Tinder hook-up. Awkward and completely unnecessary.

"I don't think it's my mother, anyway."

"Neither do I." The pathologist has joined us to stand over the body. He must have been wearing crepe-soled shoes for me not to have noticed him walking up. Or maybe I'm losing my touch. He's got greasy grey hair in a comb-over, and dandruff clings to the red turtleneck he's got on under his lab coat. He's bent over a clipboard held in age-spotted hands. They must have pulled the old guy out of retirement to cover for the skinny chick I dealt with last time. Malone said she was away on stress leave. From what I remember of her skeletal frame, that woman needed a good meal way more than a holiday.

"What makes you think that?" Malone asks the pathologist. "You said the blood matched. And I thought you couldn't do any further analysis until she, you know, warmed up." Malone looks over at me, worried she's being indelicate. But standing over a body in a morgue with its face peeled off isn't any time to get dainty with the facts.

"I analyzed a hair sample taken from the scalp," the old guy tells her. "I found traces of hair dye with 4-MMPD in it."

"What the hell is that?"

"4-methoxy-m-phenylenediamine," he says, consulting his clipboard with a pair of Mr. Magoo specs. "It's a carcinogen. Linked to bladder cancer."

"It doesn't look like this one died in a hospice, Doc."

"I agree," he says. "Most likely the cause of death was blunt force trauma to the base of the skull."

I'd noticed that. You don't need a medical degree to see that most of the back of her head is missing.

"Then what's the significance?" Malone asks him.

"4-MMPD was discontinued in the eighties in the United States. And in most countries not long after that.

If this woman was using it to dye her hair, she must have died somewhere in that time frame. I'd say this body has been in situ for at least thirty years."

Malone looks surprised, but she's nodding, making some sort of connection that I'm not.

"What you're saying is this body is too old to be Angela Starr," she says.

"Hold on a second." I turn to Malone. "You know my mother did a runner when I was a kid. If the body was dumped in the eighties that would actually make a lot a sense." I often wondered if my mother's complete lack of interest in me might have been because she was dead. It's hard to send a birthday card when you're stuck in a freezer. Maybe this *is* Angela and she's just shrunk a bit from being in cold storage.

"Your mother didn't die thirty years ago, Candace."

"How can you be sure?"

"Because she crossed the border into Detroit from Canada last month."

"How the hell do you know that?"

"We've kept tabs on her over the years, Candace. Law enforcement has a vested interest in the Scarpello family. You know that. And there's something else. I wanted to talk to you about this earlier, but —"

"Are you telling me that you knew where my mother was all this time and you didn't tell me?" I step closer to Malone, into her personal space. Because, shit, this *is* personal.

"Dammit, Candace. You told me you couldn't care less where your mother was, remember?"

And I had. But I still can't believe Malone didn't tell me.

"I need to get the deceased back into refrigeration," the pathologist says, interrupting our stand-off. "As I told you, Detective, the thawing process has to be strictly controlled."

"Understood," Malone says, stepping away from me, then lightly biting her lower lip. This means she's thinking hard, probably trying to figure out what my mother's blood is doing on the clothes of a woman who's been dead for three decades. A question I'd like answered myself. Just then, the double doors of the examination room fly open, and a girl runs into the room. She's chased by a flustered matron of a uniformed cop who looks remotely like my Aunt Charlotte.

The girl strides across the room on long legs, knocking the old pathologist out of the way to get a closer look at the body on the gurney. His glasses fall off his nose and onto the clipboard.

"I'm sorry, Detective Malone," the uniformed cop says, leaning on her well-padded knees, out of breath. "I couldn't stop her."

Her is pretty tall. Almost my height, and whippet thin. She has a blunt ice-blonde pageboy without a trace of pigment in it, and a wicked widow's peak. Huge round retro-seventies glasses take up only slightly more real estate on her face than her big brown eyes do. She looks like what might happen if Velma from *Scooby Doo* and Draco Malfoy had a baby. I always liked that nasty Slytherin kid more than Harry Potter. And this *is* a kid, I realize now, regardless of the height — early teens at best.

The girl walks around the gurney, inspecting the corpse from all sides. Once she does a full 360, she looks up at Malone, pushing her big-ass specs up her cute button nose.

"This is not my mom," she says.

The pathologist covers the corpse with a sheet and starts wheeling it out of the examination room, faster than any old man ought to go.

Malone coughs before she speaks, clears her throat.

"I told you there was something else."

CHAPTER 3

MALONE USHERS US INTO A ROOM that serves as a holding tank for the recently bereaved. There are purple and white plastic mums instead of poinsettias and two sofas set around a coffee table with a jumbo-sized Kleenex box in the centre. Airbrushed pictures of fields at sunset and ocean views are framed on the wall — the type that usually have sappy motivational messages written on them. *Goals are just dreams with deadlines. Live, Laugh, Love!* I guess someone decided those weren't appropriate sentiments if you'd just finished identifying a grandmother who'd been run over in the bingo hall parking lot.

"Let me get this straight," I say, still standing. "You're telling me this is my sister?"

"Half-sister," the girl with the pale blonde hair says, plunking herself down on the couch opposite the one Malone is sitting on. She looks down at her shoes, white high-tops with rainbow polka-dots. They're Converse knockoffs but still pretty fly.

"I told you, Candace, the department has kept records on your mother over the years, due to her connection with certain organizations."

"Mom was in the Mob," the girl says, still fascinated with her high-tops. I notice that despite the Aryan Nations hair, her skin betrays a deeper, olive tone, much like my own.

I look over at Malone, wondering how much the kid knows, and how much she should know.

"Janet is familiar with her mother's history," Malone says. And by *her* mother she means mine, too. Janet doesn't sound like a name Angela would pick. It's way too traditional. I only got the name Candace because they misread her handwriting on the birth registration where she'd written Candida, like the yeast infection. My middle name is Paco, for fuck's sake.

"Well, if Janet is so familiar, maybe you'd like to fill me in?" I tell her.

Malone outlines what my mother has been up to for the last three decades. Initially, she'd moved to a commune in California, but she got thrown out for attacking another hippy during some sort of peyote enlightenment ceremony. After that, she drifted across the country, getting pinched for small-time thievery here and there. They'd lost track of her for years at a time, but she always popped up somewhere, doing something either illegal, crazy, or both. She never did any real time, though. That's until she got nabbed for creating a disturbance in the middle of Macy's in New York City. Apparently, Angela walked in off the street and started losing it on a saleswoman about an underwear purchase. An act that wouldn't usually end up getting the attention of the police, but the saleswoman was a mannequin, and when it came to underwear, Mom wasn't wearing any. She wasn't wearing any clothes at all.

"They sent her to Bellevue," Malone says.

"That's where she met my dad," Janet chimes in, her big brown eyes lighting up behind the owl glasses.

"That's right," Malone says, smiling back at her. "Your father was a nurse there and also a Canadian citizen. Once she'd been stabilized on medication, she moved with him to Canada. Not long after, you were born."

Shit. My mother must have been hauling her bipolar ass around the country for a while before she settled down with her Canadian nurse. There had to be twenty years between this kid and me.

"How old are you?" I ask Janet.

"Thirteen," she says. Angela was eighteen when she had me. I do the math in my head. That means she was thirty-nine when she had Janet. That's pushing it on the viable childbearing years. But there are women freezing their eggs and not taking them out of cold storage until they're practically on Social Security these days. The chilly subject of cryogenics gets me thinking about the Popsicle woman on the gurney.

"So, how do we explain my mother's blood being on freezer girl's shirt?"

"Our mother's blood," Janet corrects me. Not many people try to correct me, but given she might be family, I let it slide.

"I can't explain it," Malone says. "Maybe ..." she starts, but doesn't finish the thought.

"You think Mom had something to do with that woman's death," Janet says before I can. "My mom would never do something like that." I wish I could be as sure as the kid is about what Angela might do.

"I didn't say that, honey." Malone adopts her social worker smile. It's something they teach you in cop school when you're dealing with vulnerable groups. That's what Malone calls anyone under sixteen, as well as women who have been sexually assaulted. As if being jumped by a bunch of gangbangers rips away a better part of your maturity. But I guess it sort of does, and I guess I would know. It's one of the reasons I drink.

"Listen, I'm not sure what this has to do with anything, anyway. That woman is not our mother." Wow, does that possessive pronoun ever feel weird in my mouth. "And given that she's been literally cooling her heels in a freezer since before this kid was born and when I was still eating paste in kindergarten, I doubt we can give you any information."

This is not entirely true. I never went to kindergarten. Well, I did for one day, but got thrown out for thumping the teacher with a Tonka truck during circle time. Luckily, my dad and I lived with a retired librarian who had trouble paying his gambling debts at the time. The old guy never did learn to win at the ponies, but he taught me how to read before the truant officer hauled my ass back to school in first grade.

In any case, I'm done with being creeped out in this fucking morgue. I have no problem with dead bodies, but the idea that the girl sitting on the couch shares a mother with me is freaking me out. A mother who, unlike me, she actually got a chance to know. Enough to be sure even without a face that the body on the gurney wasn't hers.

"Well, there are some other complications," Malone says. Now she's reserving her social worker smile for me. "It appears that Angela hasn't been heard from since she crossed the border into the U.S. from Canada last month."

Janet's looking down at her high-tops again.

"We had some trouble even finding out where Janet was initially," Malone adds.

"Wasn't she with her dad?"

"My dad's dead," Janet says.

"Oh," I say. "So is mine." Another thing we share.

"Janet was staying with a family friend."

"My Aunt Stacey," Janet says. "But she's not really my aunt."

Holy shit, will the similarities never end? Soon I'll find out this teenybopper knows how to snap a guy's larynx and carries her own hip flask.

"Aunt Stacey drove me down here," Janet says. "To see if it was Mom."

"Which it isn't," I say, turning to Malone. "So, unless you've got something else. I'm thinking we're done here."

"We still don't know where she is," Janet says.

I feel for the kid, I really do. But it is not like Angela doesn't have a history of taking off and leaving people behind. I don't want to get involved.

"We're working on finding her, Janet," Malone says.

"How hard?" Janet asks. She stares Malone down from behind her big glasses, her mouth a taut line. She has spunk, I'll give her that. But I can see the shadow of a tear forming behind the thick glasses. I turn away when I should probably offer her the Kleenex box. I never was any good with emotions. They're a liability, just like getting to know this kid might be.

"We are doing everything we can, Janet," Malone tells her. "We're working with the Canadian authorities, as well. You need to be patient. When your Aunt Stacey comes back, we'll talk more about what to do next."

"When she comes back?" I ask Malone.

"Yes," Malone says, clearing her throat. We're having a little trouble locating her at the moment."

"She dropped me off this morning, but she didn't want to come in," Janet explains.

"You're kidding me?" What kind of fly-by-night fuck-up did Angela leave her daughter with? Who would drive off and leave a thirteen-year-old alone to identify the corpse of her own mother?

"I knew about you," Janet says, changing the subject. "Mom told me."

This surprises me. If I were Angela, I would have kept the fact that I'd abandoned my eldest daughter to myself. But then I remember the rumours about my mother's loose lips.

"Really," I say. "What did she tell you?"

"That you kill people." Straight to the goddamn point. I like that.

"Did she tell you she left me practically as soon as I could walk?"

"Yes," Janet says. "She was sorry about that."

"Sorry, fucking sorry?"

"She wasn't well. She had a mental illness."

"She had a coke habit where her maternal instincts should've been." I am making this part up. I don't know why Angela was such a lousy mother to me, or whether she had any addictions to blame it on. I also don't know why I'm taking it all out on this pale-haired girl, with her big brown eyes. Or maybe I do, but I'm not proud of it. Jealousy is another emotion fraught with liabilities.

Malone steps in. "I'm sure both your Aunt Stacey and your mother will turn up soon, Janet," she says. "In the meantime, I've talked to Social Services. And they've got a place for you until we locate one or both of them."

Social Services. The bogeyman of my childhood. My father generally managed to stay one step ahead of them. Every time some well-meaning woman with a battered briefcase and an ill-fitting pantsuit showed up at the door, he'd make sure to turn on the charm, convince them he was providing a home life conducive to raising a child. Which he did, in his own way. He loved me and looked out for me, and that's about as conducive as you can get given our special circumstances.

But there was the one time when he got held for a week of questioning on a hit they wanted him for. I was ten years old, and they knew I was home alone. At first, I thought it might be fun, staying in a group home with a bunch of other kids. Most of my childhood had been spent around adults. I couldn't exactly bring friends over when there might be some guy tied up in the basement. But the first night in my bunk bed, a fifteen-year-old boy crawled in under the Hello Kitty sheets with me. He only touched himself, but he made noises worse than the pigeons on my E-Zee Market apartment roof. I grabbed my things the next morning and spent the rest of my father's detention sleeping inside a Salvation Army box.

"Can I talk to you, Malone?" I say. "Outside."

I open the door to the hallway.

"We'll be back in a minute, Janet," Malone says before she follows me into the hall. When she shuts the door behind us, I let her have it.

"How could you know about this kid and not tell me?"

"I only just found out about Janet, Candace. It's not like your mother was part of my usual caseload. When we got the DNA hit, I looked up her file. I'm as surprised as you."

"You can't send the kid to a group home," I say.

"I don't have a hell of a lot of choice, Candace. Stacey Bunnaman dropped Janet off at the door and didn't even say where she was going."

"Don't you have a phone number or something?"

"Only for her place back in Canada, and there's no answer there. Like I said, we're working with the local police, but there's a lot of hoops to jump through with the international component."

"Canada is not fucking international. It's like the fifty-first state, for God's sake. Can't you just drive her up there and find a real family member to take her?" The father is dead, but he must have relatives. Not everyone is like me, alone in the world when it comes to relations. Well, I guess I'm not exactly alone anymore.

"It's not that easy, Candace. The father died a few years back. Cancer. Surveillance didn't focus too much on him. It'll take a while to track whether he has any family members willing to foster Janet. It could take weeks."

"What about this Aunt Stacey?" I say. "Maybe she'll show up."

"Even if she does, she's not legally in a position to take care of the child," Malone says. "Honestly, I don't even understand how she was able to get across the border with her."

The Canadian border used to be a joke to cross before 9/11. When I was young, Uncle Rod and Dad used to drive to a back road straddling the U.S.-Canada border and hike into a hunting cabin in Ontario so we could go fishing there. Nowadays, if you try to drive on that road, you'll have a Homeland Security helicopter following your ass in under a minute.

"Come on, Malone. That kid wouldn't last a day in a group home. She couldn't take care of herself. She's not, you know …"

"Like you?" Malone says.

I think about the big eyes and the shadow tear. She may have some attitude on her, but I can tell my sister has lived a charmed life up there in Canada compared to me. And the truth is, I hadn't even lasted a full twenty-four hours under the care of the state. I make a quick decision. One that I'm sure I'm going to regret.

"I'll take her," I say.

"Oh, come on, Candace."

"No, seriously. I'm a family member, a blood relative. You've got the fucking DNA to prove it."

"What do you know about taking care of a young girl?"

"I'm not stupid, Malone. I'm not going to drop her on her head or take her to a peeler bar or something and leave her in the coat check. I am capable of being responsible for another human being." But even as I say this, I'm not so sure that I am.

"I don't know whether it's a good idea, Candace."

"I don't see where you have a choice."

"I do have a choice. I'm police, Candace. The girl is officially in my care."

"Then do it as a favour to me," I say. "As a friend." I'm playing the friendship card. Not something I'm in the habit of doing. And Malone knows it.

"I don't know, Candace."

"I do," Janet says. Malone and I turn around to see her standing in the open doorway. "I want to go with Candace."

"See?" I say, looking back at Malone. "She's made her choice."

I go to stand with my new half-sister.

"And she's choosing me."

When I come back from the restroom at Denny's, Janet is dipping the French fries she ordered in a combination of ketchup and mayonnaise. I remember hearing that makes you either artistic or a psychopath. Looking at what the kid is working on in the sketchbook she has out on the table, I'm wondering if it's both.

"That's, um, disturbing," I say, sitting down in the booth. She's got talent, I'll give her that. The drawing she's outlining with a collection of dark coloured pencils has a dilapidated haunted house in the background. Standing on the path to it is a young girl wearing a cloak, her mouth wide open. She looks like a cross between Little Red Riding Hood and the ghoul in Edvard Munch's *Scream*.

"I copied it," Janet says, still concentrating on getting the shrieking mouth of the girl in the picture just right. "It's from a graphic horror novel."

"Nice," I say, opening my flask and pouring some of the hooch I picked up on the way into a cup of black coffee.

"I want to be a writer," Janet says, reaching for another French fry off the plate. "And an illustrator, obviously."

Before starting on the fries, she'd polished off the Christmas turkey special, complete with congealed gravy and stuffing. The turkey special is just one of the sad festive offerings available at the restaurant. A Santa doll with a dirty white beard peers over the waitress station. Above my head, a shaggy silver garland droops down worse than a past-it peeler's tits.

"Well, don't quit your day job," I tell her. "There's no money in writing."

"It's not about the money," Janet says. "It's about art."

"It's about living in subsidized housing and having to sell a vital organ to pay the rent."

"You sound like my guidance counsellor," Janet says with a sigh. "He wants me to do the advanced STEM program when I go to high school."

"What's that?"

"Engineering and crap like that. I won the science fair, and I'm good in math."

"That's got more coin in it than horror books," I say. Unless you're Stephen King, I guess. But when they made that whacked wordsmith, they broke the mould.

Janet closes the sketchbook and slips it back into the shoulder bag she has with her. On the flap it says, *I love*

Oxford. Except the "love" is a big red heart. I wonder where she got it. I don't see a kid making trips over to England on a dead dad's nurse's pension. But she tells me she got it in a thrift store along with the bowling team–style top she's wearing.

"Why do you think Mom's blood was on that lady's shirt?"

"I have no fucking idea," I say, taking a large gulp of my spiked java. The old biddy at the next table gives me a disapproving look. Maybe I should cool it with the f-bombs around the kid. But that'd be hard. My language matches my life, and neither would be rated PG-13.

Janet shifts uncomfortably in a big puffy coat that dwarfs her Kate Moss frame. It makes Deep's Canada Goose parka look like a spring jacket. She's unzipped it but hasn't taken it off since we left the morgue.

"Maybe they made a mistake," she suggests. "With the DNA."

"I may not have won the science fair, but I don't think they make too many mistakes about that sort of thing."

"Yes, they do," Janet pipes up, bristling in her colossal coat. "I read about a case in Europe where they were looking for years for this serial killer called the Phantom. It turned out the DNA found at all the murder scenes actually belonged to a woman working in a cotton swab factory. She hadn't used latex gloves when she was packing the boxes they used for forensic collection."

"Was she the killer?" I ask.

"No, she just contaminated the swabs," Janet says, sighing like I'm an idiot, or an adult, which I suppose is the same thing to a thirteen-year-old girl.

"Did Angela have a job sorting Q-tips?" I ask her.

"No."

"Then I don't think that's much of a possibility then."

"I'm just saying, they make mistakes," Janet says, furiously dipping another French fry into the mayonnaise-ketchup mix.

I am starting to think it was a mistake to have taken this girl with me, to have insisted to Malone that it was a good idea. I don't have any patience. And I am starting to recall that a person requires a lot of this particular virtue when dealing with this age group. The sooner they find Angela or that Stacey character, the better.

"Where do you think she is?" I ask her. "Your mother." I'm still having trouble with the *our*.

Janet pushes a pale strand of hair behind one ear. I can't get over the colour or the silky straight smoothness of it. My own long honey-brown mop springs out from my head like Medusa snakes on acid. I don't know how we can be related.

"I'm not sure where she is," she finally says. "But I know where she was going."

"Enlighten me."

Janet bites her lip, pushes her big glasses up the bridge of her nose. "I didn't want to tell the police," she says. "I didn't want to get her in trouble."

"I'm not the cops, Janet."

"I know that."

"I'm about the furthest thing from the cops you're going to get."

She raises an eyebrow at that. I see the faint hint of a grin.

"So, where was she going?"

She pushes the empty plate of fries away, puts her hands in the pockets of her jacket.

"She said she was going to see her grandfather. In Detroit. She said he was sick."

I sense we both know who she means. But I say it, anyway. "The old Don?" Then in case she doesn't get the terminology. "Her Scarpello grandfather?"

"Yes," Janet says. "She's not supposed to see them, her family. My dad always told me that. I thought maybe it was a condition of her release from Bellevue or something. But she went, anyway."

"Why?"

"I don't know," Janet says.

But I think both of us know. From what I'd been told about Angela, she'd never give up the opportunity for a payoff. Maybe she thought the old man would feel bad about the family ostracizing her all those years ago and leave her something in the will if she did the bedside vigil thing. Although I don't know how she would expect sentimentality from the man who'd blown up her parents with a car bomb. The old Don had run the Scarpellos with tight reins right into his nineties, only loosening his grip when he was diagnosed with prostate cancer last year. He'd finally handed those reins to his grandson Alex, the progeny of his youngest son, skipping the generation before him, sort of like the Queen's expected to do. Alex Scarpello is my mother's cousin, even though he's the same age as me.

"Well," I say, downing my coffee and waving for the cheque, "I'm sure she'll be coming back soon." But looking at the young yet clearly not stupid girl across the laminate table, I figure she's got to be thinking the same thing as me.

If our mother went into that lethal den of Sicilian vipers, she may not be coming back at all.

CHAPTER 4

WHEN JANET AND I MAKE IT BACK to the E-Zee Market, Majd, the owner, is using a power drill to fasten a wreath above a display of Slim Jims. His eight-year-old niece sits on a stool holding his toolbox.

Majd is a Syrian refugee and the most excellent of landlords. He provides me with a constant supply of samosas and allows me to live virtually rent-free above his store in exchange for covering the cash when he goes to visit his mother on the other side of town.

His niece, Rima, used to be a nephew. She'd insisted she was as a girl since she could talk. A bunch of behavioural issues followed, worse than me with the Tonka truck. When they'd allowed her to finally present as the gender she wanted, the behavioural issues stopped. I'd asked Majd once how his family reconciled this with their religious beliefs, not thinking being transgendered was strictly halal. He'd said he'd seen what men were capable of in this world, the violence, the war. "There's no shame in a girl," he had told me. And there isn't. But not all men are brutal, nor all women blameless. I am the long-legged walking proof of that.

"Hi, Majd," I say when he's finished with the wreath. He turns around and sees me with Janet, does a double take.

"This is my friend," I say, not knowing how best to explain the situation.

"I'm her sister," Janet says, not having the same problem with explanations.

"I am pleased to meet you, Candace's sister," Majd says, eying her with curiosity, no doubt taking in the similar height and skin tone but perplexed by the Nordic hair. He looks back at me. "You didn't tell me you had a sister," he says.

"It's sort of a new thing," I tell him.

He nods without saying anything. Majd is cryptic at the best of times, having come from a country where loose lips can seriously shorten your life span. I notice he doesn't mention that Malone came by looking for me. Either he wants to stay out of it, or he figures that since I've just shown up with a new sister in tow, I have enough on my plate. Rima doesn't have the same history as her uncle to hold her back.

"That lady was looking for you. The pretty one with the badge."

"Thanks, Rima," I say to her. "Cool threads, by the way." She's wearing a sparkly, ruby-red peasant dress with hiking boots. A true lady always knows how to dress for the occasion.

"Can I use the drill now, Uncle?" Rima asks, ignoring me now that she's delivered her important message.

She's got a serious love of power tools for a kid who once begged the Tooth Fairy to take her penis away. But that had been a few years ago. These days she begged the tooth fairy for a fiver, just like everybody else.

I leave Majd and his niece to their bonding moment over the cordless Dewalt and usher Janet up the back stairs to my apartment. It's basically an oversized storage room with a three-piece bathroom and a hotplate. It also has a fridge. I open it and pull out a cold Budweiser for me and a bright orange Powerade for Janet. I have them for my workouts on the weight bench that's shoved into one corner of the room. I like to keep myself in fighting form, mostly because I never know when I'm going to have to fight.

Janet takes a seat cross-legged on the mattress on the floor, leaving the only chair at the small kitchen table to me. I sit down with my beer. I watch her unfold her legs and shuffle over a bit to avoid a rebel spring.

"Do you like living here?" she asks me.

"Would you like living here?" I ask her right back, taking a mighty swig of the crisp Bud.

"I don't know," she says politely. Then exclaims, "Oh my God, you have a VCR?"

This ancient bit of entertainment technology had been lifted from my Uncle Rod's place before he went to prison. It sits across from my mattress next to an old TV that Majd gave me.

Janet gets up off the couch and starts to look through the stack of VHS tapes.

"*Legally Blonde*?" she asks me, holding one up in her hand.

"I've got a thing for chick flicks," I tell her. "Comes from growing up in a house full of men." In addition to the aging librarian, my father and I'd also lived with a bookie named Rodney and a burly teamster who let me ride on his back strapped in my car booster seat. Even when my dad had his own place, my Uncle Rod was always around. Mike Starr never lived with a woman again after my mother left, though many had tried to get him to shack up. I guess once fucked over by the opposite sex, twice shy.

Janet picks up a copy of *Fried Green Tomatoes*. That movie always turns on the waterworks for me, I'm not going to lie. "I know what you mean," Janet says, studying the dusty cover.

"How would you know what I mean?" I ask her. "You had Angela." And I didn't, I want to add. But I realize that's not Janet's fault. But I could have used a mother in those years to show me the ropes of becoming a woman. So I didn't have to learn from the likes of *Mean Girls* and *Confessions of a Teenage Drama Queen*. Maybe with a different influence I wouldn't have spent half my life as a cold-hearted killer. Although it's hard to blame that on poor old Lindsay Lohan. That chick has enough to contend with.

"My dad sort of raised me," Janet says, leaving my video collection to sit back down on the mattress. "He worked the night shift, so he was home during the day." She lies down and stares up at the fraying plaster ceiling. "Mom was okay when she was taking her meds, but she didn't always."

"What happened when she didn't?" I ask.

"Oh, you know, the usual bipolar thing," Janet says. One day she'd grab me and drive seven hours north to Sault Ste. Marie to go blueberry picking." She rolls over on the bed and props herself up on one elbow to face me. "The next, she couldn't get up off the couch."

"That sounds a bit rough," I say. Maybe I was better off with Lindsay Lohan.

"She was really good when she was well," Janet says, getting defensive. "She used to take me tobogganing. She loved the snow. Even tried to ski with my dad and me once. But she was really bad at it. She'd keep losing one ski, and come down the hill on just the one, you know, like slalom. Falling and laughing her head off."

I am trying to think of all the nasty stories I heard about Angela from my father and Uncle Rod, and not in even one of them can I picture her skiing — or laughing, for that matter.

"Then we'd all go for beaver tails," Janet says. "They're these big, round flat pastries, covered in sugar and choc-olate." This idyllic Canadian family ski trip scenario is starting to stick in my craw like a broken ski pole. But I don't want to be a sore sibling.

"That's how I know there's something going on with Mom," Janet says. "When she's away, she always mes-sages me our code word, *slalom*, so I know she's okay. She hasn't sent me that message in over three weeks." She starts tugging gently on her lower lip. I'm thinking we better change the subject here.

"Tell me more about your dad," I say.

"He was great," Janet says, releasing the lip." Since he was home during the day, we played together a lot. We used to dress up in costumes and act out fairy tales and stuff. I'd always get to be the princess or whatever, and he'd be all the other parts."

I remember acting out similar one-acts with a mangy terrier we had for a while. But I tended toward pirate themes. The dog bit me one day when I tried to put an eye patch on him.

"Is that who you got the hair from?" I ask. "Your dad?"

"Yeah. Mom has hair like you, but darker," she tells me. "Dad's grandparents were from Denmark. They had a farm in Manitoba way back."

"Is that where his family is now?" I'm wondering if I can get some of this information faster than Malone can.

"I don't know. We always lived in Ontario, so my dad could work at the addiction centre in Guelph," she says. "Dad didn't talk about his family. They never came around. Mom said they didn't like her."

What's not to like about a crazed Italian girl fresh out of Bellevue? I'm thinking. But I have the sense not to let my wise-ass tendencies have a voice in this case.

"When he got cancer, I thought they'd come," she says. "But they didn't. Then it was just Mom and me."

"When did he die?" I ask. "Your dad."

"When I was ten," she says. The fairy tale games ended early for her. At least I had my father into adulthood. Although hearing your dad has washed up on the shore with a Mexican necktie isn't easy news for a daughter to handle at any age.

Janet gets out her sketchbook from the Oxford bag, flips over onto her stomach, and starts drawing like she did in the diner. This is a different picture. A woman claws at her throat with her eyes bugging out, her skin coming off in jagged strips.

"Did you copy that from the graphic horror novel, too?" I ask the back of Janet's head.

"Different book, same author," she says. "It's about a woman who gets eaten alive by her own skin cream."

"Was it eye cream?" I ask, remembering Malone and her lack of wrinkles. I've got to get into this anti-aging stuff. I've managed to hide a lot behind the tanned olive tone of my skin, still passing for twenty-something, but I can't stave off fucking Father Time forever.

Janet ignores my question, keeps shading the woman's disintegrating skin with a salmon-coloured pencil. "What was your dad like?" she asks me.

"He was a good dad, too," I say, draining the last half of my beer. "But not the most conventional guy. He spent time with me when he could. We used to go camping together sometimes." I remember sitting at the campfire with my dad and Uncle Rod, my first time out of the city. Listening to the loons. Thinking it was crack addicts howling for a fix.

"Mom said he killed people for a living, too," Janet says, still sketching.

"What the hell is that supposed to mean?" He did of course, but it sounds like trash talk coming from her after the whole Dad-and-the-fairy-tale play-acting story.

"He did," she says, turning to look up at me from the mattress. "My dad told me. He said that's why you ended up doing the same thing. It wasn't your fault. You had a bad example."

I don't dignify this comment with a response. Instead, I get up from the table and pop open another Bud. I like to think I came by who I am through my own designs. But these days I find myself getting soft, no longer thrilling to the killer instinct, wondering almost how I ever did. Maybe Janet's right. Maybe being a killer was something I was assigned rather than my true nature. Regardless, my half-sister's comment irks me. People possibly being right can do that to you.

"At least my dad stuck around. Unlike my mother," I say.

"Our mother," she says.

"Whatever."

Janet slams the sketchbook shut and sits up on the bed.

"You could find her, Candace. You could find Mom. I know you know people."

I do, in fact, know people. People who would chew this kid with the glasses up and spit her out again.

"I'm not going looking for Angela, Janet. The cops are doing that. Plus, your Aunt Stacey is going to show up. She wouldn't just leave you here."

"The cops don't know anything," Janet complains. "And I don't think Aunt Stacey is coming back. She was really freaked out about my mom."

"But it wasn't her in the morgue," I say. Damn, is this kid ever ruining my Bud buzz.

"It doesn't matter," Janet says. "When Mom dropped me off at Stacey's, she said she'd only be gone a week at the most. It's been a month now. And I told you about the slalom thing."

"She'll come back," I say. "After all, you're the daughter she stuck around for."

"That's why you won't help me find her, isn't it?" Janet's voice goes up an octave, her glasses starting to fog up with the heat of her tween fury. "You're still mad because she left you. But it wasn't her fault. She was sick."

"Seems she got better," I say. "Set up a cozy little home in Canada with your dad and you, and chocolate beavers singing on the ski slopes and whatnot." I'm raising my own voice now. "But she never came back."

This is, even by my standards, a fucking insensitive thing to say. Since the implication is that her mother won't come back for her, either. But I'm thinking it's been going on thirty years since Angela left me at a bus stop with no change, or whatever the circumstances, so maybe this kid better get used to the waiting. I'm afraid she might cry, but instead she opens up her sketchbook again and starts drawing on a blank page.

"Listen," I say, trying to think of something to smooth things over, "maybe we can find your dad's people. I've got a friend who is good at that sort of thing." I'm thinking of Deep and his hacker abilities. How hard can it be to find a few Norwegians in a country with less people in it than California.

"You're trying to get rid of me," she says, scribbling so hard I think she's going to break the tip off her pencil.

"No, I'm not," I say. But I am. I don't know whether I'm cut out for this big sister caper. I get up, leaving my latest beer on the table.

"I'm going out for a bit," I say, grabbing the jacket I'd hung on a nail at the front door. "You'll be okay, right?"

"Are you going to help find my mom?" she asks, looking up at me.

"No, Janet. I'm not."

"Then fuck you," she hisses, returning to the pad. She adds a backhanded finger gesture in my direction to punctuate her point.

"Right," I say, opening the door. I turn to her before I leave. "Don't touch anything and don't go anywhere. I'll just be across the street."

She doesn't answer, just scribbles angrily on the pad. The smell of samosas drifts up into the hallway from the E-Zee Market below, along with the insistent whir of power tools.

"I wouldn't want to touch any of your gross stuff, anyway," Janet says, as a parting shot. I've never let anyone get away with talking to me the way this kid does, but I don't take the bait. She wants me to stay and continue the argument. But I'm smarter than that. I walk out the door, slamming it behind me. Marching down the stairs, I ignore Majd and his niece, who must have overheard us shouting. They're busy fixing a piece of plastic mistletoe onto the drop ceiling.

Hands shoved into my pockets, I cross the dark street to The Goon, thinking I was right earlier.

I don't have the fucking patience for teenagers.

When I get inside The Goon, Lovely Linda is behind the bar adjusting one of her fake eyelashes in a dingy Jack Daniel's mirror. She turns around when I sit down on a stool, one eyelash still curled up like a furry centipede at the corner.

"Are you flush or flat broke?" she asks, knowing the drill.

"Flush," I say, feeling bills from the Murder Ink gig burning a hole in my pocket.

"Hendrick's it is," Linda says, pulling the top-drawer gin from a hidden shelf under the bar. She pours a generous amount into a glass tumbler, splashes a bit of tonic on top. I pull the drink toward me and take an angry swallow. It burns on the way down my throat, like a velvet flame.

Linda sits on her own stool. She's getting older and can't handle standing all day behind the bar like when she was a fresh young thing. She's worked here for as long as anyone can remember. Which is not that long given the memory of dive bar drinkers. She's known for turning a quick trick or two in the gents when things get slow. But I don't judge her for that, and neither should you. Linda's good people.

"I hear you got your sister at your place?" she says.

"News travels fast."

"I was in the E-Zee Market earlier getting some fancy cocktail napkins."

This is definitely bullshit. The Goon doesn't serve fancy cocktails and it doesn't have napkins.

"Or maybe you saw me walk in with her and got curious," I say, taking another hard pull on the gin and imperceptible tonic.

Linda throws up her hands. She's got fake nails to go with the fake eyelashes. They're painted blue and have little white snowmen at the tips. I wonder if she got it done at the Vietnamese place around the corner. I go there myself when I've got the cash, for the pedi rather than the mani. I may not be in the business anymore, but I'm not above taking a job to rough someone up who needs it. I rely too much on my hands in that line of work to worry about ruining a French tip.

"You got me," she says. "Guilty as charged." She winks the eye with the wonky lash.

"Did Majd tell you?" I ask, surprised. Like I said, he's not usually a squealer.

"No, the kid did," Linda says. "The one holding the power drill. You'd think they'd find her more age-appropriate toys."

I am not sure what age-appropriate toys are. When I was six, my dad taught me how to use a wire splicer so I could crawl on the roof and steal cable from our neighbours. I don't even know if it was appropriate to leave Janet alone. But I'm keeping my eye out the front window, watching the door of the E-Zee Market across the street. I'll see if she tries to do a runner.

"Yeah, well, she didn't lie. She's my sister. Or half-sister, I guess."

"Your dad's?" Linda asks. My dad was known to be a lady's man back in the day. Lovely Linda and him might have even had a hook-up in the restroom for all I know.

"No," I say. "My mom's."

Linda purses her strawberry-glossed lips and lets out a whistle. "Well, that's fraught with thorny possibilities." Linda has a way with words. I hear she actually went to college. But I don't think she finished. Much like myself.

I'd been on a different career trajectory then, but life tends to abhor straight lines, much like nature does with vacuums.

"I'm just taking care of her," I say. "Until Angela comes back."

"You saw your mother?" Linda asks.

"No," I tell her. "I didn't." I down the rest of the drink, throw some bills on the bar. Linda pours me another without being asked. I tell her about Malone's phone call and the morgue — about the woman without a face who somehow got Angela's blood on her. Then the revelation of a sister, the group home threat, and finally my bone-headed decision to take Janet home with me.

"Now she actually wants me to look for that crazy bitch," I say.

"That crazy bitch being your mother."

"She may have given birth to me, but she wasn't much of a mother," I point out, but Linda already knows. Angela is a bit famous in these parts, even after all these years. One time, she showed up at the bar with a teddy bear instead of me strapped into her BabyBjörn baby carrier. My infant ass had been left behind at the toy store, hidden in a stuffed animal display, just like E.T. "Seems like she managed to take care of my sister, though."

"Hmm," Linda says.

"Besides," I say. "Who knows what weird shit she got herself into with the Scarpellos. I don't need those kind of complications."

Linda blinks, maybe in agreement, or maybe because she is trying to set the fake eyelash back into place.

"Your sister's dad passed away. Isn't that what you said?" she says, changing the subject. Or so I think.

"Cancer," I tell her.

"So, Angela's all she's got."

"Yup." I flip some of my springy hair out of the way. One long twisted strand of it falls forward and drops into my drink.

"Sort of like you and your dad," Linda says.

I raise one eyebrow across the bar at her.

"Yeah, sort of like that, I guess." I don't like where she's going with this.

"Gotta be pretty scary for a thirteen-year-old girl, being without her only parent," Linda says. "Even if they're not perfect."

I pull the hair strand out of my glass then suck the gin off my fingers.

"It's not the same, Linda."

But I suppose it is. My dad hadn't been perfect, either, but he'd been my whole world. When he died, I felt like a tattered but crucial rug had been pulled out from under me. I've been trying to get my footing ever since.

"You're thinking I should help her find Angela," I say to Linda.

"I'm saying you know what it's like to be alone, Candace."

"I like being alone," I say, pushing the empty tumbler toward her. But she doesn't refill it. Another couple of customers have walked in, and she gets up off her stool.

"You keep telling yourself that, Candace." Then she's gone to serve two other dive bar lost souls, and I'm left there, staring at my empty glass.

I take a long walk to clear my head before I go back to my room above the E-Zee Market. A few flakes of snow are falling, but it melts the second it hits the gum-splattered pavement. It's supposed to be seventy degrees tomorrow. Global warming's a bitch, but at times an enjoyable one.

When I get back to my apartment, Janet is still sketching. The new picture is of a tall woman in a leather jacket with her mouth open in the same huge O as the *Scream* girl she was working on at Denny's. Long spirals of honey-brown hair zigzag out of her head like a witch. It's a pretty good likeness just the same.

I throw a jumbo bag of barbecue-flavoured chips on the table. "I brought you some snacks," I say, in lieu of an apology. That's the best she's going to get from me. I'm not good at saying I'm sorry. I'm going to let Frito-Lay do the talking for me.

She gets up and opens the bag, crams a big handful of chips into her mouth. The red barbecue dust glistens on her lips like Linda's strawberry lipgloss.

"Want to watch a movie?" she asks, indicating the ancient VCR.

"Okay," I say.

I pop in a dusty tape of *When Harry Met Sally*, and we settle down on the mattress to watch it, propped up on pillows and her big puffy jacket. Kids blow hot and cold at this age. Much like the weather. She falls asleep before we even get to the fake orgasm in the diner scene. I get up from the mattress and look out the window.

There's a car parked across the street. It's been there since before we started the movie. A cream-coloured Chrysler sedan with a black car bra stretched across the hood, the cracked vinyl mottled with road salt stains. The driver's window is halfway down, but I can't see who's inside. It's too dark and the streetlight out front of The Goon has been broken since the summer. I watch for a while, not moving a muscle, mindful of the gun I have tucked in my jeans. But whoever's in the car must have clocked me standing in the lit window, because before I can go down and check things out, they drive quickly away.

I'm not sure what Angela has gotten herself into, but the possibility of a tail tells me it cannot be good. Earlier, when the light was better, I'd noticed the plates of the car weren't local. Blue lettering on white, like they have in Michigan. Like they have in Detroit. I look at the girl asleep on the mattress. Her ponytail's come undone, and her hair has crumbs of crimson chips caught in the uber-blonde strands.

I'm not about to go off to Detroit looking for Angela, but I can make a few inquiries. Like my sister said, I know people.

I pick my phone up off the kitchen table. There are two text messages from Charlotte. I'd set it to vibrate, silencing the whales.

Did you get my package? the first one says.

What did Detective Malone want? asks the other.

I ignore both questions and tap the new number I find in my Contacts. It takes a couple of rings, but he picks up.

"Good evening, Candace," he says with that wrong-side-of-London accent. I don't need his hacking abilities, but I do need someone I can trust. Something tells me the man on the other end of the phone is worthy of that. Call it street smarts, or a sixth sense, or just the lack of another viable fucking option.

"Turns out I need something after all," I say into the phone.

And without even hearing what it is, Deep says okay.

CHAPTER 5

WHEN DEEP PULLS HIS FLASH CELICA UP in front of the E-Zee Market, Janet is still arguing with me.

"I don't see why I can't go," she whines. But I'm not having it. I've spent the whole day playing the big sister, waiting until Deep finished with his day job and could come pick her up. After a late breakfast at a House of Pancakes, Janet and I had gone to the science museum, but not until she agreed to pay for it. My Murder Ink funds are starting to dwindle, mostly from feeding my sister's three-hundred-pound trucker appetite. She'd eaten a stack of waffles at the restaurant and still needed a "snack" of honey-garlic chicken wings at the museum cafeteria once we were done looking around. Neither of us was too impressed with the place, since it seems like they haven't received any new funding since the Clinton administration. One of the exhibits was a talking typewriter, for Christ's sake. The average two-year-old has better technology than that at their disposal.

"You want me to figure out where Angela is or not?" I say, opening the passenger door of the Celica after Deep has popped the lock.

"I still don't understand why I can't come with you," she says.

"And I don't understand nuclear fission, but I guess we all have to live with the mystery," I say. "Now get in the car."

Janet throws her Oxford bag over the passenger seat and gets in. I lean into the car once Deep's made sure she has her seatbelt fastened.

"This is Janet," I say.

"It's lovely to meet you, Janet," he says. My sister just sneers. We really do have a lot of things in common besides our mother.

"I'll be back tonight," I tell him. "Touch her and I'll pour sulphuric acid on your balls."

"It's nice to see you, too, Candace." But Deep still smiles. I sense he is enjoying the intrigue of all this. Probably beats crunching code all day long.

I stand on the sidewalk outside the E-Zee Market and watch Deep drive away. Malone would probably string me up for entrusting the care of a minor to a guy I picked up at a Murder Ink meeting, but I can't have a kid tagging along with me while I make my inquiries. And while the Chrysler that was parked outside last night hasn't come back, you can't be too careful. Janet will be safer out in the suburbs with Deep.

I pull the keys for Charlotte's car out of the pocket of my leather jacket. They're attached to a big dangling red pom-pom that I hate, but it keeps me from losing them. I go into the E-Zee Market and call out to Majd.

"I'm taking the car out today."

Majd nods his head. Comes over and locks the

front door of the E-Zee Market and puts up the "Back in 5 minutes" sign. We walk through the storage room that doubles as his office and into the alleyway, where Charlotte's orange hatchback sits, looking like it should be up on blocks. You'd think the colour would hide the rust, but it doesn't.

"I think I am getting too old for this," Majd says, rubbing a shoulder.

"Nah," I say. "You're not."

I get into the car, put the stick shift in second, and shout to Majd through the rolled-down window of the driver's seat. "Okay, now!"

He shoves all his weight into the back bumper of the car, and it slowly begins to move. Once we've gained some momentum, I pop the clutch. The car starts on the first try. A good day.

I turn onto the street, driving with the window kept down. As promised, it's warmer than any day in December should be. It feels more like early summer, and that's a good thing, since the heater in Charlotte's car doesn't work. I don't close the window until I hit the interstate, where I drive the speed limit only because Charlotte's hatchback can't go any faster without something falling off of it. The trip odometer sits at twenty-three miles. I set it at zero each time I gas up, since the fuel gauge is busted. I know I can get about twenty-five miles to the gallon, and I do the math to figure out how far I can travel before I'll be running on fumes.

The city falls away behind me. I find some of Charlotte's CDs in the glove compartment and pop one in. By the time I pull up in front of the Tudor-inspired low-rise an hour later, I've sung along to the entire soundtrack of *9 to 5*, enjoying the open road and the weather. After parking the car, I enter through the arched front doors of the rest home. I try to be polite to the nurse at the front desk who sits next to a plastic Christmas tree sprayed with fake snow.

"I'm here to see my grandfather," I tell her.

She asks me to wait, which I don't do very well, but before long an orderly shows up and leads me to a common room that smells like Lysol and grilled cheese. A large picture window runs along the far wall. Through it, I can see a deep valley dotted with real-life versions of the fake tree by the front desk, minus the snow.

"Candace," the old man sitting at a checkerboard says. *"Bellissima!"*

"Roberto," I say. "It's good to see you."

Roberto Scuderi is not my grandfather. He's an old-timer from The Goon who I've gotten to know over the years, one of the few patrons at that local watering hole who can talk about my mother and the Scarpellos from firsthand experience. Unlike the other barflies of that fine establishment, he's got class. Even here in the nursing home, with a blanket over his knees, he wears a button-up cashmere sweater and black dress shoes polished to a gleam. His signature white fedora sits perched slightly askew on his head, but I don't say anything about it. Getting old sucks.

"Leave now please, Reginald," he says to the man sitting opposite him at the checkerboard. "Can you not see I have company?" Reginald looks up at me through rheumy eyes. Before this, he'd picked up one of the checkers and covertly tried to slip it in his mouth. Roberto signals for the orderly, and he comes and escorts Reginald to a puzzle table in the corner, with no regard for the possible choking hazard.

"Sit down, Candace. Sit down," the old man says. "Did you bring the small favour I asked for?"

I make sure the orderly is busy, then reach into the inner pocket of my jacket and hand Roberto the water bottle that I've filled with one-hundred-and-twenty-proof grappa. He pours some into the dregs of his orange juice and takes an appreciative sip.

"Ah," Roberto says. "This will kill me, but I will enjoy the dying."

"How are you settling in?" I ask him.

"The food is too bland and the nurses too skinny," he tells me. "But it is a necessary evil. And there are worse places for an old man to be." He's right on that one. Roberto must have had a good-sized stash put away to afford this place. The state-run nursing homes are like *Night of the Living Dead*, but with more bedpans. There's a graphic horror novel Janet should write.

"But I do not think you come all this way to inquire after my settling," Roberto says, pouring himself some more grappa.

"No," I say. "I didn't."

I tell him about my sister showing up, but not the why of it. He doesn't need to know about the frozen body in the morgue, or the fact that it had Angela's blood on it. Where Roberto comes from, everything is on a need-to-know basis. You don't ever want to have more knowledge than can be successfully beaten out of you. But I am here for information, and I hope the grappa and his age may loosen his tongue.

"Angela went to see the Scarpellos," I say. "Just before the old Don died. She hasn't been heard from since. I'm trying to locate her. You know, for my sister."

Roberto nods, politely picks up a napkin and dabs the edges of his lips.

"I had heard this," he says. "That she had come to see her grandfather." Roberto may be in a home, but he still has connections. A made man never really retires. I bet they even have a special LinkedIn for them on the dark web. "The old Don was pleased to see her."

"Really?" I say.

"Reaching the end of life changes the perspective," Roberto says. "A man looks to make amends to others and to God." Roberto makes the sign of the cross, surprising me. He had renounced his Catholicism years ago, after his daughter was found dead in the stairwell of a crack house, her corpse violated more than once post-mortem. But looking around the room, I can see how a person's beliefs could change in a place where the prospect of death hangs heavy. There are no atheists in foxholes or nursing homes, I suppose.

"Yes, her grandfather was happy to see her," Roberto says. "Not so much the new Don, I understand."

"Alex Scarpello," I say.

"Yes," Roberto takes another gentlemanly sip of the grappa. "He took over the family affairs last year when the grandfather first became ill. Some say for the better, others say not."

"Tell me about him."

"He is not of the old school," Roberto says. "More like his mother's people. In the eighties, there was much uncertainty, many arrests, the Cosa Nostra was crippled by law enforcement and informers. A marriage was arranged between the old Don's son and a young Russian girl. An alliance, to ensure the future. Many were not pleased. But it turned out to be a good match, one that maintained the family during the difficult years."

Roberto is not giving up anything new here. I had heard most of this at the Murder Ink presentation — how a power marriage was set up between the Scarpellos and the Russian Mob. My mother's uncle would've been pushing forty then, while his new wife would've been barely old enough to vote. She couldn't have had much say in the matter. But it had been a good investment for the future, just as Roberto had said.

"Alex was the only kid they had, right?"

"Yes. It took some time to produce a child. It was fortunate it was a son, of course. Anya, his Russian wife, went back to Moscow to have the baby. Her husband was killed while she was away. By the time it was safe for Alex and his mother to return to America, he was a young boy. A sickly child, many visits to the doctor. But I think he outgrows this."

"Why do you think he was upset about my mother visiting with the old Don?"

"As I said, there are those who are not pleased with Alex Scarpello. If he did not have the backing of the Russians, he may not have held on to his power after the grandfather died. His methods are ... unorthodox.

Some had hoped Angela might have gone on to produce a son, an heir to contend for leadership in his place."

"But she didn't," I say. "Have a son."

"Perhaps," Roberto says. "But your mother is one to be full of surprises. I do not think Alex Scarpello is a man who enjoys much to be surprised."

I think about all those years my mother wandered around the country. The large pockets of time that even Malone and her contacts couldn't account for. She could have had another kid — another child squirreled away somewhere. And it could have been a son. My sister and I are no threat to the Scarpello dynasty, on account of our sex. But a son would have been different. The Mob is still a fiercely guarded patriarchy. Most of the world is, if you think hard enough on it.

"Do you really think if Angela had a son he could have unseated the new Don?"

"If he had the backing of the grandfather before he died, he might have. The old Don was never a great supporter of the alliance. It was a means to an end." He picks up one of the checker pieces and moves it to another square.

"Maybe Angela was just trying to get back in with the family?" I say, moving my own checker. I picture Angela, the prodigal Mob daughter returned, burrowing in like a tick to suck the blood money out of her connected relatives. That would have pissed Alex Scarpello off.

"I think there is more to it than this," Roberto says. He clears his throat after another shot of grappa. "There have been rumours."

"What kind of rumours?"

He hesitates, but the grappa seems to be working its tongue-loosening magic. Roberto lowers his voice. "They say your mother had some claim on the Scarpello fortunes, or, at the very least, was making the hints that she did. Asking questions. This did not make the new Don happy."

"But what claim could she have?"

He doesn't answer me, just moves a checker ahead another square.

"You think she did have a son, don't you?"

Roberto waits for my move, but I don't make one. He casts his gaze out the picture window to the pine-dotted valley below, like it's a TV show he'd forgotten was on. Then he turns back to me.

"I think that Alex Scarpello is a vicious man, Candace. Unpredictable. *Il maniaco.*" He whispers the Italian words like a curse. "He has not the honour of the old Don. Some say this is the new way." In between those lines is a warning, but I'm not going to heed it. I lean across the checkerboard.

"Where is Angela, Roberto?"

The old man pours himself a little more grappa, smooths the plaid blanket he has in his lap.

"I do not know, Candace," he says. "But I wonder whether it is wise for you to ask such questions." He jumps over my checker and pockets it under his blanket, possibly to keep it away from the guy who likes to eat them. "Where we come from, the answers, they can be very dangerous things."

I get the orderly to give me a push-start out of the parking lot, after I siphon some gas from the nursing home short bus. I had spent another hour playing checkers with Roberto before I told him I had to go. When I left, he kissed me on both cheeks. The sour plum perfume of grappa still clings to my hair.

I take side roads driving back to the city. One of the headlights is burned out on the car, and it's dark now. I can't afford to be pulled over by the cops. The busted light wouldn't be a big deal, but not having a driver's licence or insurance would.

When Charlotte's hatchback coughs to a stop on the side of the road, I haven't seen another car for miles. I check the odometer. I should have had more than enough gas to make it home. It must be something else besides lack of fuel. I pull out my phone to call Deep for a lift in his more reliable Celica, but the charge on my phone is as dead as the car's engine.

I wait in the driver's seat for a while before I decide no one's going to come by that I can flag down for a ride. I'll have to wait until the morning, when the commuter crowd avoiding the traffic of the highway starts up. There is no way I'm sleeping in the car, though. I have trouble fitting my lanky frame into Charlotte's compact at the best of times. Every time I unfold myself out of the driver's door, Majd says it reminds him of a clown car. I didn't know they had the circus in Syria, but I suppose dancing bears and trapeze artists have their own cross-cultural appeal.

I pull an old car blanket out of the back. Charlotte keeps it stored where the spare tire should be. I lock up and look around. There's a moon out tonight, so I can see well enough to make out a murky depression in the trees next to the road. When I get closer, I find the remnants of a farmhouse foundation, the fieldstone walls of the basement lining a large rectangular hole in the ground. There are still intact stairs, made of cast iron, that lead down into the pit of it. Down there, I find the usual leftovers from teenage bush parties — discarded beer bottles, cigarette butts. A used rubber gets stuck on my boot, and I have to kick it away.

There's a small opening in one of the walls, to a cold cellar that would have been built under the earth rather than the house itself. This is what they used in the days before refrigeration. I manage to crawl inside and make a nest in the corner with the blanket. I'm careful to check for condoms and broken glass, but it looks like the kids stay out of this room. Not surprising, since it's got a *Blair Witch Project*-feel to it. But there's an earth roof above it, and it's better than waking up bent over like fucking Quasimodo after a night sleeping in the car. It's a good thing the weather has changed, or I would end up tomorrow morning covered in frost worse than that chick in the freezer.

I'm almost asleep, with the help of the bourbon in my flask, when I hear a twig snap. I open my eyes, keeping them trained on the doorway. It allows me a partial view of the forest above. I wait, not moving, except for a slow reach toward the gun tucked into my jeans. That's when I see a pinpoint of light moving through the trees. One of those flashlight apps you can use on your phone. It bounces through the branches and shines itself into the basement foundation when it gets close enough. The moon must have gone behind a cloud, because I can't see who or what's behind the tiny beam. I watch it move like Tinkerbell along the edge of the foundation. Its disembodied brightness starts a careful descent along the stairs, the old cast iron creaking with every step. I slowly pull the gun out from under the blanket that I still have wrapped around me.

It could be kids, similar to the ones who left the beer bottles behind. But maybe I hadn't been paying attention in my rear-view enough after I left the old folks' home, too preoccupied with the information Roberto had given me about Angela and the wisdom of questions. I could have been followed. When the light is halfway down the stairs, I have to make a decision. I don't want to shoot some pimply teenager carrying a six pack and looking to get laid. But I am also vulnerable here in the cold cellar, with no exit point other than the doorway I crawled through. If this is the person who sat outside my place last night in the Chrysler, I need to create a distraction, then find a way to get out in the open.

I train my Ruger on the rise underneath the stairs, unlatching the safety. When I let the hammer down, the shot echoes off the stone walls of the old foundation and leaves a hole in Charlotte's blanket before I throw it off. I do a commando roll out the doorway to the basement proper and crouch down tightly beneath the last few steps of the stairs, waiting to see what the light does next. Soon, I hear a car engine start up, the squealing of tires. I take the rickety metal stairs two at a time, but when I get back to the side of the road and Charlotte's broken-down hatchback, all I can see are the red tail lights as they disappear around the next bend in the road.

CHAPTER 6

THE NEXT MORNING, I CATCH A RIDE with a lady in a pink car on her way to a Mary Kay conference. She tells me they always have a great time there, comparing sales figures and checking out the new product line over cocktails. She's really looking forward to the unveiling of a new long-lasting lipstick. Apparently, you practically need a sandblaster to get it off before you go to bed at night.

I ask her about under-eye cream, and we pass the next half hour discussing serums and collagen boosters. When she drops me on an exit ramp just on the outside of town, she hands me a business card the same colour as her car.

Now, I'm in the backseat of a Honda. The two guys up front reek of dope. The driver looks like Cartman from *South Park*, that prime time cartoon that isn't for kids. His ballooning gut barely fits behind the steering wheel. The one in the passenger seat has dirty-blonde dreadlocks and a grey-and-black Mexican jerga hoodie. They call me "dude," even though I'm not one, and giggle inappropriately a lot. A girl can't be too picky about a ride when she's covered in dirt and smelling of leaf mould. After my run-in with the cellphone flashlight, I'd found a nearby ravine and covered myself with the blanket and a heap of leaves. Cramped space aside, I hadn't wanted to risk the exposure of sleeping in my fishbowl hatchback of a car, or the trapped possibilities of the *Blair Witch Project* cold cellar.

When the stoners pull up in front of the E-Zee Market, they start giggling again. I thank them for the ride, then go to open the car door, but the little fuckers have put the child locks on.

"You want to open the door?" I say, pulling a twig out of my hair.

They giggle some more. "You sure you don't want to stick around, ragamuffin?" the one with the white-guy dreadlocks says with a sad attempt at a patois accent. Someone should tell this moron that no amount of hairstyling is going to make him Jamaican.

"Yeah," says the Cartman look-alike. "Ass, gas, or grass, baby. Nobody rides for free."

I could use my gun, but I don't. Instead, I pull Charlotte's car keys out of my jacket pocket, reach forward, and press the pointed end of one of them into his jugular. The red pom-pom on the chain swings back and forth above his huge gut.

The door locks pop open. When I get out of the car, their beat-up Civic speeds off faster than the car with the tail lights did last night.

I open up the E-Zee Market front door, and the bell jingles over my head. Majd looks up, but then sees my face, creased and cranky from a night on the forest floor. He goes back to sorting the lottery tickets he has spread out on the counter.

When I get back inside my apartment, I take off my jacket, kick my jeans off, and throw them in a corner along with my shirt. The gun and holster I hide in an emptied VHS box set of *Sex in the City,* Seasons 1–6. I've watched enough of Carrie Bradshaw's hijinks to last me a lifetime. After I tuck the box back with the other tapes, I connect my dead phone to the charger on the kitchen table and step into my coffin-sized bathroom.

Majd likes to call this ceramic cubbyhole a three-piece, but there is no separate shower. Instead, the walls and ceiling are covered in white subway tiles, and there's a spray nozzle hooked up at about the height of my nose. I have to turn it on and crouch under the weak stream of water without falling into the toilet when I shampoo. But at least the water's hot. After about fifteen minutes, I finally begin to warm up. I wash the smell of the forest out of my hair, watching the stray leaves as they gather at the drain in the floor. My mane, now fully saturated, reaches all the way to my ass. When it dries into my signature spiral of mad curls, it only comes to the middle of my back.

Once I towel off, I brush my teeth and floss. I'm particular about my mouth. My bite's come in handy in the past. I've got a great smile when I choose to show it, which is not very often. A somewhat clean pair of jeans lie crumpled under my weight bench, along with a State U T-shirt. I slip both of them on, then sit down at the kitchen table with a bottle of pre-mixed rum and egg-nog. I bought it at a service station when the Mary Kay lady stopped for gas. The phone on the table, which now has a few bars of charge to it, has a full screen's worth of messages.

Most of them are from Deep.

J and I watching Dr. Who. When u getting back?

Wondering where u r. Getting late.

After midnight. J asleep. All ok?

GN. J has eaten all the bacon. Where the fuck r u?

But it's the text from Malone that catches my eye. She must have gotten my number when I called her from Deep's place. She's my friend, but for a variety of reasons, I keep my contact details vague. Most of them to do with the fact that I don't like to be contacted.

Call me right now.

I phone her back, figuring they may have found Angela, or perhaps Aunt Stacey, who, with a little arm-twisting, Malone might be convinced to let me unload Janet on. I like the kid well enough, but I'm not cut out for the caregiver role. Already, I've left her alone with a guy I barely know who has a limited supply of bacon. Something tells me Malone wouldn't approve.

When she picks up the phone she sounds pissed.

"Did you see my text?"

"Of course I did. Why else would I be phoning you?"

"I sent it hours ago."

"I've been a bit busy."

"With what?"

"Best you don't know."

Silence on the other end. "Where's Janet?"

"I sent her around the block to get milk."

"You live above a convenience store, Candace."

"Majd was all out."

I'm enjoying our little back and forth. I used to love twisting Malone up like this when we worked together. Well, I guess, she was the only one really working. I was just trying to look like I was. But I'd saved her life during that unlikely partnership, so I guess I earned my keep.

"She's just a kid," Malone says.

"And I'm taking care of her," I say. "Have you found out anything about her dad's family? Janet told me he might have relatives in Manitoba."

"No," Malone says. "We don't have any further intel on that."

"And Aunt Stacey is still MIA?"

"She hasn't contacted us, no."

"So, what's with the urgent text, Malone? You just checking up on me?"

"We've got some more results back, from the pathologist."

"And?"

"The woman we found in the freezer is not your mother."

"I thought we figured that out already."

"Yes, well it's confirmed now," she says. I can sense there's more, though. And there is.

"We found amniotic fluid on the woman's scrubs."

"Amniotic fluid? Like the stuff a baby floats around in before it's born?"

"Yes," Malone says. "Amniotic fluid has the same genetic code as the fetus it carries. It was preserved because of the low temperature. It gave us another DNA match."

"To who?"

"To you, Candace," Malone says. "It appears this woman was present at your birth. Probably as a nurse."

Wow, that body *had* been in the freezer for a long time. That explains the blood on her being a match for my mother. My father told me it had been a difficult birth, so there could have been a lot of blood. Although Dad wasn't around for my delivery, off at a job out west to get rid of a pesky police informant. Still, this doesn't explain why a nurse got whacked.

"There's more, Candace," Malone says, while I'm still trying to process what she's told me.

"Jesus, what more can there be?"

"It wasn't just your amniotic fluid we found."

"What are you saying?"

"You have a twin, Candace." This is something my father definitely didn't tell me.

"That can't be right," I say.

"We double-checked the results, Candace. The other baby was definitely your twin."

This is all the world needs, I think. *Another one of me.* But I still can't get my head around it.

"We're working on getting your birth registration," Malone says. "But there's all sorts of red tape to go through. You can't just ask for access to private information like that. You've got to get the right paperwork, and even then, they can fight you on it."

"Wait," I say, my well-oiled wheels spinning. "If it was a twin, then the DNA would be exactly the same as mine. How could you tell one from the other?"

"It was fraternal twins, Candace. Each fetus has its own amniotic sac in that case. Its own distinct set of DNA."

"So, you're saying I have another sister?" I can't believe I started off this week with no sisters and now I might be saddled with two.

"No, Candace. The DNA shows the other twin was a boy. You have a brother."

I sit down hard on the mattress on the floor.

Angela, it seems, had a son after all.

I get Lovely Linda to drive me out to Charlotte's broken-down car. She'd been working on clearing air out of the draft beer pipes when I crossed the street to The Goon, my mind full of what Malone had told me. The bar didn't open for a few hours, so after I'd helped her get the brews flowing again, she'd grabbed her 204-piece socket wrench kit and driven us here. Right now, she's under the orange hood of the hatchback with a pair of greasy gloves on to save her snowman nails. I lean against the fender and hand her tools when she needs them from the case opened up on the ground. Not far in front of me, I can see fresh skid marks on the tarmac, no doubt from whomever was following me last night when they hauled ass after I shot at them.

"I can get it going," she says, grabbing another wrench. "But it'll only be temporary. You really need to take this to a mechanic."

Linda grew up with an uncle who owned a garage, learning her way around an automobile from an early age. I often wonder why she didn't apprentice. I would've thought overhauling engines would be better work than slinging beers. But we all have our reasons for how we end up making a living.

"I just need it to get me back to the city," I say. And back to Deep's to pick up Janet. It's not that far out of the way.

Linda drops the hood with a thud, puts her gloves away.

"What were you doing all the way out in the sticks?" she asks.

"Visiting a friend."

"Who do you know around here?" Linda asks, not buying it.

I tell her about going to visit Roberto, and why. After all, it was her advice that got me looking for Angela in the first place. I don't tell her what Malone said, about having a twin brother. That information's too hot to handle, or to share at this point.

"How's he keeping?" Linda asks. She's always had a soft spot for Roberto. Mostly because he was one of the few customers at The Goon who left a tip bigger than a nickel.

"He's old," I say.

"He was old before they put him in the home," Linda says.

"Yeah," I say. "But he's older now."

I get in the car, put one of the keys from the ring with the dangling pom-pom into the ignition. The engine turns over on the first try.

"You're a fucking genius, Linda," I say.

"I know," she says, putting her tools back into the trunk of her car. "But you're one of the few people who appreciates it."

I take the back roads to Deep's, not because I'm trying to evade a police check, but because I'm concerned the hatchback won't be able to handle the speed limit of the highway a second time. I put my phone on speaker and drop it on the passenger seat after pressing Charlotte's number.

"Can't come to the phone right now. Leave a message," her pert voice says from the passenger seat. I wait for the tone.

"Hey, Aunt Charlotte, it's Candace." I'm not sure what to say next, so I keep it simple. "Call me, it's important." That'll get the old girl's panties in a knot. She can't resist a good mystery. I reach out with one hand and press disconnect, returning it quickly to the shaky wheel to steady it.

Charlotte wasn't around when I was born. She and my Uncle Rod don't go that far back. But she'd spent enough years with him to have learned a thing or two about the past. Rod might have known about the twin thing, being as close as he was to my dad. And my dad must have known. He may have been across the country when my mom went into labour, but surely he would've been wise to his wife carrying two babies instead of one. That's something they tend to pick up, even with the most pathetic of prenatal care.

Then again, Angela might have not told him. I wouldn't put it past her. Maybe she'd always planned to give one of the kids up for adoption — figured she couldn't handle two kids with her untested maternal skills. Hell, she couldn't handle one it turned out. She wouldn't have wanted my dad to know about that plan. Never leave a man behind, was Mike Starr's motto. I'm pretty sure that would have included a son. But maybe by the time he got back, the baby had already been signed over to new parents. Or maybe Angela left my twin brother on a doorstep, like she left me in the toy store that time with the stuffed animals.

In any case, Charlotte is my only possible link to that murky past. Like I said, Uncle Rod and I don't talk anymore. Plus, I don't think he would tell me anything if we did. He's not one to divulge information without putting up a fight. My dad said he once got his jaw broken in custody, refusing to give up so much as his address. A son of Angela Starr's, formerly Scarpello, would have further-reaching implications than a man's street number right now.

Angela might have used one of those adoption registries where they reunite grown-up kids with the parents who ditched them. Although, I suppose that's not fair. There are lots of parents out there who shouldn't have a minor in their possession. It's the right decision to make, I suppose, if you're not being selfish about it.

Of course, the situation would be a little different for Angela. If she'd managed to make contact with my long-lost twin brother, it would have given her a major bargaining chip when she showed up in Detroit. Although trying to cash that chip might have cost her her life. And where was my brother in all this? Poor unsuspecting sap could be buried in a shallow grave right alongside his birth mother.

Distracted as I am with these thoughts, it takes some time before I pick up on the tail following a fair distance behind me. I tilt the rear-view to keep an eye on their progress, but otherwise don't give anything away. The car is still following about fifty yards behind me when I pull into Deep's driveway. I get out of the hatchback and quickly double back into the woods, so I can wait in a ditch by the road. Sure enough, along comes the Chrysler sedan I saw outside my place Monday night when Janet and I were watching our chick flick. I recognize the salt-stained car bra. It pulls to a stop on the shoulder a few feet ahead of where I'm hidden. The driver's window goes down with an automated hum before the engine turns off. Wispy smoke from a cigarette floats up and out before being blown across the roof by a weak wind. I can see a blonde head of hair above the headrest in the driver's seat. There doesn't appear to be anyone else in the car.

I carefully pull out my gun, train it on the blonde head, clicking the safety off. I'm about to make my move, when I see a shadow stretch out over the ditch, cast from behind. I roll over onto my back and pull the trigger without looking. The car engine starts up, and I hear the Chrysler burn rubber as it takes off down the road. Above me, Deep holds a hand vacuum in the air, still smoking from the hole I just blew through it.

"What the fuck?" Deep yells, dropping the vacuum to the woodland floor. He quickly begins stomping on it with his thick-soled hiking boots, possibly worried the dried fallen leaves will catch and start a forest fire. I look over my shoulder at the road. The car is long gone.

"What the hell did you think you were doing?" I shout back at Deep. "Sneaking up on me like that!"

"I saw you pull in," he says, still stomping. "Then you disappeared into the trees. I thought you might be in trouble."

"And you were going to save me by vacuuming someone to death?"

"I just grabbed what was handy," he says, making one final stomp on the smoking hand vacuum. His long hair hangs free and a strand gets caught on a low-slung branch.

"Well, next time, find a handy baseball bat," I say, standing up and brushing the leaves off my jeans. "I thought you were descended from a race of warriors. I doubt your ancestors rushed into battle with electric brooms."

He did come to defend me, though, rather than hide out in the house. I had to give him that.

"Who was in that car, Candace?" Deep ignores my ancestral taunt.

"I don't know."

"And yet you were prepared to shoot them."

"You know what they say about asking questions later."

"Yes, I do. And if you hadn't been such a crappy shot, I might have never been able to give an answer again."

"I am not a crappy shot," I say. "I hit that fucking Dustbuster head on." I don't appreciate having my marksman abilities mocked by a guy who arms himself with household appliances. Plus, I'm annoyed that the Chrysler got away before I could see who the hell has been tailing me.

I step past Deep and start off back through the woods to the house. He doesn't follow me at first. Maybe he feels I've insulted his manhood along with his choice of weapon. Or maybe he just can't get his hair disentangled from the branch. But after retrieving the vacuum, he catches up and rushes to stand on the front steps of the house, blocking my way in.

"Where the hell have you been, Candace?" he asks.

"It's a long story."

He sighs and looks off down the road to where the Chrysler disappeared. His hair blows across his face in the breeze that's picked up, and he tosses his head slightly to move it out of the way before turning back to me. Then he steps aside and opens the front door, gesturing with the gutted hand vacuum. The nozzle falls off and shatters on his well-swept concrete steps.

"Well, then," he says. "I reckon you better come in and tell it to me."

CHAPTER 7

WHEN I WALK INTO THE HOUSE, I find Janet propped up on the couch with her sketchbook balanced in her lap. The man in the picture she is drawing has dark skin and hair that fans out behind him like a Middle Eastern mermaid. In his hands, he brandishes a frying pan and a spatula, threatening a small group of demons on the opposite page who have bacon where their arms should be. She's got earbuds in, listening to music on her phone. The tinny foreign lyrics of K-pop leak out from under her ice-blonde hair. She wouldn't have heard the gunshot, and that's probably for the best.

"Hi," I say, waving my hand in front of her face to be noticed.

She takes the earbuds out, pausing her playlist. "You find Mom?" she asks me, not pulling any punches.

"No," I say. "I didn't."

"Great," she says, the sarcasm laid on heavy. We both hear Deep outside, cursing as he cleans up the broken vacuum from the front steps. Janet raises an eyebrow, but then goes back to drawing, although she doesn't put the earbuds back in. I wait a bit, but she keeps on sketching, saying nothing. I suppose she's mad at me for not coming back last night, but I don't mind the silent treatment. I've got a wicked headache.

I walk over to the fridge and pull out a cold beer, pop the cap, and take a long swig before I spew it out in the double sink under the window. Fucking near beer. More like near crap. I leave the bottle on the counter and sit down across from Janet in an armchair, the bad taste still in my mouth.

"So, there's been some developments," I say.

"I should say there bloody well have been," Deep says, walking in from outside. He hangs what's left of the hand vacuum in a wall mount by the front door and then chucks the shards of the broken nozzle into the garbage under the sink before joining Janet on the couch. She puts down her sketchbook on the coffee table and scooches over to make room for him.

"Your mother *was* in Detroit to see the old Don," I say.

"Tell us something we don't know" Janet says with a smirk.

So I do. I tell them about the amniotic fluid they found on the frozen broad's scrubs and the DNA that proves I had a twin brother and everything else Malone filled me in on.

Two sets of brown eyes stare at me from across the coffee table. I couldn't have got a more stupefied reaction if I told them I was abducted by aliens.

"That's crazy," my kid sister says, having lost both her sarcasm and her smirk.

"Yes, it is," I agree. I turn to Deep. "You got anything stronger than fake beer around here?"

"In the kitchen, above the refrigerator," he says, still stunned. Janet just sits there with her rosebud mouth hanging open.

I walk over and open up the cupboard, pull down a bottle of Rémy Martin and a cut crystal lowball glass stored next to it.

"You fancy pouring me some of that?" Deep asks from the couch.

I grab another glass and bring it over to the coffee table, where I measure out two fingers of brandy each. Deep takes a healthy gulp. I down the whole thing and pour myself another. My headache immediately improves with the top-shelf booze.

"But how did the nurse end up dead in a freezer?" Deep asks, putting down his glass.

"Your guess is as good as mine."

"But I don't understand," Janet says. "Mom didn't tell me anything about a brother."

"She didn't tell you why she was going to see the Scarpellos, either," I say, then wish that I hadn't.

"What do you mean?" Janet asks. "She wanted to see her grandfather. He was dying."

"Yeah, that's right," I say, trying to backtrack. "Don't know what I was thinking." I don't want to let on what Roberto told me, about Angela making waves for Alex Scarpello. Ones that possibly got her pulled out to sea to sleep with the fishes. The kid is freaked out enough.

Janet narrows her eyes at me. "You know something," she says. "You know something about Mom."

"No, I don't."

"Yes, you do," she says, jumping up off the couch, her hands in tight fists. One of them still holds a coloured pencil, and for a moment, I think she's going to stab me with it. "You know something, and you're not saying."

"Now listen, you just have to trust me on this —"

"I don't trust you. You didn't even come home last night when you said you would." She's shaking now, raising her voice.

"My car broke down," I say, trying to keep my temper in check. Not something I excel at even under normal circumstances. "I slept in a ravine for fuck's sake. All to find your goddamn mother."

"Our mother!"

I shift my position in the chair, ready to twist the arm holding the pointy pencil behind Janet's back if the situation calls for it.

Deep stands up and makes a motion with his arms, like an umpire calling an out.

"Okay, let's just all calm down here," he says. "Why don't I fix us something to eat."

"Are you kidding me?" I say.

Janet plunks herself back down on the couch.

"How about I make you another one of those strawberry protein shakes you liked so much," Deep says to Janet, all composed and reasonable. Two traits that annoy me at the best of times.

My sister throws her pointy pencil onto the table, crosses her arms. "Fine," she says, refusing to look at either of us.

"How about you, Candace?" he asks.

I grunt something in the affirmative. I'm pretty hungry. The last time I ate was a stale Jamaican beef patty I lifted on my way out the door of the E-Zee Market yesterday.

"Two strawberry protein shakes coming up," Deep says, heading toward the kitchen island. From a cupboard, he pulls out a food processor the size of a small outboard motor. Janet and I sit in silence in the living room. Both of us cringe when he pushes the power button. A set of vicious blades whir to life, liquefying in seconds the kale and frozen strawberries he's dropped into it. Honestly, you could get rid of an entire corpse with the power of that thing — pour the body down the drain when you were done.

"I just want to find Mom," Janet says, all the fight gone out of her. I can barely hear her over the blender.

"I know."

She picks at a thread from Deep's couch, worrying it between her slim fingers. I can see now that her eyes are reddened behind her thick glasses. She probably didn't sleep well last night, worried about where I was, as well as her mother.

"You think I'm a baby, but I'm not," she says.

"I don't think you're a baby." But I do. She may be tall and smarter than most her age, but I have underwear older than this kid.

Janet gives the thread a final violent tug. It comes off with a snap. "If something's happened to Mom, you have to tell me. I deserve to know. If she's, if she's —"

"Straws?" Deep blurts out, placing two insulated tumblers filled to the top with a pink froth on the coffee table. In his hands he holds a couple of shiny silver tubes. Why hadn't he grabbed those earlier? Metal straws would have been a whole lot more lethal than a vacuum. Janet looks up at him and then drops her face into her hands.

"Did I miss something?" he asks.

"Yes," I say, grabbing the straws and dropping them in the drinks. "You missed putting vodka in mine."

He sits back down with Janet, ignoring me. That's okay. I was only joking. I hate vodka with milk.

"Listen, Janet," I say, leaning across the coffee table. "It's nothing like that." Although it might be something like that. Something like Angela being dead for trying to stage a coup in the Scarpello dynasty with a son she pulled out of the woodwork. But the woman hasn't lasted this long without being a crafty survivor of dangerous circumstances. I bet after a nuclear holocaust she'd still emerge from the mushroom cloud, fully intact and covered in cockroaches.

"Then what is it?" Janet asks, looking up from her hands, managing to hold back the tears that threaten behind her big glasses. "What did you find out?" She stares me down, waiting for an answer.

Deep tilts his head at an inquiring angle, also waiting. I feel more pressure from these two earnest faces than I did after eight solid hours of questioning without a pee break in detention. I realize I'm going to have to give up the conversation with Roberto after all. I suppose my sister has a right to know.

"Okay," I say. "There've been rumours."

"What kind of rumours?"

"Rumours that Angela was making trouble for Alex Scarpello."

"What could Mom have done to get in trouble with him?"

"If Angela started telling people she had a son. She wouldn't have been too popular with the guy in line to be the new Don," I tell her.

"Why?" Janet asks.

I'm trying to find a tactful way to explain to her the often-violent succession rules of a Mob family, when Deep beats me to it.

"He could have challenged Alex Scarpello for leadership."

I take a long slurp of the strawberry protein shake through the metal straw. It tastes like Lovely Linda's strawberry lip gloss smells. Which is pretty damn good.

"But how could that get Mom into trouble?" Janet asks. "Wouldn't they just be after her son, not her?"

Deep and I exchange a look, both knowing that Mafia families are not fans of loose ends. Every dangling string attached would have to be tied up, if only for appearance's sake.

"It may not be that simple," Deep says. That's about the kindest way you can say that your mother may have been whacked by her own family to keep her quiet.

"I don't understand," Janet says, shaking her head.

Just then my phone starts vibrating in my pocket. I take it out and look at the call display. Malone again. I throw the phone to Janet on the couch.

"Here," I say. "You gotta answer this. Make sure you tell Malone you were out getting milk earlier. And about the science museum. But *nothing else*."

Deep gets up from the couch and motions me toward the bedroom. Something tells me it's not to take advantage of me now that I'm relatively sober. I sit down on the plump white comforter spread out without a wrinkle on the bed. He closes the door behind us.

"Who was in that car, Candace?" he asks me, still standing.

"Thanks for looking after Janet," I say, leaning way back on my elbows, so my boobs are thrust forward. It's a cheap trick, but you can get guys to ignore a lot with much less.

"Stop taking the piss," Deep says. I've watched enough of *Fleabag* to know this means he thinks I'm screwing with him. Which, of course, I sort of am.

I sit up straight again on the bed. "I'm not sure, okay? Someone's been following me."

"Since when?"

"Since the night before last."

He digests that for a bit. "Is it the Scarpellos?"

"Maybe," I say. "But I think if it was them, they'd have made a move by now." Truthfully, they did make a move, on the side of the road last night. But if it had been hired muscle from the family, they would have brought a gun into the open basement of that farmhouse, not a bouncing phone flashlight. Still, you never know.

"But just in case I'm wrong, maybe you should take the kid for a few more days. Until I figure it out."

"I'm not a babysitting service, Candace."

"I get that."

He comes to sit beside me on the bed. "Do you reckon your mother really was aiming to have your brother made the new Don?"

"I don't know. I figure Angela must have given him up for adoption when he was born. But she could have found a way of locating him."

"How?"

"She's not stupid, Deep. There are ways to find these things out." Angela had the shrewd intelligence that fucked-in-the-head people often possess. At least that's what I'd been told. "Your mother was no idiot," my father was fond of saying, "except when it came to keeping her yap shut."

"If she convinced your brother to make a bid for leadership, it would have meant a big payout, both for him and for her. He'd need to have the right background, of course."

"You mean a criminal background."

He nods.

"Take a look at my family, Deep. There's a pretty strong genetic argument for him being a felon."

"It's not all about genetics."

"Whatever."

"But if there have been people questioning Alex Scarpello's right to lead for years," Deep says, "why would Angela have waited so long to get your brother sorted?"

"I don't know. Like I said, I don't even know if that's what she was up to. Or if that's what got Alex Scarpello pissed at her. This brother bullshit may be a red herring or whatever you call it. My twin could be living in Topeka in his adoptive parent's basement for all I know."

"Then where's Angela?"

"I don't know."

"It doesn't sound like you know much of anything, Candace," Deep says, then adds, "despite being gone all night."

"My car broke down."

"So you say."

"For Christ's sake, Deep. I didn't even find out I had a twin brother until this morning, or a sister until the day before yesterday, so pardon me if I'm not up on all the details of my entire fucking family tree."

I get up off the bed and open the door to retreat from Deep's interrogations. In the living room, I find Janet stuffing a pile of her T-shirts and one of the metal straws into her Oxford bag. She is no longer wearing her glasses. Her eyes seem even more massive now that they're unleashed. They draw you in, make you think she's older than she is. Maybe I shouldn't be leaving her with Deep after all, gentleman or not.

"Listen, you may not want to pack that bag too fast," I say. "It might be a good idea to lay low here for a few days while I take care of a few things."

"I'm not staying here," Janet says. "I'm going to Detroit."

Deep has come up to stand beside me. "I don't think that's a good idea, Candace," he says close to my ear.

"Of course it's not a good fucking idea," I say to him, then turn back to my sister. "You are not going to Detroit, Janet."

"Yes, I am," she says, grabbing her sketchbook from the kitchen table and cramming it into her bag. "And you can't stop me."

"I sure as hell can," I tell her. "I've made a goddamn career out of stopping people."

"So, what are you going to do?" she says, turning to face off with me, her hands on her skinny hips. "Kill me?"

"No, Janet, I'm not going to kill you."

"Well, then, I'm going. Detroit was the last place Mom was and that's where we should be looking for her."

"No, you're not."

"You think I'm not capable, you think I can't handle myself? How do you think I got over the border with Aunt Stacey?"

I remember Malone wondering about this. "How?" I say.

"I used a fake ID, that's how. Says I'm eighteen, old enough to travel without a parent."

"Where the hell did you get that?" She would need something pretty sophisticated to fool a U.S. border guard. You can't just liquid paper over the birth year on your library card for those guys.

"I bought it online," she says. "Through the dark web."

"The fucking dark web?" Jesus, the things a kid can see on there could put them into therapy for years. Not to mention that she might have found my stats.

"What I'm saying is, I know how to take care of myself, Candace. And I'm going to Detroit."

I can't believe she's trying to play me with this little teenage rebellion fit. She may think she's a badass, but she wouldn't last a second with the kind of vultures that start to circle around a thirteen-year-old girl on her own in that city. I imagine her, trying to hitch a ride with those two stoners looking for *ass, gas, or grass,* and the strawberry smoothie starts to curdle in my stomach. I don't like being concerned enough about someone to be given indigestion. I see my phone where she has discarded it on the kitchen table, and I hit her with the worst threat I can think of.

"I'll tell Malone to put you in Social Services," I say.

"I'll run away," she counters.

"Fucking hell," I shout, kicking one of the discarded hard drives on the floor with my cowboy boot. It flies across the carpet and comes to rest on the leg of the wood coffee table, leaving a dent.

I can't let this kid go to Detroit on her own. And as she points out, I can't kill her. I am uncomfortably out of options. Or else I wouldn't make the offer I'm about to make.

"I'll go," I say.

She looks up at me. "You'll go to Detroit?" she says. "You'll talk to the Scarpellos?"

"I can't believe I'm saying this, but yes." Roberto said that answers could be dangerous in the family. But better me than my sister walking into that particular minefield.

"Fine," she says. "But I'm going, too."

"Aw, c'mon Janet. Just stay here with Deep. Let me handle things."

I'm sure I can convince Deep to keep her. I'll turn on the charm again. I'll get him some more bacon.

"Why don't we all go?" Deep says.

"What?" This I hadn't been expecting, and it doesn't work for me. Bad enough to be saddled with a thirteen-year-old, but I don't need some guy in chinos and a neat streak cramping my style.

"I can look after Janet there, while you check into things," he says to me.

"I don't need looking after," Janet fumes.

"I could help you, Candace," Deep says, still pleading his case. "I can get you information where most people can't. And I don't have to beat it out of a person to get it. I just have to use a few keystrokes. I could even find out where your brother is."

I think about this. It's true. Data is the newest weapon of mass destruction. If Deep can get access to the birth registrations and adoption records without the hassle and delay Malone has to go through, it could help a lot. If we found my brother, it might lead us to Angela, and my sister wouldn't have to spend her life as an orphan, like me. Hell, if we found my twin, maybe the two of us could stage our own coup on the Scarpello leadership, sharing the spoils. I've sworn off killing people for a living. But if I had the Mob behind me, I wouldn't have to. The Mafia usually farms that shit out now.

"Can you hack into birth registries?" I ask Deep.

"I can hack into just about anything," he says. "And I have a car. That deathtrap of yours won't make it out of the county."

I'm suspicious. Nobody helps someone like me out of the kindness of their hearts. He's got to have his own agenda.

"I don't get it, Deep. What's in it for you?" I ask him. But he's already getting something heavy down out of the hall closet.

"Adventure," he says, coming into the living room with two hardside Heys suitcases in matching Easter-egg blue. They both have little wheelies on the bottom. He starts packing his computer equipment, careful to include a bottle of nasal spray and a fidget spinner he had sitting on the desk. "I don't get a lot of that."

"I bet you don't," Janet says. She rolls her eyes at me, but she's smiling. It's the first time I've seen her do that since I came back to the house.

While Deep packs, I take the bottle of Rémy Martin and go sit on the front steps. The cold of the concrete on my ass makes a nice contrast with the warmth of the brandy. I watch as the high branches of trees sway in the wind, listen to the sounds of birds I'll never know the names of. I may be a city girl, but I can still appreciate the outdoors. At least when I'm not sleeping in a ravine.

I look down the long driveway toward the road and wonder whether the Chrysler will come back. It could be an agent of the Scarpellos in that sedan. If Angela was planning what we think, they may have gotten rid of both her and my brother, then decided to come for me. But if that's the case, they shouldn't have bothered.

Because it looks like I'll be coming to them.

CHAPTER 8

WE'VE BEEN ON THE ROAD A FEW HOURS when I see the
Gun Superstore coming up on the horizon. I remember
it from a trip my dad and I took once for an out-of-town
gig. We had to snuff a serial pedophile who got freed on
a technicality and make it look like an accident. All the
parents on the soccer team he used to coach had taken
up a collection to pay our fee. The guy ran into traffic
running away from us and got hit by a Pepperidge Farm
truck. I still can't look at a box of Goldfish crackers without feeling smug.

"Pull over," I say to Deep.

"What, here?" Deep asks me, taking in the huge neon
shotgun that flashes like a Las Vegas stripper sign on top
of the flat gravel roof.

"Yes, here."

Deep signals and turns into the parking lot. One
storey high and sprawling, the superstore looks like a
large strip mall with no windows. We have to search a
while for a place to park, despite it being a Wednesday
afternoon. Crowds of people walk in and out in a steady

stream, with grocery carts empty or full depending on their direction. There's a hot dog vendor near the entrance, with a line-up, mostly parents with kids who keep pushing each other. The place is busier than god-damn Costco on a Saturday.

Deep follows a guy dressed in head-to-toe camo back to his car in order to take his spot. We wait in the Celica while the man empties his shopping cart into a double-cab pickup, throwing three pistols and a box of Smith & Wesson–inspired Christmas ornaments into an empty car seat in the back. I am impressed by a redneck such as him getting his holiday shopping done so early. Deep pulls carefully into the space after the camo guy drives away.

"Can I have a hot dog?" Janet asks from the back seat.

"That sounds like an excellent idea," Deep says. "You fancy a hot dog, Candace?"

"We're not here for fucking lunch," I say, getting annoyed at the family-road-trip feel that seems to be settling in with both of them. "We're here to get a gun." I have already been subjected to three rounds of I Spy and one of Punch Buggy that Deep will not be repeating now that he realizes shouting "No punch backs" doesn't work with me.

"You already have a gun," Janet says. "I saw you put it down your pants yesterday morning at your apartment." The kid is observant, I'll give her that.

"The gun's not for me," I say.

"Then who's it for?" Deep asks, still checking in the centre console of the Celica for change to help buy the hot dogs. When I don't answer, he looks up and sees the serious set of my face.

"Oh, no," he says, shaking his head. "I don't want a gun."

"If I'm going to leave you with the kid while I take care of business, you should have one," I say. "You said you wanted to take care of her."

"I meant making sure she eats her veggies and doesn't get hit by a bus," he says.

Janet sighs from the back seat. "You people really think I'm pathetic, don't you?"

"Sorry, Janet," Deep says.

"Listen, we might stir up some shit looking into all this, Deep," I say, getting him back to the point. "You said you were looking for some adventure. Well, sometimes adventure comes looking for you, and it's carrying a Glock."

"I'm not going in there, Candace."

"You have to go in there," I say. "I'm a registered felon. There's no way they're going to sell me a gun. The moment they run my ID through the system, my record will pop. It's got to be you who buys it."

I can see my sister looking at the people coming out of the automatic sliding doors with their full shopping carts. One guy is wearing pyjama bottoms instead of pants and is missing most of his teeth. Another has a tattoo of a tear under one eye and a biker jacket warning us that he is part of the one percent, and that doesn't mean he's a millionaire. "Doesn't look to me like they're too fussy," she says.

"You don't understand," Deep tells me, running one hand through his hair.

"I understand that you're being a wuss," I say. This is America. Not England, where you're too candy-assed to even give your cops a gun. It's a wonder the criminals don't run the whole damn country."

"You do realize the U.S. has a hundred and sixty times more gun deaths per year than Britain."

"And we've got way more people, too," I say, defending my country and its gun violence statistics, when really, let's face it, there is no defence.

"Not a hundred and sixty times more," Deep says.

"Actually, the United States has only six times the population of Britain," Janet pipes up from the back seat.

"Really?" Deep asks, turning around in the driver's seat to smile at my sister. "I didn't realize that."

"I did a project on it for school."

"For fuck's sake, I don't give a shit about population density," I shout, slamming my open palm on the dash. "And I'm not arguing about this anymore."

Deep and Janet look at me the same way they did when I broke the "no punch back" rule. But I'm not having it. I can't always be around, and if I'm leaving Deep with my sister, he'll need more than his fidget spinner if the Scarpellos come around.

"I can't buy a gun, Candace."

"Are you twenty-one years of age or older?"

"Yes."

"Are you under the influence of alcohol or drugs?"

"No."

"Then you can buy a gun in the state of Ohio," I say, opening up the passenger door and stepping out into the unseasonably warm sunshine. Tinny Christmas music squawks from speakers in the parking lot. If I'm not mistaken it's a Chipmunks version of "Ave Maria."

Deep gets out of the car along with Janet, and the two of them follow me through the sea of parked cars to the sliding front doors of the Gun Superstore.

"Does this mean I don't get a hot dog?" Janet asks.

I let out a sigh, wondering how I ever agreed to take a teenager with a hollow leg and a limey pacifist to see the Mob.

But I still wait with the grocery cart, while Deep buys them both lunch.

"Is there a washroom in here?" Janet asks once she pops the final end of her hot dog bun into her mouth. Deep is still working on a foot long with sauerkraut.

I look up and down the bowling alley of a gun store. Display cases full of boxed ammunition line both of its long sides, with the counters attended by smiling customer service reps in cherry-red T-shirts with name tags. The guns are hung on long metal prongs behind them, sorted like batteries at a supermarket checkout. The rifles cover one side of the store, the pistols are on the other. In the centre are bins full of every accessory a discerning Second Amendment shopper could want, but we appear to be in the toy section. Deep has just picked up a Mr. Potato Head packing a Colt 45.

"What do you need a washroom for?" I ask Janet. "We just stopped twenty minutes ago at the gas station." Deep had insisted on filling up, even though we were above the halfway mark on the gas gauge. For a guy who has dropped everything to accompany a criminal and her underage sister on an adventurous road trip, he's still fairly cautious.

"I need to take my contacts out," she says.

"Right now?" I've been waiting behind a young mother with a baby strapped to her chest for the last ten minutes. She can't decide between a Remington pistol and a Kel-Tec 9mm, no matter how many times the sales clerk lets her hold each gun in her hand and pull the trigger. Behind me, a lady with salt-and-pepper hair and a great figure for her age waits her turn, as well. I'm not interested in losing my place in line to help Janet go in search of the ladies'.

"My eyes are feeling irritated," Janet says. And I do notice that one lid seems a bit swollen where the lashes connect.

"Okay," I say. "Once I'm done here, we'll find the washroom."

"But I need to go now," Janet says.

"I don't think your eyeballs are going to self-destruct in the next fifteen minutes, Janet."

"You don't know that," she says, getting all huffy in her big jacket. "I read once that this girl got sweat bees caught under her contacts, and by the time she got to the doctor, they were eating away at her cornea."

"What the hell are sweat bees?"

"They're bees that feed on sweat," Janet says. "Duh."

"Why don't I help Janet find the toilets," Deep says, dumping the Mr. Potato Head back in the bin.

"I don't need the toilet," Janet says loudly. "I just need somewhere to take my contacts out!"

People are turning around, looking at us. I don't need this kind of attention. I'm already nervous enough about being here. If the cops found out I was looking at firearms, I'd be up shit's creek without a parole hearing. I'm not supposed to be anywhere near a firearm, a condition of my release. And to be honest, I've never really liked them. I can usually take care of myself without resorting to the tattle-tale possibilities of ballistics. But Deep hasn't got my training, passed down from my dad or Uncle Rod, who bragged once when drunk that he had belonged to an international version of Special Ops.

"Fine," I say to Deep. "Go with her. But you have to be back here in time to do the purchase," I say. Deep heads off with Janet toward the far end of the store. I watch them disappear in the crowd of people with their baskets and grocery carts. The salt-and-pepper lady behind me smiles.

"I had six girls," she says. "Daughters, that is."

"Wow," I say. "That's a lot."

"They turn nice again at eighteen," she tells me. "Until then, I recommend drinking wine with dinner."

"I'll take that under advisement."

The baby ahead of us has started to wail, perhaps as aggravated by his mother's total lack of decisiveness as the rest of us. The store clerk finally says she'll throw in a free box of ammo if the woman gets the Remington, and that seems to seal the deal. The mother cradles her new gun and ammo up against the bald skull of her screaming baby as they head off in the direction of the conveyor belt cash.

"How can I help you today?" the girl behind the display case asks as I step up for my turn. Her name tag says *Hi, my name is Maddysin*. I've never been too sure whether these variations of normal names are a result of aggravating hipster trends or parents who never bothered to learn how to spell.

"I'd like to look at the M&P 9," I tell her.

"Sure," Maddysin says, giving me a winning smile, untroubled by phonetics.

She slides the Smith & Wesson pistol off one of the metal prongs, lays it out on the display case on a piece of felt like we're in a jewellery store.

"Now, this is a great duty gun, but hugely popular in the civilian market," she says. I already know this. The M&P stands for *military and police*, the original market targeted by the manufacturer. But the minimal controls and reliability have made it a commercial hit, as well, popular with just about everybody.

"Do you see the ambidextrous slide-stop control? And the reversible mag catch?" Maddysin says, caressing the gun's features without touching them, like Vanna White does with letters on *Wheel of Fortune*. "That means the whole family can use it, regardless of handedness."

"Hmm," I say, picking up the family-friendly gun and turning it over in my gloved hands. I hadn't thought about whether Deep was a southpaw or not. This way it won't matter.

"It's full-sized, with a standard seventeen-round magazine. You won't get anything better for the price. You can take it home today with cash, debit, or credit. Or with only six tiny installments using our Christmas payment plan."

"How about ammunition?" I say. "I saw you gave baby-on-board a deal."

"Sure," the ever-accommodating Maddysin says as she bends down to unlock the display case and take out the 9mm cartridges to go with the gun. Nobody seems to worry around here about the wisdom of giving people weapons along with the ability to load them in a store full of people. I wonder how many snipers are hiding in blinds behind the walls, ready to pick off anyone stupid enough to try something.

Deep comes up behind me, just as Maddysin is laying out the box of ammo on the counter. When she sees him, her smile vanishes.

"I'm sorry, sir," she says. "You'll have to wait in line."

"He's with me," I tell her. "In fact, he's the one buying the gun."

"I thought you were the one purchasing this firearm today," Maddysin says, confused.

"I wouldn't be caught dead with that beginner series gun," I tell her. "The damn thing is so basic it should have training wheels on it."

"I'm sorry?"

I turn to Deep. "Show her your ID, Deep." Deep looks like he'd rather show her his upper colon, but he reaches for his wallet after I give him a covert punch back.

Maddysin takes his driver's licence and Social Security card like she is picking up a live bomb.

"I have to talk to my manager," she says, and disappears through a door that pops out from the wall of guns, like one of those secret passageways through a bookshelf. She makes sure to take the gun and the box of ammo with her.

"What the hell is going on?" I say to no one in particular.

"I reckon I know," Deep says with a sigh, returning to the toy bin behind us. He pulls out an NRA-themed version of Monopoly and starts reading the back of the box, possibly in search of further ironies.

"When Maddysin comes back through the wall, she has her manager, *Hi, My name is Bob* with her. He is considerably older, and obviously had parents who knew how to spell. Deep drops the board game back in the bin and joins me at the display case again. The salt-and-pepper lady has left and is now browsing the household items section several yards away, looking at the plastic six shooters that squirt ketchup and mustard.

"So, you'd like to buy a gun," Bob says.

"Yes," Deep says. Even though we both know he doesn't.

"Well, if you would just fill out this form," Bob says, producing a six-page epic poem of boxes and fine print. "We'd be happy to submit it on your behalf. You should be able to pick up the gun in three days." Maddysin stands beside him, looking everywhere but at Deep and me. When Bob lightly elbows her, she produces a pen.

"I don't think I understand," I say, although I am beginning to. "Maddysin here was ready to pack this gun up for me to take home today, and all of a sudden we got to wait three days?"

"Yes," Bob says. "Well, as I'm sure you're aware, a NICS background check is required to purchase a firearm," Bob says.

"Of course I am. But a NICS check takes three minutes, not three days. The fucking *I* stands for instant." I know my state gun laws, and this is bullshit.

"Our computer is down," Bob says, lying his nametag ass off, then adds, "Is your friend a U.S. citizen?"

"Of course, he's a U.S. citizen!" Deep had told me this earlier. He has dual citizenship, half Brit, half Yank. "But he doesn't have to be a U.S. citizen to buy a gun in this state, and you know it."

"You do realize I'm standing right here," Deep says, but both Bob and I ignore him.

"There's no need to get irate, ma'am."

I look around the gun store, see all the people at the cash, buying pistols and shotguns despite supposed computer glitches.

"You're a licenced dealer. You can sell the M&P to him while you wait for the approval."

"At our discretion," Bob says.

"And I suppose your discretion gets a little selective when it comes to brown skin."

"Let's just leave, Candace," Deep says.

"What's going on?" Janet asks, coming up on the other side of me, owl glasses back in place, her cornea saved from bees. Behind her, I see two store security guys bursting the seams of their wannabe cop uniforms, making their own beeline towards us.

"I'm not sure what you're implying ma'am, but we —"

"Screw this," I say before I storm away from the counter, losing myself in the tangle of shoppers that has surrounded a store employee standing on a platform. He's demonstrating the proper cleaning technique of an M16.

Deep and Janet join me back at the car with two toasted almond bars they bought from a guy roaming the parking lot on his Good Humor ice cream bicycle.

I'd have thought a guy like that would have packed it in for the winter, but the warm weather we've been having must have made him dust off his fudge bars.

"I can't believe that fucking asshole wouldn't sell you a gun," I say, still fuming.

"I can't believe that fucking asshole called you ma'am," Deep says.

We get back in the Celica without saying anything further on the subject. Janet, sensing the tension, pops in her earbuds and starts listening to music I can't hear.

We've been back on the highway for a quarter of an hour before anyone speaks. And it's Deep who breaks the silence.

"I told you I didn't want to go in there," he says.

"How did I know they would be a bunch of racist pricks?" I say.

"How did you know they wouldn't be, Candace?"

"Oh, c'mon, Deep. I know some people are assholes, but not everyone gives a shit about stuff like that." Although, living above the E-Zee Market run by Majd these last few years has taught me how many people actually fall into the shitty asshole category. This includes the lowlife who tossed a Molotov cocktail through the store window one night, shouting crap about ISIS. I guess he hadn't gotten the memo that those bastards killed half of Majd's family back in Syria.

"You know I went to MIT, right?" Deep says.

"Yeah, what does that have to do with anything?"

"Where do you think most graduates of MIT go after graduating in the top one percent of their class, Candace?"

"I don't know." But I do.

"NASA, Candace. Or the CIA." He turns on the windshield wipers. It's starting to rain. Though in December it should be switching to snow. "But for some reason, neither of those government agencies would hire me."

"There're lots of people of colour at NASA. Didn't you see that movie about those black chicks?"

"Bloody hell, Candace. It's not about colour. It's about ideology. And because a bunch of nutter extremists who look like me are screwing with the world, no one wants me anywhere near their state secrets, or even a train schedule for that matter."

"But those are Muslims, not Sikhs," Janet says from the back seat, one ear bud taken out. She'd been listening after all.

"It doesn't matter. It's all about optics," Deep says. "That's why I work behind the scenes, where I'm Hardy Bains with the English accent who people only talk to over the phone. I have to avoid background checks, too. As soon as they discover my dad was born in Kashmir, nobody returns my calls."

I can't say much in response to that. I can't pretend to know what it's like to be Deep, but I do know what it is to be judged unfairly. People always expected the worst from me, even before I did anything wrong.

Deep puts on the acid jazz we'd listened to before. Janet puts her earbuds back in. We don't talk anymore or even play I Spy. Eventually, I fall asleep in the passenger seat.

When I wake up, the rain still hasn't turned to snow. Now, though, it's coming down in sheets, making the lights of the city streets of Detroit blurry through the window. I can see an old cemetery coming up on the right, illuminated by floodlights that threaten to wake the dead. They must be worried about vandals. Tree-lined paths meander through the tombstones that range from Gothic overkill to Victorian creepy. A lower corner of the cemetery has flooded in the rain, and the gravestones are partially submerged. The tops of the stone markers rise up out of the water like the tips of grey fingers.

"Where are we?" I ask Deep after we've left the cemetery behind.

"Indian Village," he says.

I look out the window for a good Tandoori or maybe some place I can get samosas as awesome as Majd's. I haven't eaten since I had that strawberry protein shake at Deep's place. But all I see are residential streets with big old houses on them. Some look like they were built by the same stonemasons who did the cemetery. When we reach a more commercial strip, there are none of the sari shops and sweet paan joints I'm used to seeing in Little India back home. I ask Deep what kind of self-respecting Indian Village wouldn't have a decent kebab house. He points at a street sign as we pass it. Seminole. And the next one. Iroquois Avenue.

"Wrong kind of Indian," he says, checking his blind spot before changing lanes. His raglan-sleeve T-shirt exposes his strong forearms, held firmly at ten and two o'clock.

That's when I realize he'd taken his coat off and draped it over me when I was sleeping. No matter what village you find yourself in, that makes him the *right* kind of man.

CHAPTER 9

WE PULL INTO A MOTEL ON THE EDGE of Chandler Park in the East Village. A nice enough neighbourhood, but the place is a bit of a dive. Deep and Janet had wanted to stay at a 3-star not far away, but I need a place with direct access to the street from the rooms. If you get caught out in a hotel hallway, you might as well be at the wrong end of a shooting range with a bullseye stuck to your chest.

"You in town for the beatification?" the small Asian lady behind the check-in desk asks. She's from South Korea she'd told us, before, when Deep showed her his passport and she realized he, too, was born overseas. Although East London is a far cry from Seoul. South Korea is the good Korea, she said, just in case we might be confused and think Kim Jong-un was her uncle or something.

"What beatification?" Janet asks, taking her glasses off to rub at one tired looking eye. She's held up fairly well on this trip, but the whole thing with Angela missing must be taking its toll on her. I know it has on me.

"For Father Murphy," the little lady says, beaming. "It will be at the cathedral on Sunday afternoon. Only rich people get seats in the church, but they will have a big TV outside for the crowd to watch. After Father Murphy is venerated, they will make him a saint. First one in the United States!"

"I thought there were already some American saints," Deep says. "There was that nun."

"And the Mohawk chick," I add, remembering Indian Village.

"St. Tekakwitha!" Janet says. "I read about her. She was being forced to marry some warrior she didn't like, and she ran away and became a Catholic instead."

"Aren't they all being forced to marry some warrior they didn't like in those legends?" I say. "It's like every story about a Native American princess involves jumping off a waterfall to avoid a shotgun wedding."

"Except this one jumped into a baptismal font," Deep says, chuckling.

"This is not the same!" the South Korean lady shouts, interrupting our banter. That's okay. I'm not big on debating the damsel motif. If you don't want to marry a guy, then chuck him in the goddamn waterfall yourself.

"Father Murphy is a *man*," she continues. "Those other saints. All women. This could be first man saint. From right here in Detroit."

This is somehow different for the lady behind the counter. I want to point out that even if this Father Murphy makes it into the Catholic canon big time, it's still three-to-one for the ladies in the saint department here in the U.S. Maybe there's a reason men don't get remembered for their miracles, while women sing with the angels. But what do I know? I had my wings clipped a long time ago.

Deep pays for two rooms with his credit card. I feel bad about that. I don't like handouts, but I don't have the scratch for this place. After all, it wasn't my decision to bring these two with me. If I were on my own, I'd have found an abandoned building to sleep in and left it at that. Detroit's got more of those than it has motels since the downturn.

Our rooms are adjoining. After we've ordered a party-sized pizza, Janet goes for a shower. I've been listening to the steady stream of water for ages now, flopped out on one of the two twin beds. Five more minutes and she'll have used up all the hot water in the motel, and if the pizza hasn't come by then, it'll be free. I knock on the flimsy door shared between Deep's room and ours. There's a bit of shuffling inside before he opens it.

"Sorry," he says. "I was just sorting out some of my equipment."

Some equipment appears to be almost the entire set-up from his living room back home. He hasn't brought all the disemboweled hard drives that he mines for spare parts, but just about everything else sits on the dresser opposite the two double beds. He's moved the motel-issued widescreen TV onto an armchair in the corner to make room for it all. Two extra laptops are stacked on the floor.

"How are you going to do anything with this?" I ask. "The motel doesn't even have Wi-Fi."

"There's no guest Wi-Fi. But I noticed the lady at reception had a password protected one. She was using it to play online Boggle when we came in."

"How did you figure out the password," I ask. "Some fancy hacker algorithm?"

"More than twenty-three million users have the password 123456, Candace. A few more million actually use the word *password*. People aren't too hard to figure out."

"What was her password?" I ask.

"Murphy," he says. "The almost-saint. I cracked it on the third try." He leans over to connect a cable behind the monitor that replaced the TV. He's wearing a pair of faded jeans rather than the chinos he had on when we met, but they still fit in all the right places. A person can see why I agreed to go home with him the night of the Murder Ink presentation. Even after a few drinks, I can recognize a superior cut of beefcake when I see it.

"What's the plan?" he asks once the cable is re-attached. He's sitting on the bed opposite me now, using a tiny screwdriver on a motherboard.

"I figure we'll eat the pizza and get some shut-eye," I say. "I'm fucking beat." The nap in the car was not enough to make up for my ravine sleep under the stars last night.

"I meant tomorrow," Deep says. "How do you plan on looking for Angela?"

"Well, I suppose I have to start where she was last seen. Chez fucking Scarpello."

Deep puts down the screwdriver but leaves the motherboard on his lap.

"What are you going to do, waltz right in there and ask for her?"

"I haven't figured that part out yet."

"Wouldn't that be just a little bloody suicidal?"

"Not if you do it right," I say. "You've heard that thing about keeping your friends close, but your enemies closer?"

"Sure, but wasn't that phrase coined by a bloke who eventually got his head blown off by an enemy?"

"Very funny," I say. "But if I start digging around elsewhere, it'll get back to them. And that wouldn't be considered going through the proper channels. The Mob is all about respect."

"The Mob is all about putting people into concrete galoshes and dumping them in the river," Deep says.

"You watched all the *Godfather* movies, didn't you?" I say.

Deep nods and puts the motherboard down on the bed. "Even the third one."

"I just have to find an *in*," I say, thinking how that third Corleone flick really was a disappointment. "A way to introduce myself."

"How are you going to manage that?"

"Like I said, I'm still thinking about it."

Deep returns to fixing the motherboard. "What about the Catholic thing?" he asks after a little while.

"The Catholic thing?"

"You heard the lady at the front desk telling us about the beatification. Catholics will be turning out in droves for that. Alex's mother, Anya Scarpello, is known for being very devout. She attends almost every Mass they have at St. Clare's Catholic Church."

"You really are serious about your research, aren't you?"

"I am when daft people like Murder Ink are footing the bill."

"Still, I can't believe you know the church my great-aunt goes to."

"Everybody knows that church, Candace. It's been serving Sicilians in Detroit for over a hundred years."

"Anya's Russian."

"She's still a Scarpello. And probably the most innocuous one for you to try and chat up for information about Angela." Deep puts the motherboard down again and stands up from the bed. He types at the keyboard in front of the monitor, moves the mouse around. The website for St. Clare's Roman Catholic Church flashes up on the screen.

"It says here there's a Mass at seven thirty a.m. tomorrow," Deep says.

"Shit, is God even awake at that time?" I go over to the mini bar and grab a few mini bottles to replenish my flask. This fleabag may not have toilets with lids on them, but it has enough booze in tiny plastic bottles to stock The Goon at happy hour.

"It would be a smart way to get access to Anya Scarpello and make it look casual," Deep says. "Maybe she can tell you where Angela is, and you'll never even have to deal with the rest of the Scarpellos."

"Yeah, I guess so," I say, thinking it will probably not be that easy. But Deep is right. The mother of the current Don would probably be the least lethal member of the family I could connect with initially. The mini bottle of Jack Daniel's I'm trying to pour into my flask starts to

spill down the sides. I could really use a funnel. I wonder if Deep has one in his bag of tricks.

"We *are* looking for Angela here, aren't we, Candace?
Not just trying to find her son so you can somehow gain
from it?" So, he's figured out that angle the same as me.

"Do those two things have to be mutually fucking
exclusive?"

"They might be for that thirteen-year-old girl in the
other room. She looks up to you, Candace, you do realize that?"

"If you're telling me to be a good example, I think that
bird has flown," I say, licking the spilled Jack Daniel's off
my fingers.

"It's never too late, Candace. To do things a new way."

"You get that from a fortune cookie or something?"

"Pinterest."

"Hmm," I say. But I've had enough of this discussion.
I get up and make my way toward the adjoining door
with my refilled flask.

"Well, if you're finished spouting social media wisdom, why don't you set your alarm to wake me at six
thirty so I can go check out this Mass or whatever."

Deep smiles. "You like my idea."

"It's half decent."

"I think I should go with you."

"No way, Deep."

"Do you know anything about how to conduct yourself at a Catholic Mass, Candace?"

I stop and think. There's only one time I was inside
a church, and that was to scout out a preacher who
thought heroin was one of the sacraments.

"I studied world religions as an elective at university. Just let me come and show you the ropes. So you don't make a balls of it in front of Anya."

"I'll think about it," I say.

"I'm concerned about you, Candace. I know the Scarpellos are your family, but ..." Deep walks over to me, so close I can smell his aftershave. Paco Rabanne, if I'm not mistaken. He must have just shaved. I tilt my head and one long spiral of hair falls across my face. Deep reaches out to brush it out of the way, but I step away quickly before he can.

"Fine, you can come to the church, to help me with this Catholic stuff. But after that, I'm the lone wolf, you understand?" I look out the window, see the pizza delivery guy pull up in the rain. I turn to Deep. "Besides, I need you to look into this birth registry thing. See if you can find out anything about my twin brother."

"That information might have gotten your mother killed," Deep says. "What makes you think you won't end up the same?"

"Jesus, Deep, I'm not exactly a newbie when it comes to handling myself." This concern for my well-being is getting old. Worrying about me in a dangerous situation is like worrying a saltwater crocodile is going to cut itself on its own teeth. "The Scarpellos know there's no love lost between Angela and me. That we haven't had contact in years. As far as they're concerned, I don't know anything about her having a son. I can play a convincing dumb when I have to."

"Somehow, I doubt that."

I open the outer door to the pizza man before the skinny guy shivering in the rain has a chance to knock.

"Nineteen dollars and fifty-three cents," he says.

"It's been over thirty minutes," I say. I grab the pizza and brown bag of canned soda out of his hands. "It's free."

After I slam the door, the delivery guy knocks a few more times. Deep tries to pay, but I won't let him. "Thirty minutes or free," I tell him, blocking the door. "I may not know much about religion but that's like one of the ten commandments of take-out delivery."

Deep shakes his head and goes to the bathroom to wash his hands before dinner.

I fetch some ice from the motel lobby and check my phone. Charlotte hasn't returned my call. She must be out on the water with her fisherman husband. She tells me they can't get a signal out in the bay. I don't want to leave another message or she'll completely panic. I fill the plastic bucket under the distrustful eyes of the lady at reception. I don't think she's forgiven me for suggesting that American women were winning in the saint department. After dodging cold rain as I run through the parking lot, I join Deep and Janet back in the motel room. Deep has been busy filling my sister in on our plans for the next day.

"I want to come, too," Janet says, grabbing another piece of greasy pizza from the box. She peels a couple of slices of ham off the lid, where they were stuck, and adds them on top before taking a bite. "She's Mom's aunt. I want to meet her."

"This isn't a family picnic, Janet," I say, grabbing a piece of pizza for myself from the half without pine-apple. Janet had insisted on this tropical fruit topping that really has no damn business being on a pizza. She says everyone in Canada eats it this way. They call it a Hawaiian, which I figure must be the farthest thing from Canada a person could possibly think of.

"Deep's going, so I'm going, too," she says, taking a fierce bite out of her slice. "You can't stop me." I realize that I probably can't, but I can lay some ground rules.

"Fine," I say. "But you've got to let me handle things." I give a warning look to both her and Deep. "If I make con-tact with Anya Scarpello, the two of you have to back off."

"Why?" Janet asks. "She's my family, too."

"This isn't up for fucking debate, Janet. Either keep to the background, or I'll handcuff you to the motel mini bar." This wouldn't be a bad idea, I think, but unfortu-nately I didn't bring handcuffs.

"Fine," she says, furiously detonating her can of Coke. The brown fizz spews down the sides, and she has to run to the bathroom to keep it from going all over the already stained rug.

"I hope you know what you're doing," Deep says, sip-ping on his ginger ale.

"I do," I say. "Just make sure you keep the kid out of my way."

"I'll do my best," he says. "But she tends to have a mind of her own." He closes the box of pizza, trying to keep it warm. "She reminds me of someone that way."

After the pizza and a few rerun episodes of predictable sitcoms on TV, we all hit the sack in anticipation of the early wakeup call for Mass. Janet and I lie under the covers of our respective twin beds with the lights off. A large billboard advertising the Detroit Pistons blazes from between the cheap venetian blinds. It gives the room a murky glow that you can pretend is moonlight if you ignore the fact that it's electric blue. Like a kid from *The Waltons*, Janet calls out to me from the other bed.

"Candace, are you awake?"

"You realize that's a dumb question, right? If I wasn't awake, I really wouldn't be able to tell you."

She's quiet for a while after that, but I can hear her restlessly shifting under the stiff sheets.

"You are going to find Mom, right, Candace?"

"I'll do what I can," I say.

"I mean, it's not just about finding out about our brother, right? You're not just here to try and, you know, take advantage of that?"

"No," I say, although I'd like to point out to her that this is probably what Angela came to Detroit to do in the first place.

"Because I really appreciate you saving me from Social Services and everything. And I know she wasn't that great to you, our mother." Her voice waivers a little, becomes all of the thirteen-year-old girl that she is. "But I really need my mom."

"I know," I say, thinking about what Linda had said, about how sometimes having someone who isn't perfect is better than having nobody at all. I am about as not-perfect as they come. But right now, I'm all Janet's got when it comes to finding Angela. Deep is right. She is looking to me for guidance or salvation or I don't know what else. I roll over in the bed and try not to think about it. The weight of a thirteen-year-old's trust is not something I'm used to carrying.

Because I *am* looking to take advantage of what a brother might net me in the Scarpello fold, as much as I hope to find Angela for my little sister in the process. I am what I am. A woman used to finding the angles, out for my own gain. It's hard to change those kinds of well-worn stripes. If Deep says I need to set an example for Janet, well then maybe that's it. That everyone's got their own agenda. My little sister might as well learn that now. I sure as hell learned it from a young age.

"Are you afraid?" Janet asks me.

"Of what?" I say.

"Of the Scarpellos."

"They're family, Janet. Don't worry. Everything will be okay."

I don't know whether it's the guilt over my not-so-hidden agenda or that last bit of our conversation that keeps me awake long after Janet's soft snoring tells me she's asleep. After about an hour of tossing and turning, I get up and go to the adjoining door. Through the open crack, I can see the glow of the computer monitor. I open the door and find Deep asleep on top of the bedspread, his hair in a tumble on the pillow, just like that first morning when I woke up beside him.

I pad my way over to the monitor to see what he's been up to. On the screen are crime-scene photos. I scroll through them, each one more grisly than the next. I've seen a lot of dead bodies in my time, but there are good and bad ways to die, and every one of the people in these photos had a really bad death. Probably preceded by some serious torture and other sick-fuck stuff that makes the undigested pizza in my belly want to move back up where it came from. It takes a lot of carnage to produce acid reflux in someone as desensitized to violence as myself.

Every bad death in those pictures is the work of the Scarpellos. My blood. My inherited murderous genetic code.

The family I never had.

CHAPTER 10

ST. CLARE'S CATHOLIC CHURCH isn't much to look at from the outside, and it's dwarfed by a large stuccoed apartment building that rises up behind it. Even without that for comparison, it's a lot smaller than I would have thought, with narrow windows and a third-rate night club awning over the front door. The two tiers of the church are topped with a skinny bell tower painted a yellowy beige, piped with white around the windows and eaves. It looks like a wedding cake made out of crème brûlée. You wouldn't think I'd have much experience with fancy desserts, but Dad liked to blow his cash at upscale restaurants when he was flush. I've seen my fair share of prix fixe.

"It doesn't look like a Mob church," I say.

"It's not a Mob church, Candace," Deep says, getting annoyed with me. "It was founded by hard-working Sicilian immigrants who came to this country for a better life. The vast number of Sicilians are upstanding citizens, you know."

"Like me?"

"Last time I checked, you weren't one of their regular parishioners."

I let out a sigh. I really do work better alone. "Maybe you two should stay out here in the car."

"How am I supposed to school you in all things Catholic from out here?" Deep asks.

"I'm not an idiot, Deep. I'm not going to start washing my pits with the holy water or something."

"If you're going to fool Anya Scarpello into thinking you're here for the beatification, you'll have to make it convincing. Do you understand about taking Communion?"

"You got to eat and drink stuff. How hard can it be?"

"It's a little more than that."

"You're not in a state of grace," Janet says from the back seat.

"What?"

"You can't take Communion if you're not in a state of grace. You're supposed to have fasted beforehand and been to confession recently. Mom told me that. It's why she said she didn't go to Mass anymore."

"Because she didn't want to go to confession?" I ask.

"Because she liked to eat breakfast."

"You can't take confession in a Catholic church if you're not baptized a Catholic," Deep says.

"How are they supposed to know if you are or not?"

"They don't."

"I won't tell if you won't."

"That just might be sacrilegious."

"I'm going to Mass at seven thirty in the morning with the express purpose of infiltrating my Mafia family, and I've got a gun down my pants. I think if I'm going to get hit with a lightning bolt, it would have happened by now."

One of the heavy black front doors opens, and a bald priest steps out onto the sidewalk. He unlocks a glass-encased bulletin board beside the front entrance. After taking down a few older notices, he tacks up a new one. I can't read it from here, but it's got way too many colours and fonts going on. He looks up and down the street but doesn't seem to notice us. He's focused on two little old ladies bent over their walkers. They're making their way from the nearby apartment building, moving along the sidewalk like glaciers. He waits awhile, perhaps thinking he'll hold the door, but one of them has to sit down and take a rest on a bench, so he heads back inside. When the door closes, it almost catches on his long black robe, but he tugs it out of the way just in time.

"Okay," I say. "Let's go."

We get out of the car and make our way toward the church. At the front door, I check out the poster that the priest tacked up. It's advertising something called a "Mass Mob."

"I thought you said this wasn't a Mob church," I say to Deep, pointing at the poster.

"It's supposed to be a play on words for Flash Mob," he says. "They use social media to try and attract a younger audience. I read about it online."

I check out the two old ladies, who are both now sitting on the bench, their pantyhose bagging at the ankles above their orthopedic shoes.

"I don't think it's working," I say, opening the door.

Inside, it's fairly dark, and it takes a minute for my eyes to adjust. We're standing in a foyer of sorts. It smells like lemon wood polish and dusty upholstery. There's an archway to the business end of things, or the sanctuary, as Deep explains to Janet. He steps up to a little stone recess in the wall and dips his two fingers into the water there, then makes the sign of the cross on his forehead. Janet does the same. They both then stand and wait for me.

"You two go inside first," I say. "I don't want it to look like we're together."

Deep rolls his eyes at me before he turns and leads Janet through the archway. I see him drop to one knee in the aisle before taking a seat in one of the dark varnished pews. My sister follows suit. Christ on the Cross hangs front and centre above a raised platform, the blood streaming down His face from a nasty-looking crown of thorns. I don't know whether it's this that sends a shudder down my spine, or the idea that I am purposely trying to make contact with a family that may have killed the woman who gave birth to me. The brass pendulum of an old clock swings back and forth on the wall. The incessant ticking sounds like a bomb counting down.

I dip my fingers in the holy water and tap it on my unbelieving forehead before going in and taking a seat in the pew directly behind Deep and Janet.

In this situation, I can use all the help I can get.

I managed to get through Mass without making a total ass of myself. It's not that hard. All you have to do to fit in is mumble the words everyone else knows off by heart and stand up at the right places. I followed along with what Deep and all the others were doing. In that way, it *is* a bit like a flash mob.

I didn't end up going up for the Communion thing. The way the priest was looking at me, I thought for sure he knew I wasn't a baptized Catholic. I don't know if they have a bouncer for that sort of thing, but the altar boy had this long, heavy brass candle snifter that I imagine could give a person a serious clock to the head. So, when they were handing out the bread and wine, I stayed put like Deep and Janet and acted like I was praying. Which I sort of was, in my own way.

It looks like the whole Anya Scarpello thing is a bust, though. She never made an appearance, and the Mass is over now. Deep and Janet have already gone to shake hands with the priest, who stands at the archway as the trickle of attendees file their way out. I wait awhile, flipping through the leather-clad Bible in front of me. I don't want to be seen leaving with them. I'm standing up to go when the priest comes over, heading me off at the pew.

"I haven't seen you at St. Clare's before," he says. "Welcome. I'm Father Randolph."

"I'm Candace Starr," I say, shaking his hand, surprised that I've just used my real name. Maybe he's caught me off guard, or maybe I'm a victim of the Catholic guilt that seems to permeate this place, acting like some kind of truth serum.

"I'm just visiting," I say, explaining myself. His smile falters a little. I guess he was hoping I was one of the people under the age of seventy he'd attracted with his Twitter account. "I'm in town for the beatification."

"Ah, Detroit's own Father Murphy," he says.

"Yes." I'm not sure what to add to this. Where the hell is Deep when I need him to provide me with some Catholic 101.

"I noticed you didn't partake of the sacraments," Father Randolph says, raising a shaggy grey eyebrow. He's got a lot of hair happening on his face for a bald man. I can see a few swinging from his nostrils, as well.

"I'm not in a state of grace," I say, remembering what Janet told me.

"Well, I have a few minutes. I can take your confession if you'd like."

I look over his shoulder, hoping to find a way out of this predicament. I'd rather do just about anything than crawl into one of those creepy boxes at the back of the church where the priest listens to all your faith-based fuck-ups. My sins would take longer than a few minutes to confess. Deep and Janet have disappeared, either waiting in the foyer or back at the car by now. I'm about to make my excuses when a woman enters through the archway. She's got a three-quarter-length fur coat that easily cost more than Deep's car. She's also got two goons flanking her, both wearing shiny suit jackets that barely button up over their barrel chests. She leaves them to stand guard by the confessionals and walks up behind the priest, politely clearing her throat. Father Randolph turns around and then walks up and kisses her on both cheeks.

"Anya," he says. "I thought we had missed you today."

"I am so sorry, Father. I was delayed by a family matter. My son ..." She flits her delicate hand in the air but gives no further details. I'm quite sure that Father Randolph knows the type of family matters her son is responsible for, but he doesn't let on. Anya Scarpello looks even better kept in person than she did in the photo at the old Don's funeral — hardly a line on her face, her upswept dark hair not showing a hint of grey. A small mole dots her lower left cheek, marking her for beauty, just like Marilyn Monroe. Here's a woman I should be asking about eye cream. She looks past the priest to me, waiting for an introduction.

"This is Miss Starr," the priest says. "She is in town for the beatification of Father Murphy. This is Anya Scarpello, one of our most esteemed parishioners." By esteemed, I assume he means loaded. The amount of Anya Scarpello's offering plate donations would be followed by a lot more zeros than the old ladies in their support hose.

Anya extends one well-manicured hand. "Starr?" she says. "Are you any relation to Mike Starr?"

"He was my father," I say as we shake hands. I feel the slightest tension enter her long fingers before she let's go.

"I see," she says, then turns back to the priest. "Father Randolph. I wonder if you could find me the contact details of the caterer we used for the Communion brunch?"

"Certainly, Anya. I can forward you a link to their website this afternoon." This really is one tech-savvy priest. Or maybe they are all like this. After all, the pope is on Instagram. I hear God even has a Twitter account.

Anya smiles, but I notice her eyes don't. "I hoped you could get it for me now, Father," she says, placing a hand lightly on his upper arm. "You see, I would like to hire them for a small fundraiser," she says, "to benefit the church building fund."

That gets a fire under his cassock. Father Randolph excuses himself and races down the aisle to go get the catering brochure from his office.

Once he's out of earshot, which is where she wanted him, Anya fixes her gaze on me. She has the piercing dark eyes shared by many Eastern Europeans, eyes that tend toward a default look of mistrust. Probably comes from never knowing when your neighbour was going to rat on you to the KGB out of spite. I don't back down from her staring contest, but I also keep tabs on the goons in my periphery. For now, they aren't moving from their stations.

"Your mother did not say you were coming," Anya finally says, breaking the tension. I guess we're not pretending Angela and the Scarpellos haven't seen each other, then. Maybe she's alive after all.

"I haven't talked to my mother in almost thirty years," I tell her. "But it sounds like you have."

She nods, slowly and with assessment. "She came recently to visit with my father-in-law, before his death."

"My condolences."

"He was your great-grandfather," Anya says. "Did you know of his passing?"

"I don't live locally," I say, feigning ignorance.

"It is a shame when family lose track of one another," she says with a sigh, and I see a tiredness behind those penetrating eyes. "Your mother and I were close once. When I was first married. Friends as well as family. But we lost touch."

Friends? I didn't think my mother went in for friendship — much like myself. But maybe Anya had been the exception to that rule. My mother's very own Malone. This woman has way more class and dignity than Angela ever possessed, but there is still something broken about her. Maybe that's what brought them together. Come to think of it, the two of them are probably around the same age, given that Anya was married off young to Angela's much older uncle.

"So, you are in town for the beatification? I didn't realize you were raised in the faith."

"I found religion in prison," I tell her. I'd made up this lie beforehand. The only religion I found in prison was the Church of the Immaculate Appeal.

She nods again but stays silent. This is another trait I've noticed in people who have lived behind the Iron Curtain: their economy of words. Or maybe she's clammed up because the priest has re-entered the sanctuary, holding the catering brochure in his hand. He hands it to Anya, practically salivating over the prospect of a building fundraiser hosted by someone with her connections. You really can't blame the guy. He's not greedy, just desperate. I'd noticed the cracked shingles on the roof of this place, the damp around the windows. St. Clare's is clearly strapped for cash, struggling to keep this monument to the man upstairs from falling down around them. This priest would probably auction his own soul just to get a new furnace.

"I'd be happy to administer a private Mass for you, Anya. Since you missed this morning's," he says. "I only need to take this young lady's confession first if you would like to wait in my office."

"That's okay," I say, looking to wriggle free. "I wouldn't want to make anybody wait."

"Please, do not concern yourself with me," Anya says. I have another engagement to attend. I will come this afternoon, Father. Around threeish?" Anya must be in one hell of a state of grace to have the resident priest at St. Clare's on Mass-standby.

"That would be fine," Father Randolph says before kissing her hand goodbye. For a celibate guy, he does a lot of smooching. He takes my arm and leads me over to the confessional boxes. The two goons move over by the archway, either out of respect or because they're expecting Anya to leave. But I see she hasn't moved from where I left her in the aisle. She's still gazing up at the bloody Jesus when the priest shuts the door on me in the wooden box.

I don't buy this "Seal of the Confessional" garbage, where the priest has to keep mum on whatever you tell him. Although I know quite a few felons who have counted on it. But I'm not about to give up my criminal resumé to anyone, even if they put me in a box. I've withstood tougher interrogation techniques than that. So I stick to my sexual history in the sin department, figuring I'll give the old guy a thrill. After about five minutes,

I can hear Father Randolph start to hyperventilate on the other side of the privacy screen. I take this as an opportunity to make my exit. He doesn't come after me, probably still trying to catch his breath after my story of fucking a bounty hunter on a cluttered desk in The Goon's back office. I'd had to use nail polish remover to get the Liquid Paper off of my ass the next day.

Outside, I shield my eyes from the bright morning sun, my pupils still adjusting after the twilight of the dark confessional. Deep's Celica is gone. But a black Caddy pulls up from where it was waiting down the street. The tinted back-seat window powers down and Anya Scarpello extends her hand out to me. Between her slim fingers she holds a small embossed card. I take it from her and read the name and address. I didn't know Mafia mothers had their own business cards.

"You will join us for dinner this evening, Candace?" she asks, lilting it to be a question when really it's a statement I'm not meant to dispute. "My son, Alex, will be interested to meet you. Family should not be strangers to one another, I think." She's wearing big starlet sunglasses, hiding her eyes so I can't really tell what she thinks.

I nod. It is my turn to be short on words.

"I am so glad. I look forward to discussing the beatification with you. Please come at eight. We prefer to dine late." She motions to the driver, and the Caddy pulls away. I'm left standing on the street with only the two old ladies sitting on the bench as witnesses. They'd made it to Mass but are now taking a rest for the long trip back home.

This is what I'd wanted, a way into the Scarpello inner circle, but I'd imagined it would be a covert one, not an upfront invitation. Anya Scarpello seemed genuine enough with her talk of family and strangers, but like I said, I couldn't see her eyes. And while she'd mentioned seeing Angela, she didn't give anything away as to where she is. Maybe I'll find her sitting at the dining room table, waiting to greet me, with some simple explanation for why she hasn't messaged Janet their code word, *slalom*. Perhaps Anya is hoping for a teary reconciliation between the two of us, like they do on daytime TV. But I'm not one for tears.

I'm not one for traps, either. Even though I realize I may be about to walk right into one.

CHAPTER 11

IT TURNS OUT DEEP WAS PARKED around the corner, watching my whole Anya Scarpello encounter go down from behind a dumpster. Dumpsters are rampant in Detroit. Despite the mayor's call to rebuild, they seem to be tearing everything down. Skids covered in demolition dust are as common as streetlights. Which I understand the city didn't have enough scratch to turn on for a while.

After Deep picks me up, I fill them both in on meeting Anya, show them the card I was given. Janet is anxious for details of Angela, but other than what we already know, I don't have much to tell her. She sulks about it while we eat all-day breakfasts at a diner named after a hot dog or an island in NYC, depending on how you look at it. Denny's was too far downriver. Deep offers to take her to an art store to pick up supplies, and that seems to cheer her up a bit. Now she'll have a whole new selection of coloured pencils to draw nasty caricatures of me.

When we get back to the hotel, I go for an afternoon nap. I'm not used to such early mornings, and I'm now two nights of ugly without much beauty sleep. I surprise myself by not waking up until almost five o'clock. The sky has turned a steely grey outside the motel window — more rain, as well as dusk on its way. We're almost at the shortest day of the year after all.

Janet is propped up in her bed, watching Netflix on her iPhone with earbuds in. She doesn't look up when I stumble into the bathroom and switch on the light, too involved with the latest season of *Orange Is the New Black*. That show is such a heap of shit. Or maybe I'm just jealous I didn't think of writing a memoir about my own incarceration for fame and profit. That Piper Kerman is living large now. But then again, she was never a real criminal, not by my exacting standards, at least.

When I look in the motel bathroom mirror, I find a crease running down the side of my cheek, left there by the seam of the motel bedspread. There are swollen bags almost the size of Deep's matching luggage under my eyes. This is the problem with beauty sleep, too much of it can sometimes have the reverse effect. I try taming my bedhead hair into a messy bun, heavy on the mess, and splash my face, but I'm going to need more than this to look presentable for my dinner with the Scarpellos. I figure some ice under my eyes will take the sleepy swelling down. I've used Preparation H for the purpose in the past. A girl who dehydrates herself with as much alcohol as I do doesn't get this far without learning a few tricks. Unfortunately, I forgot to pack any, or maybe I just didn't want Deep to see a tube of 'roid cream in my bag.

After a quick shower, I come out of the bathroom to find Janet still glued to Netflix, but with a slice of pizza in her hand. They must have ordered in again. She waves at me with her free hand as I walk past. I open the door to Deep's adjoining room and close it behind me.

"I hope you didn't pay that guy for last night," I say, still towelling off my long hair. Deep turns around in the chair that he's set up in front of his huge monitor. The guilty look on his face tells me he has.

"I found a copy of the birth registration," he says, changing the subject, but also because this is probably more important than take-out. "It only lists a single birth, though."

"That would be me, I guess."

"Correct."

I drop the towel on Deep's crisply made bed. I know they don't have maid service here. These hospital corners are his doing. I lean over to pick up the ice bucket from where it sits on the bedside table next to an ancient alarm clock that actually flips over the numbers to tell time. Inside the bucket, there is only water, melted from the night before.

"So, I guess that's a dead end."

"I thought so, but then I ran the name of the doctor who signed off on it through a few databases," Deep says, turning back to the computer. "Dr. Stanley Razinski."

"And?"

"Well, it seems a bit dodgy that he was the one to sign off on the birth."

"Why?" I ask, coming to stand behind Deep with my bucket. But I can't garner any info from the screen. It's not all ones and zeroes, but it's close enough to be indecipherable to a mere mortal like me.

"Because he's an endocrinologist."

"That's glands and stuff, right?"

"Yes," Deep says. "And the hormones they produce." He brings up a photo on the monitor of a serious-looking man with a grey beard surrounded by beaming middle-aged women in caftans. "He's mostly retired now, but I found a retreat facility that he heads up for menopausal women with mood issues. It's some sort of in-patient clinic. He has a whole foundation for it."

I remember when Charlotte was going through the change. Mood issues is the polite term for when a woman starts crying over the washing machine because the Tide ran out.

"Where's the retreat?" I ask. I put the bucket down on the floor and lean over, squinting at the screen. I'm thinking it might be a good idea to pay this doctor a visit. Ask him why my twin brother didn't make the cut for birth registration sign off. As I bend down, some of my wet hair falls over into Deep's lap. It's either that or the closeness of my freshly washed skin that makes him antsy. He gets up out of the chair and grabs a piece of pizza from the box on the windowsill.

"That's the problem," he says, taking a napkin to go with his slice. "I can't seem to locate the clinic. They have a website, but they're cagey about the location. A bid to protect the privacy of their clients, I reckon. I've looked everywhere I can think of — tax records, land registrations. I can't find it. But I did find some interesting information in his foundation finances. Guess who his biggest contributor is?"

"Who?"

"Anya Scarpello."

That *is* interesting. Although, Anya is the same age as Charlotte was when she started crying over laundry detergent. Maybe the doctor helped her out.

"I still don't get what a guy who specializes in jacking women up on estrogen cocktails would be doing delivering babies."

"I wondered that myself. But it seems back in the eighties when you were born that wasn't his specialty."

"What was it?" I ask.

"Fertility."

"Jesus, Deep, Angela was eighteen when she got pregnant. That's not an age when most women need a petri dish to procreate."

"Maybe, but those kinds of interventions often result in multiple births."

"I really don't think she had any problem with getting knocked up, Deep."

"Anya Scarpello had problems," Deep says, polishing off his slice. "I ran across that in my research for Murder Ink. Maybe your mother and her used the same doctor to achieve both their pregnancies."

"I don't know, Deep. It still seems strange."

"Maybe. But even if Angela didn't need help getting pregnant, it wouldn't be so unusual that Dr. Razinski delivered her baby. The Scarpellos, like most crime families, tend to keep a select group of physicians on the payroll."

"But Angela wasn't even talking to her family when I was born."

"Do you know that for sure?"

Angela had been tossed out on her ear when my dad got her pregnant. I'd been told the Scarpellos made it clear that if anyone associated with the family contacted her, they'd suffer the consequences. It was a full-on Italian shunning, at least until recently. But you never know — maybe the doc took pity on her.

"I guess it's possible," I admit. I'm not great at admitting things. On the rare occasions I took part in childhood party games, I usually chose the dare. The one time I picked truth it made me break out in hives.

Deep nods while munching on the pizza. "Oh shit," he says. "I'm sorry, did you want some?"

He gets up and holds the grease-stained box out to me. I see Janet has forced us to get fucking pineapple again.

"I have dinner plans," I say to him. "Remember?"

"About that Candace. Maybe —"

"We've already discussed this, Deep. We're not discussing it again."

Deep isn't too keen on me going behind enemy lines at the Scarpellos'. I'd pointed out to him that they're not the enemy, they're my relatives. But I suppose those two can sometimes be the same thing.

Deep sits back at his makeshift desk. He knows I'm not going to budge on my decision.

"I'll keep looking for the location of that retreat," he says. When he clicks on the mouse, he smears a little red tomato sauce on it, but he doesn't seem to notice.

I pick the bucket up off the floor. Those eye bags aren't going to get rid of themselves.

"I'm going to get some ice from the lobby."

Deep nods but doesn't look away from the monitor, sucked in by his latest search. He doesn't even seem to notice the cold air that blows into the room when I leave. Between him and Janet, I've got two zombies stuck to their screens now. I bet I could set up a cardboard cut-out of myself by the mini bar, and nobody would notice the difference.

As I cross the parking lot, I feel my wet hair start to go crunchy with the freezing effects of the falling temperature. It's still pretty warm during the day when the sun is out, but once that bright-yellow ball starts to go down for the night, you remember it's almost officially winter. By the time I reach the motel reception, I'm wishing I'd put on my leather jacket for this little trip. I close the door to the outside and look around the small lobby. The Korean lady must have gone in the back room to eat her dinner because she's not at her post. I can hear the sound of the evening news on the television, and the smell of freshly steamed rice with veggies wafts up and over the reception desk from her quarters out back. I'm almost finished filling my white plastic bucket with ice when I feel a vibration in the front pocket of my jeans. I put the bucket down on the linoleum and take my phone out, briefly snagging it on the gun wedged under my pants. I forgot my jacket but remembered to pack my trusty Ruger. A girl has her priorities.

"I got your message," Charlotte says when I answer. "Is everything okay? Is it something to do with the call from that detective? I've been so worried."

"Nothing to worry about, Charlotte," I say. "I've got everything under control."

The little South Korean lady peeks her head around the corner when she hears my voice. I give her a nod with the phone at my ear and raise the ice bucket to show her my intentions. She goes back to the news and her dinner.

"But what did Detective Malone want, Candace?" She's really worked up. She hasn't even asked me about her Christmas package yet.

I tell Charlotte about the corpse in the morgue. How they thought the dead body was Angela, but it wasn't. I don't tell her about my new sister and supposed twin brother. Or about me being in Detroit looking for Angela among the Scarpellos. If she'd been worried before, that news would send her right off the charts on the stress meter.

"That must have been hard," Charlotte says. "Thinking it was your mom."

"We weren't close, Charlotte. You know that."

"I know," she says. "But she's still the only family you have."

I think about how untrue that is, given the events of the past few days, but of course, Charlotte doesn't know about any of that. Or maybe she does.

"Did Uncle Rod ever say anything to you about how I was born?"

"I think you know full well how that happens, Candace."

That's my Aunt Charlotte, a real card.

"I don't mean that. I'm talking about my actual birth. Did Rod or my dad ever say anything about it?"

"Why are you asking about this?"

"Just humour me, okay?"

"Well, you know men don't talk about these things much. Especially men like your father and Rod."

It's true. The two of them had no trouble cutting a body up into pieces for easy disposal, but any discussion of my period and they'd collectively start looking for the exits.

"Your father was away for months on a job. He wasn't there for your mother's labour or most of the pregnancy. Angela wasn't very good at taking care of herself while he was away, I heard. I don't think she had the best pre-natal care. It was a difficult birth. It was a good thing it took place in a private clinic."

"How did she afford a private clinic?"

"Oh, she didn't pay for it. I remember that. Your father had been angry about that."

"Who paid for it?"

"Her people."

"The Scarpellos?"

"Yes, that's why your dad was so mad. He didn't want her to have anything to do with them. But she was close with one of them. An aunt, I think."

"Anya Scarpello?" I ask. Anya had said she and Angela were tight back in the day, not just family, but friends.

"Rod never told me her name," Charlotte says. But she arranged for everything. Really, honey, why all these questions now. Is there something —"

I disconnect the call with Charlotte in mid-sentence, drop the ice bucket to the linoleum floor. I'm not usually rude for no reason. At least not to Charlotte. But out the window of the motel I've just noticed a car pull into the back alleyway. It's the Chrysler with the tatty car bra. I drop down behind the motel check-in desk and crawl my way into the Korean lady's living room. She's sitting with a tray balanced on her lap, eating her dinner.

"Is there a back way out to the alley from here?" I ask her, still on all fours.

She blinks a couple of times before pointing in the direction of a hallway, then returns her gaze to the announcer on the TV giving details on the latest fake news. Because fake news is real news these days. She seems to have the same problem with screens as Deep and Janet.

When I reach the end of the hallway, I open the heavy fire door a crack and peek out into the alleyway, see the blonde head leaning on the headrest of the Chrysler parked to my left. The driver's window opens halfway, and a hand reaches out and flicks the ash off a cigarette onto the asphalt. There's no one else in the car. I do a quick scan of the area. There's no one on foot, either. The building bordering the other side of the alleyway is crumbling to the ground. There won't be any nosy neighbours to see me and call the cops. I pull out my gun and stay crouched down low until I'm at the open car window, where I stand up and train my Ruger on the temple of the blonde head.

"Get out of the fucking car."

The blonde head complies. A petite woman wearing an ugly Christmas sweater gets out of the car, cringing, her hands in the air. I close the driver's door and step in front of her. She looks up, takes in the full height of me. Her pale blue eyes are framed with spiky mascara lashes, clumped into multiple triangle points so sharp they could cut glass. I level the gun at her chest, smack between the antlers of the Rudolph the Red-Nosed Reindeer sewn on the front.

"Who are you, and why are you following me?" I ask.

"I'm a friend of your mother's," the pint-sized blonde says. Like that's going to endear her to me.

"Name?" I ask.

"Stacey Bunnaman," she says. The elusive Aunt Stacey. "I don't want any trouble. I was just worried about Janet." Her eyes plead with me through her pointed lashes.

I walk around to the front of the car, still keeping my gun on her. The licence plate is blue lettering on white, all right, but it says Ontario, not Michigan. I return to stand in front of Stacey, blocking her way out of the alleyway just in case she gets any ideas about legging it.

"If you were so worried about Janet, why did you take off?" I ask.

"I was worried about the police," she says. "I run a grow-op back in Canada. Jesus. Please, please don't shoot me."

"Pot is legal in Canada." I lower the gun a bit, aiming it at Rudolph's big red pom-pom nose now. "What do you care about the cops?"

"I didn't know what Angela had gotten herself into," Stacey says. "I can't afford to be associated with any-thing criminal. They take away your licence to sell can-nabis in Canada if you so much as jaywalk." Her arms start to slacken above her head a bit, like a sail in need of a good breeze.

"So, my mother left her kid with a drug dealer," I say, raising the gun again. Stacey's arms shoot back up to full mast.

"It's not drug dealing in Canada," she says, getting defensive. "It's like having a vineyard. I was only concerned about Janet, I swear." Big fat tears are forming at the corner of her eyes. One drops, and the black mascara runs like a dirty stream down her cheek. "Please, can I put my arms down?" she asks. "I've got a bum rotator cuff."

I nod and lower the gun a little, but I don't put it away.

"Pot's still a drug, even if it's legal," I say.

"It's better than having it get to young people through thugs and criminals," she says, wiping at her snotty nose now that her hands are no longer in the air. "Shit, no offence."

"None taken," I say. "But you still supply to addicts."

"We're not like that in Canada," she says.

"You have the highest fucking opioid use in the world," I say. Canadians are an anesthetized lot. That's probably what makes them so laid back and polite.

"Well, I'm not like that," Aunt Stacey says. She's more relaxed now but still hasn't taken her spiky lashed eyes off of the gun.

"Shit, it was you," I say. "The other night. At the side of the road."

"Yes," Stacey says, biting her lip. "I just wanted to talk to you. Find out what happened with Angela." She sniffles a little, pulling the snot back up into her nose, then wipes with the back of her hand at the melting mascara. "And you shot at me."

"You should know better than to creep up on people in the dark," I tell her.

"You could have killed me!" she says.

"If I was aiming to kill you, you'd already be dead."

Aunt Stacey swallows hard, thinking about that, starts fiddling with the silver *S* pendant around her neck.

"But how did you follow us here?" I can't believe this woman could have tailed me all the way to Detroit and I never picked up on it.

"I used the Find My Phone app on Janet's iPhone," she says. Technology, the ultimate tail. "Is she okay?"

"Yes," I say. "No thanks to you."

"Was it her?" she asks me. "The body in the morgue? Was it Angela?"

"No," I say. "It wasn't her."

"Oh." More fiddling with the silver-plated *S*.

"Where did Angela say she was going when she left Janet with you?"

"She said her grandfather was sick," Stacey says, dropping the pendant. "That she had to go see him. That's all I know."

Her eyes, now resembling the classic raccoon, shift off to the left, away from the gun. She could be looking to see if some crackhead in the crumbled building next door will come and rescue her, or she could have just lied to me. I raise the gun up to her chest again.

"What else did she say?"

"Nothing, I swear." But those raccoon eyes shift off to the left again.

"Tell me what else she said."

"I don't want any trouble," Aunt Stacey says, repeating her earlier mantra.

"You're going to be in a hell of lot of trouble if you don't tell me what you know."

"Your mother made me promise not to say anything," she snivels, a snot bubble inflating at one of her nostrils.

"And she promised she'd come back for my sister, but she didn't. So, fucking spill it." I take the safety off the gun. The loud click makes Stacey jump and Rudolph's pom-pom nose bounces in-between her small boobs.

"She called me," she says, her lower lip quivering.

"Who?"

"Angela," Stacey says. "About a week after she left."

"I'm listening."

"She said her grandfather told her something. About her son."

"My twin," I say.

"You know about that?" Stacey asks, her doe eyes go wide within her disintegrating lashes.

"I know a lot of things," I say, still not putting the safety back on my gun. "What else did she tell you?"

"That it could be worth some money," she says. "What she found out."

So, it was as we'd suspected. With so much dissension in the ranks about Alex Scarpello taking over the family business, Angela had been ready to cash in on her boy.

"Where did she say he was?" I ask her.

"Who?"

"Her son."

The blackened doe eyes get wider. "What do you mean?" Stacey looks perplexed. "He wasn't anywhere.

He died." This does not make sense. What could a dead son be worth to Angela in the scheme of things?

"When did he die?" I ask.

"When you were born. Angela knew she was having twins, and the Scarpellos made her go to a private clinic with their own doctor. They had to do a C-section. When she woke up from the anesthesia, they told her you were okay, but the boy had been a stillborn."

The wheels are turning in my head, clicking all the facts into place. My father hadn't been at the birth. But I bet someone else had. Someone who was a good enough friend to stay by your side while you tried to push out two kids in some Mob-sponsored private clinic. Someone who really needed a boy child or the Scarpello-Russki alliance would all go to shit. A woman who'd left the country and then come back with a son the same age as me. Who was still paying the bills for a doctor who'd delivered Angela's twins more than thirty years ago.

"Who told her the boy died?" I ask Stacey. But I know before she tells me.

Anya Scarpello did.

CHAPTER 12

I LET AUNT STACEY GO IN THE END, after getting her to confirm that Anya Scarpello had arranged for the private clinic for Angela's delivery and had been there when the whole thing went down. Anya knew that my mother was having twins, even if my dad didn't. And with him away, it was a perfect opportunity for a woman who couldn't seem to produce *one* baby to take advantage of a friend with the fucking nerve to come up with two. Stacey said that Angela never saw the son she gave birth to, that the doctor had whisked him away to save her the trauma of seeing his dark and still little face. But it was more than possible that Anya Scarpello had whisked my perfectly healthy twin brother off to Russia with a faked passport instead. If she told everyone she'd been pregnant when she left, the age difference when she came back would have been only a matter of months. It's kind of brilliant when you think about it. No one would have been any the wiser. Except maybe her Russian relations, who also had a vested interest in making sure the Scarpello alliance went as planned.

Maybe the nurse in the morgue wasn't down with kidnapping another woman's newborn, and that's what got her sent to the deep freeze. The doctor must have known better, trading his scruples for a lifetime of cash infusions from Anya Scarpello. A pretty good deal when you consider the alternative.

When Stacey leaves, she takes off out of the alleyway with a squeal of tires worse than the night I shot at her. Back to Canada, I suppose. She didn't want to take Janet with her, still too worried that whatever shit Angela had got herself into might hit the fan and blow back on her legal right to sell dope. I swear, I could throttle that woman. If I'd known it was just a mascara-mad cannabis dealer following me when my car broke down, I'd have tackled her on the steps of the abandoned farmhouse and demanded a ride back to town. Then I could have slept in my own bed.

I go back to get the ice bucket from where I'd left it in the motel lobby, bypassing the Korean lady's inner sanctum and entering through the door off the parking lot. I can still hear her television. But the evening news has now been replaced by Alex Trebek asking for answers in the form of questions. I'm sure that little motel lady has some questions of her own. But she's smart enough to stay in her room and not ask them. I send a quick text to Charlotte, tell her I'd had to run because I have a new job doing mall Santa security and one of the elves got out of line. I'll talk to her later.

Deep and Janet are waiting for me when I return, finally torn away from their respective screens.

"What took you so long?" Deep asks me, looking concerned.

"There was a bit of an incident," I say, adjusting the gun, which is now slipped back down the front of my jeans.

"How can a trip to the ice machine cause a bloody incident?"

I put the ice bucket down on the table next to the now empty pizza box.

"I ran into Aunt Stacey. We had a little discussion," I tell both of them. "It was her tailing me all along."

"Aunt Stacey? Janet jumps up and pulls aside the curtain to look out into the parking lot. "Where is she?"

I sit down and pick up a piece of ice from the bucket, hold it under one of my eyes to try and deflate the puffy bags. "She had to leave," I say, casting a knowing look at Deep.

Janet turns away from the window. "She's not coming back for me. Is she?"

I think of Stacey trembling by her car at gunpoint in her ugly Christmas sweater, her snot dripping down onto Rudolph's pom-pom nose.

"No," I say. "I don't think she is."

"That's okay," Janet says, coming away from the window and plunking herself down on the bed. "I never liked staying at her place, anyway. It was really hot, and it smelled funny." But you can see the pain of rejection dart across her face. First her mother, and now Aunt Stacey, leaving her behind.

"What did she say?" Deep asks me.

I could keep this all under my hat, instead of tipping it to let my suspicions be known. But Deep is already aware of Anya Scarpello's fertility issues, as well as the connection with the doctor who'd signed off on the fake single birth registration. And despite what I'd said, it was possible that Aunt Stacey might come back and spill the baby beans to Janet about what Angela told her. Neither Deep nor my sister are stupid. They'll eventually connect the dots, just like I did, about who my twin brother might be. I decide it's better if the information comes from me. The medium may be the message, but it also has more control over what gets said. I relay most of my conversation with Charlotte as well as Aunt Stacey, leaving out the piece where the latter conversation was held at gunpoint.

"So, you reckon Alex Scarpello is your brother?" Deep asks when I'm done, showing his dot-connecting abilities are much as I'd expected.

"Our brother," Janet corrects him, having made her own connections.

"It sure as hell looks like he is," I say, switching the ice to my other eye. "The old Don told Angela something about her son when she went to see him. I'm thinking he must have known about the baby-snatch caper and had an attack of conscience before he bought the farm." Like Roberto said, there's nothing like impending death to reset a man's moral compass.

"The timing and Alex Scarpello's age lines up," Deep says, closing the top on the pizza box and stacking it carefully in the corner for recycling. "And that would explain why Angela didn't start causing problems for Alex Scarpello until now."

"It would," I say, picturing Angela's reaction to the old man's reveal. She wouldn't have been able to see straight for the dollar signs dancing in her head if she found out the son she thought died was really the heir fucking apparent for the Scarpello fortunes. Of course, I've been thinking about those monetary possibilities myself. Like mother, like daughter, I suppose. Although, it makes me cringe a bit to think about those sort of comparisons. But having the current Don as my twin brother brings up a whole new avenue of exploitation. One that doesn't involve a messy coup. He could be asked for favours if he were amenable. Blackmailed about the information if he wasn't. Maybe I won't have to live out the rest of my days in a room above the E-Zee Market after all. This could be the fucking "brother lode" for me.

"Of course, there could be another explanation," Deep says.

"Like what?" I'm on a roll here, and I've never liked debates. Except the ones for the presidential election a few years back. Clinton vs. Trump. Now that was entertainment.

"Her grandfather could have told her something else about her son," Deep says.

"Something that was going to net her a bunch of cash? Stacey said there was a payoff involved."

"Maybe they messed up the delivery," Janet says. "And that's why the baby died. She could have sued for malpractice or something."

"There's a statute of limitations on stuff like that," I tell her. "It's not like murder." This is something I know about. "And besides, how would that piss off Alex Scarpello?"

Neither of them has an answer for that, but they still don't look convinced.

"Listen, Anya is the one who told Angela the baby died. She was there at the clinic. And, conveniently, that same year she comes up with a son over in Russia, where no one can verify that he's actually hers. The doctor who signed off on the birth registry is on her permanent payroll, and the maternity nurse was put on ice for three decades. The whole thing stinks of a cover-up."

"Alex Scarpello would lose a lot if the Russian side of his lineage was called into question," Deep says, coming over to my side. "His major supporters are from the Eastern European gangs. With people already concerned about his fitness to lead, something like this could definitely cause a war."

"But he wouldn't hurt Mom, would he?" Janet asks with hope in her eyes. "If it's true, then she's his mother, too."

I'd like to mirror Janet's hope, for her sake. But Roberto had said Alex Scarpello was vicious, unpredictable, possibly unbalanced. Still, you'd have to be one hell of a cold bastard to bump off your own birth mother.

"Let's just take it one step at a time," I say. "I'll meet up with them tonight and see what happens." I drop my piece of ice back into the bucket, wipe away the melted tears it's left on my cheeks with a napkin left over from the pizza. "In the meantime, Deep, how hard is it to hack into some Russian birth records?"

"Hard," he says. "But I'll see what I can do.

"It could give us some leverage, if we had proof." It could also keep me from getting killed, I'm thinking. Right now, all we have is a damn good theory. Theories can be snuffed out with the person who speculates about them. Documented facts have a life of their own.

"I still don't like the idea of you going there tonight," Deep says.

Janet doesn't look too happy about it, either. As much as she wants to find Angela, the idea of me disappearing into the void her mother was last seen entering has got to be causing the kid some anxiety. I try to reassure them both.

"If things get hot, I'll just tell them I already have documents proving Alex Scarpello is an Italian-Pole changeling. That if anything happens to me, it'll go public. You know the drill. You've seen it in the movies."

I stand up. It's getting late and I need to get moving if I'm going to make it for dinner at eight.

"What if he isn't?" Janet asks.

"Isn't what?"

"A changeling," she says.

"Then he has no good reason to kill me now, does he?"

The address that Anya gave me is in the Indian Village that isn't, but not on one of the streets that ripped off its name from Native Americans. I get the Uber driver to drop me off about a block away, so I can get a feel for the place. Deep had wanted to drive me, but I convinced him to stay with Janet. I left the two of them in the motel room, playing Risk, that board game where each country tries to destroy each other and take over the world. Deep had brought it from home. That goddamn game goes on forever. Much like the real-life version.

At first, I think I'm in the wrong neighbourhood. On the main road, there are a bunch of sketchy-looking low-rise apartment buildings fronted by a strip mall that has not one but two pharmacies sporting rusty metal bars across the windows. There's also one of those cheque cashing places used only by the desperate, or by naive stooges tricked into sending money to Nigerian princes on the lam. I'm feeling damn cold, although the temperature is still probably a few points above the freezing mark. I jam my hands into my leather jacket and start making my way down a residential street, wishing I'd brought my gloves.

After I get to the other side of the sketchy low-rises, the real estate abruptly changes to large homes, all built from old money, but with significant injections from the newer variety. Restored turn-of-the century mansions line the street, sitting on big-ass lots. Some of the houses are framed with multiple strings of flashing Christmas lights, enough to induce a small seizure. They look like life-sized Victorian dollhouses gone Vegas.

When I get to the address Anya Scarpello gave me, I cross to the other side of the street and deke into the shadows behind a low stone wall covered in ivy. I crouch down behind it to conceal myself, which isn't easy on account of how tall I am. What's the point of building a wall in front of your property when it's this short? It doesn't keep anyone out, including the ivy. The house behind me looks empty, no lights on, even though the sun went down hours ago. It's a good enough place to hide and observe for now.

I check out the Scarpello compound across the quiet street. It's Alex's place, but Anya lives with him, according to Deep's preliminary research. I count four chimneys and a turret with a witch-hat roof. I don't know what they call this kind of architecture, but it reminds me of the house perched above the Bates Motel in the movie *Psycho*. That's if Anthony Perkins's character had spent his time fixing the place up instead of mummifying his mother and stabbing women in the shower.

There are CCTV cameras mounted under the eaves rather than Christmas lights here. A goon in a puffy parka like Janet's is patrolling the edges of the property. Each time he comes around the side yard, I can see the glowing end of a cigarette tucked in his gob as he smacks his gloved hands together to keep them warm. There's a significant bulge under the front of his heavy jacket, visible despite its bulk and his own. The bulge looks too big for a revolver, too small for an M16. Most likely an Uzi. I hate those Israeli submachine guns from hell. Not because they're Israeli but because they have a twenty-five-plus round capacity that will cap your ass before you even have a chance to kiss it goodbye.

Either his shift is over or he was only out for a smoke break, because the patrol eventually knocks on the side door of the four-car garage, and another man lets him in. I'm about to come out from behind the wall and cross the street when my phone shudders in my pocket. I pull it out and look at the screen glowing in the dark. Fucking Malone. I better answer it. She'll want an update on Janet, and if I don't give her one, she might show up at the E-Zee Market and find out my sister hasn't been there in two days.

"Hey, Malone." I try to act all laid back and natural, and not like a woman skulking under the ivy across the street from a Mafia stronghold.

"Is it true you took Janet to the science museum?"

"Yes." Not sure where she's going with this, but I'm okay to play along.

"I didn't think you had it in you. To do something normal like that."

"Would it help if I told you we scammed public transit to get there?"

"No."

"Then we didn't." I've been jumping turnstiles into the subway since I was ten. Janet wasn't too bad at it when I showed her how it was done. She said she did hurdles in track at school, cleaned up in her age category on account of her height.

It appears that Malone has only called to chat. Since she is technically my friend, this isn't entirely suspicious, but it still feels alien to me.

"Any news on the Angela front?" I ask, eyeing the house across the street. Still no replacement for the goon on patrol. I guess they can't be out there all the time, or the neighbours would complain.

"We know she was in Detroit to see the old Don before he died. We're focusing our inquiries there." I guess Janet needn't have bothered to keep that bit of intel to herself. The cops already knew. But then again, they've been monitoring the Scarpellos for years, so I suppose it makes sense.

"We're still working on getting your birth registration. It should tell us who attended the delivery. We might be able to get a name for our Jane Doe. Or find out what happened to the other child." She sighs. "What I can't understand is why the Scarpellos would bash a woman's head in over it all."

"The Scarpellos? What makes you think it was them?" I try to sound my best approximation of surprised. I know the Scarpellos put that nurse in the freezer so she wouldn't be able to tell the tale of two babies. But I don't get how Malone figured it out.

"The warehouse, where we found the body," she says. "We still haven't gotten anywhere on the ownership. But our records show it was a Scarpello safe house back in the day."

"Wasn't too safe for the chick in the freezer."

"No, it wasn't."

"What are the Scarpellos into these days, anyway?" I ask her, all causal, as if we're just talking shop. Back like we did when we worked on the Brent murder case together. I'm ace at making people feel at ease when I want to. It's easier to snap their necks that way.

"The usual," Malone says. "Extortion, money laundering, the lot. Although they've branched out. They're more into cybercrimes lately. Bilking old people out of their life savings with phishing emails. But right now, the feds are interested in a high-stakes poker game they've got running. No one knows how the money gets moved around, but there's got to be a lot of it." Malone pauses, remembering now that she's not talking to a colleague, but a criminal.

"Why do you want to know?"

"No reason," I say.

"You're up to something. I can tell," Malone hisses into the phone. "Listen, Candace. Leave this one to us. You don't want to mess with the Scarpellos. We'll find Angela, or a relative up in Canada to take Janet."

"Ah, Malone, you misjudge me," I say. "I wouldn't have it any other way."

A light goes on across the street. Someone is standing at the window. "Listen, I have to go," I tell Malone.

"Why?"

"I'm in the middle of playing Risk."

After I get off the call with Malone, I delete her number from my phone before shutting if off to save the battery. If the Scarpellos got a hold of it, it wouldn't be kosher having a cop in my call history. I come out from behind the shadowy stone wall and stride up to the Scarpello's front steps, pressing the old-style doorbell. It sets off a succession of deafening chimes worse than Westminster Abbey. I flick a leaf of ivy off my leather jacket, just before the door opens.

One of Anya's security detail from the church stands there gawking, as if he hadn't thoroughly checked me out on the video feed long before he came to the door. He frisks me right there on the front step, but I'm clean. I left my piece back at the motel, knowing they'd just confiscate it, anyway. I tried to give Deep a brief lesson on gun mechanics and how to shoot, but he refused to touch my Ruger, offended by its violent un-Britishness. He'd claimed this was a real word, like un-American.

But I think he made it up. I'd left the Ruger in the bed-side table for him just in case, next to a Gideon's Bible and an escort service flyer someone had left behind. Or maybe Deep got lonely when I went for my nap earlier.

"I'm Candace Starr," I say once he's done giving me the once over with his massive hands.

"I know," he grunts. "Angela's brat." He stands aside so I can walk through the doorway. "The Scarpellos are expecting you."

I cross over the threshold into what might be my brother's house.

And just like that, I'm one of the family.

CHAPTER 13

THE SCARPELLO FOYER IS A LARGE ONE — marble floor, spiralling staircase, the works. The guy who answered the door has left me here under a tear-drop chandelier with instructions to wait. For what, he didn't say. A large antique mirror reflects a tarnished image of me from where it hangs on the wall. It looks like the one that bitch of a stepmother used to screw over Snow White.

"Candace, I'm so glad you have come."

Anya Scarpello is at the top of the curving staircase, dressed in a classy below-the-knee skirt, topped by a quilted jacket in gold and silver paisley. I thought you weren't supposed to mix those two metals, but on her, it looks good. In my black jeans and scuffed cowboy boots, I guess I'm underdressed. Even the bozo who answered the door was decked out better than me.

Anya descends the staircase, caressing the polished mahogany banister with her fingertips. When she reaches the bottom, she throws her jacketed arms around me in an honest hug. Usually, I hate that sort of thing, but she smells of Chanel N°5 and hair spray, and there's something comforting about this combination of aerosol scents. Must be a throwback to the years my dad and I spent living above that drag bar on the strip when I was a kid. Those queens were always nice to me, babysitting me in their dressing room while my dad was out on a job, fussing over my hair in their size 14 platform heels.

Anya stands back after the hug and holds me at arm's length.

"You look so much like your mother," she says.

"Yeah, I've heard that." Angela was a looker, from all accounts, so I don't mind being compared to her too much in this way. But if this woman understood anything at all about who and what I am, she'd realize it's my father I take after.

"She's not here, is she?" I say. "It's just I'm not that anxious to see her." I figure this is a way of asking after Angela without seeming like I care. Which in some ways I don't.

Anya takes a step back, smooths her skirt with her hands. "She was, but she has left." I knew it wouldn't be that easy.

"Oh, well. That's good then," I tell her.

"I am disappointed to hear you say that, Candace. Family, as I've told you, is very important. Especially for us."

Her earlier warmth with the hug has dropped a few degrees. I've disappointed her. I decide I better play a different tactic if I want her to trust me. Trust, I have learned from experience, is most easily gained when you mirror back what the other person wants most to see reflected.

"Don't get me wrong," I say. "I just don't think I'm ready to see her just yet, you know? But I want to, I really do."

Anya nods, not convinced.

"Besides, looks like she didn't want to see me, either. Otherwise she'd be here." I jut my lower lip out a bit. I'm trying to play the pity card here, hoping it'll force Anya to show her hand. The play works. Her face and her stance soften a little.

"Angela would be here to see you if she could, Candace. I am sure of it." She seems really sincere and earnest about this. It makes me wonder if she knows my mother at all.

"Then why isn't she here?"

A shadow passes over her face, brief but still betraying a darkness. She steps over to the Snow White mirror and checks her hair, patting down errant strands that don't exist.

"Your mother was very distraught after the death of her grandfather. She can be ... unstable. I don't know whether you are aware of that."

"I am."

She turns from the mirror to face me. "Alex thought it best that she get some professional care. There is a retreat, for women of a certain age, not far from here. The doctor who leads it is a close friend of the family. It is very reputable."

I remember the retreat for women going through the change that Deep found in his research. The one run by the doctor who'd delivered Angela's twins and then lied his ass off about it on the birth record.

"There is no contact with the outside world there — no phones permitted, or internet connection," she says. "A digital detox, I believe they call it. That is why your mother isn't here, and why she doesn't know that you are."

"Oh," I say. "I guess that explains it."

She steps away from the mirror, takes my arm, and leads me down a long hallway with fake candelabra burning brightly on the walls. One of them crackles and snaps as we walk by, a tapered bulb threatening to blow.

"I am so glad you are open to seeing your mother, Candace," she says, her warmth returning. "Mothers and daughters have a special bond. You are aware of the saying — it is an English one — a son's a son until he takes a wife, a daughter's your daughter for the rest of your life?"

"Well, I guess that means you still have your son," I say, remembering the Murder Ink presenter's comment about Alex being far from the marrying type.

"Yes," she says, staring down the long hallway in front of her as if she were still looking into the darkness of the mirror. "I do have that."

Dressed in a charcoal-grey suit tailored on the slim side, Alex Scarpello stands up from the head of the table when Anya and I walk into the formal dining room. He looks to be about the same height as me, same colouring, although his hair is darker. The curls we share have been cropped short since the picture I saw, accentuating his face. He has full lips, and heavy-lidded fuck-me eyes, like Mick Jagger or that Irish guy from *Peaky Blinders*. I can see where he'd be popular with the ladies, with his long lashes and limbs, and more than a hint of danger about him — a predatory pretty boy. Although I've never been into that stormy androgynous look myself. A faint hint of acne scars marks his cheeks, but not too badly. He could be my brother, but he could also be my cousin once removed, like he's supposed to be. He smiles at me in a catfish way. You know those people online who try to pretend they're something they're not. It's fucking unsettling and makes me wish I still had my gun.

"Well, the infamous Candace Starr," he says, indicating for both Anya and me to take our seats at the table. Our place settings have been laid out at the opposite end from him. The table is so long, it wouldn't fit in my apartment, even if I kept the door open to my shower/washroom as well as the hallway. The seating arrangement is designed so he can literally keep his distance.

"It's nice to meet you," I say, not knowing how else to react to my *infamy*. I follow Anya's lead and take my spot in front of the fancy dishes and silverware set up for me. There are way too many fucking forks. Alex sits back down again and steeples his long fingers.

"First your mother and now you. We really are being treated to a Starr family reunion these days."

"My mother wasn't much for reunions," I say. Despite how I played it with his mother, I can't let him think I'm too interested in what happened to mine. Or let on any of my real intentions for being here. Otherwise, I might end up being shipped off to a mysterious retreat myself.

"Do you know where she is?" he asks me. This surprises me. I turn to Anya, but she only looks back at me with a red lipstick smile.

"No," I say, retuning my focus to the head of the table. "I haven't known where she was for most of my life."

"No need to be coy, dear," Anya says to me, then addresses her son. "I've told Candace that you sent Angela to the doctor to recover."

"Ah yes, the Razinski Clinic for Women. An excellent retreat. It was for the best."

Alex has a way of talking that comes from either a deep-seated need to look like he's got class or from watching too many episodes of *Downton Abbey*. He hasn't got the British accent of a lord, only the highbrow affectations of one.

"Yeah," I say. "But I don't know where that is."

"It's probably best that you don't, Candace. But if you do hear from your mother, I'm sure you will tell us. She was quite unstable before she left here. We were all very concerned."

I bet they were. Concerned she'd blow their cover. This whole story sounds rehearsed, with both Alex and his mother working from the same script.

"Candace is in town for the beatification," Anya cuts in. She covers her wine glass when a guy in a penguin suit comes around with a bottle of chianti. I make sure my glass is open for action, even get the penguin to top up his original pour so it goes right to the top of the crystal goblet. I'm surprised an underworld boss would go in for this much flash. But I suppose he has enough legitimate businesses to launder his wealth. The Scarpellos own several casinos in the area, of which there are many, propping up the cash-strapped city of Detroit with their hefty sin-tax dollars.

"Yes," Alex says, taking a sip of his wine. "The beatification. I hadn't realized you were so devout."

"I found religion in prison," I say, keeping with the story I'd told Anya.

"So my mother tells me."

The penguin returns, this time with a serving bowl that looks like a Victorian chamber pot. No one speaks while he doles out a thick brown soup with a silver ladle. Only when he leaves does conversation start up again.

"Alex and I will be attending the beatification at the cathedral on Sunday night," Anya says, daintily starting in on her soup. I dig in, as well, but the slop tastes like a bunch of root vegetables left to ferment, and there's way too much yam for my taste.

"It's difficult," Alex says, ignoring her, "to remain faithful in the world we live in. Don't you think, Candace?"

"I suppose."

"Come now, we're all family here," he says. "The line of work we're in can be at odds with, shall we say, traditional Catholic values."

"I don't think so," I say, knowing this is a test.

"No?"

"Well, if the meek are inheriting the earth, I guess we're in the wrong business," I tell him, putting down my spoon. It leaves a shitty brown glob on the white tablecloth. "But you have to do what you can with the gifts you've been given. It's a sin not to, right?" I don't know whether it is, but it sounds like what a devout criminal would say.

"And the gift you've been given is your ability to kill people?"

"I don't do that anymore."

"Nor do we," Alex says, putting down his spoon, as well. "Well, not ourselves at least. It is important to out-source the more menial tasks."

"Menial tasks?" I'm slightly offended. While I may no longer off people for a living, I had always considered my previous vocation a skilled trade.

"Anyone with access to a noxious substance in a spray bottle can remove a target these days, Candace." He's right. Two Vietnamese chicks had managed to take out the brother of North Korea's Kim Jong-un using a discreet squirt in the face with a nerve agent. "If you hadn't retired, the amateurs would have driven you out of the market."

I hadn't thought about this, the idea that my former career as a personal assassin has been made redundant. Who needs a professional for a hit when you can pass someone death in a spray bottle?

A woman comes to collect our soup bowls while the penguin starts laying out the main meal. Quinoa and zucchini topped with that Middle Eastern cheese that squeaks like rubber when you chew on it.

"I'm a vegetarian," Alex explains, digging into his meal, "as is my mother."

"Yes," she says, eyes down. I gather our discussion on the compatibility of killing and Catholicism has caused her some amount of distress.

"Still," Alex says after the staff have left the room, "I could use someone like you in my organization."

"Someone who knows how to kill people without a spray bottle?" I ask, trying to saw through the rubbery cheese.

"Someone who is both attractive and lethal."

I suppose that's a compliment.

"I told you, I don't kill people anymore."

"You don't need to kill people to get results, Candace," he says. "Threat and intimidation are all that is necessary to run an organization like ours."

"Threat and intimidation are necessary to run any organization. Haven't you read that Steve Jobs biography?"

He stares at me with those heavy-lidded eyes. Anya looks up nervously from her dinner. Then her son starts to laugh, so heartily I think some quinoa might come flying out of his full lips.

"I like you, Candace," he says, recovering himself. He dabs at the corners of his mouth with a red linen napkin. "I really do."

Anya smiles. I guess she's glad he likes me.

"I have a private function tomorrow night where I could use you in a professional capacity. Are you interested?"

It would be a clever way to bury myself further into the Scarpello fold until Deep digs up those Russian birth records. "I could be," I tell him.

"Of course, you'd need to find some appropriate clothing to wear. This is a high-end event. My female staff are expected to dress," he pauses for effect, "attractively."

"I don't do the hooker thing," I say flatly. Sex for money is not my thing. There are too many more valuable things you can trade for it.

"Oh, we don't endorse prostitution!" Anya startles me with this earnest outburst. She's been pretty subdued until now.

"You misunderstand me," Alex says, after giving his mother a hard look. "I only mean that this is an upscale event we're planning. A gentlemen's game of cards. I like all my security detail to dress formally. It's important to keep up appearances." The gig sounds like the high-stakes poker game Malone was going on about.

"Are you going to make me wear a tuxedo, like the penguin over there?"

The waiter has returned with a trolley, the top of it a dull metallic surface that sizzles when he drops some beads of water on it. A portable hot plate. But he doesn't put any food on it to keep warm. If he's offended by my comment, he doesn't let on as he scurries out of the room.

"What I have on is about as formal as I've got," I tell him, which is true. I'd taken the time to pick out a T-shirt without a rip in it for the evening.

"I could take you shopping," Anya exclaims from beside me, startling me again. She really was more poised in the church earlier today. I get the impression her son makes her nervous. Hell, he makes me nervous.

"We could go tomorrow, after Mass," Anya says.

Shit, another early morning. I hope I don't have to go to confession again.

"Sure," I say, picturing me and Anya Scarpello in a store sorting through form-fitting little black dresses.

Maybe I can convince her to let me wear a suit like Alex's. Something I can still drop kick a guy in if he tries to pull a card from up his sleeve. But I sense she's itching to pimp a more feminine ride on my rough trade carriage, her chance to play dress-up with the daughter she never had.

The waiter returns, this time with a chopping board and a meat cleaver, which he places in front of Alex on the table. This seems strange, since he's a vegetarian. He hands Alex a red-and-black smoking jacket. Alex stands up and slips it on, doing up the belt around his lean waist. The waiter retreats to the back of the room, a towel draped over his arm. I hear a commotion in the hallway, some grunting and scuffling, before the two goons I saw in the church earlier come in with a skinny guy by the arms. He's got a gag in his mouth, and his eyes bulge wildly like a horse I saw in a parade once when a Shriner car backfired.

"As I said, Candace, appearances are everything. For instance, this gentleman here thought he could steal from me, skimming a little off the top of one of my casino's nightly draws. Not a lot, but it doesn't make for a good impression."

The goons hold the skinny guy's forearm down on the cutting board.

"Perhaps we should leave the men to their business," Anya says, getting ready to stand.

"Don't be silly, Mother," Alex shoots her a look that speaks louder than the muffled screams coming from the gagged man's mouth. "Candace is family, after all. Besides, I wouldn't want either of you to miss out on dessert." Anya settles reluctantly back into her seat.

When Alex Scarpello brings the meat cleaver down, it makes surprisingly little mess. He only takes the one hand. The goons slam the bloody stump onto the trolley hot plate to cauterize it, so it doesn't have time to bleed much. As the guy's wrist sizzles, the stench of burned flesh fills the oversized dining room, which smells much like singed hair, if you've ever got too zealous with your flat iron. A lot of people don't know that. But this isn't my first barbecue.

"Threats and intimidation, Candace. I'm afraid that for appearance's sake, sometimes one or the other must be carried out."

The waiter runs up and throws his towel over the oozing hand on the cutting board. He carries it out of the room like a dead rat. The goons follow, dragging the gagged guy, who appears to have passed out.

"You'll stay overnight with us here this evening," Alex says as the woman in charge of cleaning up clears away our dinner plates. He hands her his smoking jacket, darkened by a fine spray of blood on the lapels. I guess he hadn't wanted to spoil his suit. "You can get an early start with my mother for your shopping expedition tomorrow."

Anya nods obediently. Underneath the table, I can see her smoothing her linen napkin over and over again with her delicate hands, as if to reassure herself that she's still got two of them.

The penguin brings in dessert. It's crème brûlée. But I've sort of lost my appetite.

After dinner, Alex says he has work to do in his study. Once he's left the dining room, Anya claims to have a headache and goes up to bed. The security guy shows me to my room, but doesn't lock me in, which means he doesn't know much about being secure.

I figure if they were going to kill me, they would have done it at dinner. I'm even a bit hopeful that Angela's still alive at this point. Maybe they did send her to that retreat. They could be holding her there while they figure out what to do with her. Alex asking me where I thought she was seems odd, but it might have been just another one of his tests.

The bed in my room is a king size. A treat for a person of my height. My feet always hang over the mattress on the floor of my apartment. I drop down on the puffy duvet and grab the remote for the wide-screen TV mounted on the wall, flipping through a bunch of reality shows about sex. Don't people get enough of that every day? Reality, that is, not sex. You can never get enough of that. I finally settle on a channel with an unlimited number of episodes of *Friends* shown back to back. Propping myself up on the bed, I watch the antics of a group of far-too-good-looking people living way too cushy lives. I let that unreal crap flow over me like waves of false nostalgia. It helps to wash away the shit I've just seen, along with other unpleasant memories. The whisky I swiped from the liquor cabinet downstairs doesn't hurt in this regard, either. That security goon really should have locked me in. I'm into the sixth episode, where Monica and Chandler are screwing but pretending they're not, when I remember my phone.

I pull the phone out of my jacket and power it up. There are no messages from Deep, which I feel a bit disappointed by. But then again, I'd told him not to try and contact me while I was here.

I tap out a quick text.

I'm in.

And then add, *You two okay?* I'm not usually one to inquire after other people's well-being. Perhaps it is an effect of the *Friends'* ensemble.

Still playing Risk, Deep texts back quickly. *R u ok?*

I'm thinking about how I might respond to this when I hear a stirring in the hallway. I wait, trying to listen over the canned laugh track. Then I hear it again, just outside my bedroom door. I delete the texts, and turn off the phone, slipping it under the king size mattress.

I don't have much to arm myself with here, not even a hand vacuum. I grab the half-empty whisky bottle in my hand and open the door a crack, listen for a while, then open it wider.

Anya Scarpello stands at the end of the hall in front of an upstairs window, looking out into the night. I can see some light snow has started to fall. It swirls in the floodlights from the backyard. I'm about to close the door and leave her to her private moment when she turns around and startles a bit at the sight of me. Which isn't surprising when you catch a six-foot-three woman brandishing a whisky bottle.

"Oh, Candace, I did not know you were still awake," she says. "I was only getting some Aspirin for my headache."

She says this, but she doesn't move to go get the pills, still casting a half glance out the window.

"I think we will forgo early Mass tomorrow," she says. "After breakfast, we will go to the shops." She looks at me again and smiles weakly, which is the only way to smile a few hours after you've seen a man's severed wrist fried on a hot plate.

"Okay," I say.

Anya returns her gaze out the window. I take that our conversation is over.

"And Candace," she calls out to me, just as I'm about to close the bedroom door.

"Yeah."

"Your mother will come back for you," she says, touching her fingers to the glass. "Mothers always do."

CHAPTER 14

WALKING INTO NORDSTROM with Anya Scarpello feels more surreal to me than walking into one of those Salvador Dalí paintings. Except, instead of melting clocks, it drips with bloated consumerism. Not unlike the Gun Superstore, but with more dog strollers and classier Christmas carols on the PA. A store employee tries to douse me with Calvin Klein's latest scent as we walk through the cosmetics department. But I manage to elbow the atomizer out of her hand before she has a chance. Anya makes some comment about me having to work on my manners, but I think this is kind of rich coming from a woman whose son performs dismemberments between dinner courses.

It's not true that mothers always come back for you, no matter what Anya says. But I suppose a woman like her can't conceive of that. She'd sent breakfast to my room this morning on a tray with a single red carnation stuck in a white vase. A buttercup-embossed notecard was propped up against it, where she'd written what time I had to be ready for our shopping trip. I tried to work the coffee press, but screwed it up and got the grounds all mixed in. After downing a couple of gritty cups that I spiked with what was left of the fine whisky, I dug into the avocado on toast. It was tasty but couldn't hold a candle to Deep's bacon fry-up, as he called it. Vegetarians are supposed to live longer, but I think it just feels that way to them because their life sucks so much without meat.

Anya helps me pick out some dresses to try on, handing each one to a salesgirl with hair slicked back in a bun so tight it threatens to cut off the circulation to her face. Anya chats to me about fabric and hemlines. Each time I try to steer her toward the men's suit section, she heads me off at the pass like a Louis Vuitton linebacker. Since she's buying, I can't really argue. I'm only tolerating all of this fussing in hopes that Anya will tell me more about where Angela is or shed some light on her violent creep of a son's parentage.

I go to the ladies' change rooms, followed by the salesgirl with the bloodless face. Each stall has an upholstered door that opens out onto a private viewing area with an overstuffed round couch. Anya sits on it and waits. I feel like a life-sized Barbie doll. She coos over every outfit I try on, insisting I model each one for her. Even the black-sequined pencil dress that binds me at the knees so badly I have to walk in baby steps to keep from falling over. I look in the three-way mirror, overwhelmed by the effect of myself in shimmering triplicate. I look like an angry backup trio for Cher.

"I don't know if it's my style," I say.

"Nonsense," Anya says, circling me. "It only needs the right shoes. What size are you?"

I look down at my black cowboy boots, worn down at the heels.

"Thirteen," I tell her. The salesgirl takes in a rush of air, which brings a momentary blush of colour to her blood-starved cheeks. My dad always told me as a kid that I'd grow into my feet, like a puppy does, and I suppose he was right. But it still makes it tough to find women's shoes in my size outside of fiercequeen.com.

"I don't think we have any heels in that size in the store," she says.

But Anya is undaunted. "I'll have a look myself, shall I?" She shoots the salesgirl a disapproving look. Then turns to me, "Wait here, dear, I'll be back in a moment."

I shuffle over to the salesgirl once Anya's gone. "Do you have anything a person can actually move in? Like maybe a dress with some Lycra or something?" She gasps again, no doubt appalled by the mention of a synthetic fibre, but reluctantly goes in search of a dress not designed to keep a woman captive.

Finally left alone, I grab my leather jacket with the phone in the pocket and lock myself in the far change room to call Deep. I never did text him back last night, too spooked after my run-in with Anya in the hall. When I power up my phone, there are multiple missed calls from him and one from Malone. She'll have to wait.

"Candace?" Deep answers the phone sounding breathless.

"Hi," I say. "What'd I take you from?"

"I was shaving," he says. I'm reminded of the smell of his Paco Rabanne, and surprise myself with a sigh that almost pops the zipper running down my back.

"I've been worried sick. What happened last night? Are you still at the Scarpellos'?"

"Nope."

"Where the hell are you, then?"

"At Nordstrom, trying on clothes."

"You're shopping?" Deep shouts down the phone, so loudly I have to pull it away from my ear. I unleash the zipper and start to shimmy my way out of the sequined strait jacket of a dress.

"Anya Scarpello made me," I say.

"Like at gunpoint?" he says.

"That's just hysterical," I say, stepping free of the dress. I kick it to the other end of the fitting room with one of my cowboy boots. "Listen, I think I have a line on Angela. They say she got all unstable, so they sent her to that retreat you were telling me about. The one run by the doctor who signed off on my birth cert."

"Dr. Razinski?"

"Yeah, that's him."

"And you believe them?"

"Maybe, but I think she may still be alive. Alex Scarpello was keen on whether I'd heard from her or not, and Anya seems to think she'll turn up. I don't think either of them know for sure where she is. Or else they're just being cautious, trying to figure out what I know. But don't tell Janet that. Just say that they sent her for some R&R. She'll just freak out otherwise."

"Okay," Deep says. But I can tell he feels reluctant about keeping things from Janet. Lying is something that doesn't come naturally to him.

"You better work on figuring out where that retreat is

just in case, though." After all, even the Scarpellos could tell the truth sometimes.

"I'll try. But they're serious about protecting the privacy of their patients. Although the good doctor is not so careful when it comes to his personal life."

"What do you mean?"

"I've found him in a few chat rooms. Online sex stuff. Live feeds. That kind of rubbish. His financials show quite a few charges for escort services."

"What a charmer." Looks like the doctor who specializes in hormones doesn't have too much trouble with his own. "Any luck hacking into those Russian birth records? Or have you been too distracted by the smut sites?"

"I've been working on it. It's not like they publish them on Wikipedia, you know. These things take time, Candace."

"So does playing an unending game of Risk."

Deep sighs. "I was trying to take Janet's mind off of the situation. The poor kid needs some normalcy in her life, Candace." I guess Deep is a better judge of what constitutes a normal childhood than I am. Waterboarding was the closest I ever got to board games as a kid. Learning how to dry drown a reluctant source cuffed to a drainpipe was a skill Mike Starr felt no young lady should be without.

There's a bit of a scuffle, and then Janet comes on the line.

"You're shopping?" I have to pull the phone away from my ear again.

"Hey, Janet."

"I thought you were looking for Mom."

"I am."

"And you thought you'd find her at the mall?"

"The Scarpellos say she's at a retreat."

"The one Deep and you were talking about run by that doctor?" Looks like she heard more through those earbuds than I gave her credit.

"That's it."

"It doesn't sound like something Mom would do."

"It's the best I have for now, Janet. Can you put Deep back on the line? I don't have much time here."

She lets out an angry huff before Deep takes back the phone.

"Are you coming back here tonight?" he asks me.

"No. I've got a job, working security at a high-stakes card game for Alex Scarpello."

"Do you think that's safe?"

"At this point the most dangerous thing seems to be the wardrobe required for it."

"I don't know, Candace. Why don't you just stick around the house. Look for some information there."

"I know what I'm doing, Deep. You just keep working on those Russki birth records and let me figure out the rest, okay?"

"Your sister's getting stroppy," he says, rather than debating the matter further.

"Tell her we'll all go out for dinner tomorrow. The kid loves to eat." I can hear Anya talking to the salesgirl outside the entrance to the change room area. "I have to go." I turn off the phone and slip it into my leather jacket.

I step out into the viewing area just as Anya and the salesgirl return to stand by the round couch. I'm wearing nothing but a bra held together with a safety pin and a men's pair of tighty-whities that I stole from Deep. My bright-silver star tattoo peeks out from above the elastic waistband, winking in the harsh change room lights. The two eye me appraisingly.

"I think we may need a visit to lingerie, as well," Anya says. The salesgirl nods before she runs away in search of silky underthings, or maybe just to get away from my deadpan stare.

Unbelievably, Anya is able to locate a pair of shoes that fit me. She got them off of a seven-foot Mrs. Claus strutting it up in one of the store-window displays. The shoes are ruby-red patent leather with six-inch metallic stiletto heels that taper to a sharp point. If you took the rubber lifts off the bottom, you could use them to pick up trash off the interstate.

For a dress, we finally settle on a Lycra-blend cocktail number that clings to my curves like crêpe wallpaper but still has enough give to allow for a drop kick if the need presents itself. Anya insists on topping it with a satin blazer, which I intend to ditch for my leather jacket tonight as soon as I leave the house.

After Nordstrom, Anya's driver drops us off at St. Clare's Catholic Church. She wants Father Randolph to give us a private Mass to make up for missing the early morning one. We're waiting for him to finish in the confessional. There's a bit of a line-up. It must be a busy week for sinners. There's a petite ash-blonde with an eyebrow piercing waiting her turn. I would probably try to get her number under different circumstances. But something tells me that snaring a hookup in a confessional queue might be frowned upon.

I'm a little nervous about doing the Holy Communion thing. If I screw up, the priest might figure out I'm not a real Catholic and give me the bum's rush. I'm not really concerned with any higher authority than that. I figure God has to be thoroughly pissed with me already, given the life I've led up until now. When it comes to endangering my mortal soul, that ship has definitely sailed, thrown anchor, and possibly sunk. One more act of blasphemy is not going to change that. Maybe I should try to pick up that girl in the confessional line-up after all.

Anya and I sit down in one of the pews up front, out of earshot of the people waiting on the priest in the booth at the back. In front of us, a collection of white stubby candles flicker in an angled tray, giving off a scent of cheap wax. Anya stares up at a statue of Mary in blue-and-white robes. Mary's hands are outstretched as she looks down at her bare feet. She's way too white for a chick from the Middle East, but who am I to judge. Mary's much easier on the eyes than her son, who hangs crucified not far away, blood dripping from His hands and feet in high-gloss red paint. No wonder she's looking down.

"I used to wait for the priest with my sister like this when we were children," Anya says, still keeping her eyes on Mary. She fingers a string of shiny black-and-silver rosary beads that she's holding loosely in her hands. I tell her I left mine at home by accident.

"In Russia?" I say. It might be good to get her talking about the old country. Maybe she'll divulge something that would help Deep with his birth record search.

"Yes. In St. Petersburg. Not in a church, of course. Religion had been outlawed by the State. But my father kept his faith. A priest would come in secret to our home to say Mass. Beforehand, he would take my father to the study for his confession. We would wait in the living room." She sighs. "Our mother died when we were babies, so it was always only Karine and me."

"Was it always this boring?" I say. I know I'm supposed to be playing the good Catholic here, but waiting for a bunch of people to unload all their sins on the padre is about as thrilling as watching the paint on the crucified Jesus dry.

She smiles but doesn't take her eyes off the statue. "We would play little games to make the time pass. Try to count the number of pieces of stained glass above the entrance to the hotel across the street. Or make up romantic fantasies about our teachers at school. Unrequited love. Scandalous affairs. Karine was a wonderful storyteller."

I should find out more about this sister. She could be a lead. Karine might have helped Anya if she showed up in Russia with a baby that wasn't hers.

"Where is she now?" I ask.

"She died," Anya says, turning her eyes away from Mary.

"I'm sorry."

"It was a long time ago. We were young women. Karine had a wild nature. One that my father couldn't rid her of. She refused to do as she was told. That romantic streak again. She ran off with a man my father had forbidden her to see. A man who could not protect her as we could."

"What happened?"

"She was kidnapped, by enemies of my father. The boy she loved was killed. Karine was forced into a brothel. Violated by strangers against her will." Anya fingers the rosary beads so aggressively now I'm afraid the shiny beads are going to break and spill out onto the floor.

"They found her a year later, in the penthouse of a prominent man. She had hanged herself with a filthy bedsheet. She was all but unrecognizable, even to me, her only sister."

"People look different after they die." I know this from personal experience. They always show dead bodies in TV cop shows looking all serene, or mildly startled, with their eyes wide open. The only thing that stays wide open after you die is your mouth. That's why the undertakers have to wire those suckers shut at the funeral home.

"I think suffering is the only emotion that survives past death," Anya says. "And my sister's suffering was written all over her broken body. The last story she ever told." She turns to me, her eyes sharp and focused, no longer dreamily contemplating the past.

"This is why we do not allow prostitution of any sort in the family's business dealings. People who want to destroy themselves with drugs, or gamble, this is their choice. My sister did not have a choice. As many young women do not. It is the only thing I ask of my Alex. To prohibit these activities. It is not my place to tell him how to run his affairs, but on this one point he respects my wishes."

Alex Scarpello didn't strike me as a guy who gave a damn about anyone's wishes, but I keep that to myself. "I'm sorry," I say, "about your sister."

"My sister brought on her own bad fortune, I'm afraid," she says. "Where I come from, a woman does as she is told. I know this is not a popular sentiment. But it is the way things work in families such as ours. Karine disregarded our father. She suffered the consequences of that." She bites her lip for a moment, putting a crack in her lipstick. "But I am afraid that I did not discourage her. I enjoyed her spirit, my little Karine. Perhaps too much. I could have stopped her, but I did not."

I nod, thinking about Janet. I kind of enjoy her spirit, too. It's different than mine. But maybe that's what I like about it.

Anya gets up from the pew and lights a candle next to a bunch of others flickering in the tray. She drops a couple of coins, which clatter into the bottom of a metal box for the privilege. Even remembering someone you love comes with a price, I guess.

Anya returns to the pew, crosses herself before sitting down.

"I am so glad you are here, Candace. For the beatification. Faith is so important. I would have been lost without mine." We sit quietly again. I study the Stations of the Cross, depicted in graphic detail on the walls of the church, in case there's a quiz later.

It's getting harder and harder to reconcile this woman with the baby-snatching villain I suspect her to be. But I know a bit about desperate times and desperate measures, and I'm sure Anya Scarpello does, too. You don't grow up under the shadow of both Stalin and the Russian Mob without learning a thing or two about being ruthless. Or maybe it hadn't even been her idea. This bullshit of women doing what they're told seems to run deep with her. I suppose her experience with her sister gave her a taste of what might happen to those in the family who didn't obey that rule. Still, I'm almost ashamed, sitting beside this woman who has provided me with her own confession, while I hide my ulterior motives. Feeling anything remotely like guilt is a new thing for me.

Perhaps I'll make a good Catholic yet.

CHAPTER 15

IT LOOKS LIKE THE POKER GAME is held on the other side of town, the rougher side. But then again, most of Detroit is rough, except for the downtown financial district, where they roll up the streets at night after all the office workers hightail it home to the safety of the burbs. We've been driving for a while when the goon at the wheel pulls into an old Jiffy Lube converted into a storefront. All the windows are darkened with thick acrylic paint. A sign above the scuff-marked door reads *Ponyboy Vapes*. I just don't get the attraction to this new way of fucking up your lungs. Smoking is bad enough. But at least you don't have to add to the stupidity of killing yourself by looking like a moron sucking on a kazoo while you're at it.

"Wait here," the driver says. "I will be back." He's got a thick Italian accent, being what the Mob calls a *Zip*, a recent immigrant from Sicily brought to America for the cause. His English vocab is good enough, though — must have studied back home in preparation for the job.

He disappears inside the vape shop. It's probably a front for one of the Scarpello lines of business. Most likely drugs. The Mafia used pizza parlours for years to distribute heroin. A scheme that would come to be known as the Pizza Connection — like the French Connection, but with more dough. But the feds got wise to that, so I guess a Vape shop makes for a better smokescreen these days, both literally and figuratively. After a few minutes, the Zip returns, drops a baggie of white powder on the front passenger seat. I so called it.

We pull back onto the darkened street. He adjusts the rear-view, trying to catch a better look at me in the back. I tug at the hem of my new black dress. When I'm sitting down, it rides up to my crotch. I'm not interested in showing my cooch to this guy, although I'm wearing more acceptable underwear since my trip to Nordstrom — a navy-blue lace number that makes my thighs itchy.

"You want to keep your eyes on the road, buddy?"

He ignores me. But he stuffs his peepers back in his head. We travel in silence. I watch out the window as the neighbourhood continues to deteriorate.

"So, where is this place, anyway?"

"It changes with the week," he says.

"So you don't get jacked?" A lot of people don't realize that the biggest risk for these underground high-stake card games is not getting raided but robbed. Changing the venue every week reduces their chances of being a target for thieves.

"That is not a problem," he says.

"Why?"

"We do not deal in the cash."

Malone had said they were having some trouble following the money on this one. I had assumed it was a cash game. Sounds like I was wrong.

"Then what do you deal in?" I ask.

He doesn't answer.

I lean forward from the back seat, close to his ear, trying to turn on the charm. I don't bother to pull down my dress when it rides up my thighs this time. "So, what do they bet with?" I ask. This information could be useful, given what Malone had said.

He pulls a half-smile in the rear-view. The teeth I can see are capped with silver metal, like that Jaws character from the Bond movies. He doesn't take care of his dental hygiene as well as I do.

"Are you Italian?" he asks me.

"Half." I'm not sure where this is going.

"We have a saying in Sicily. *La bocca è per mangiare.* The mouth is for eating."

"And what's that supposed to mean?"

"It means shut the fuck up with the questions."

I lean back against the seat again, resisting the urge to strangle this Zip with my itchy lace undies. Nobody tells me to shut up. But I've got to behave, at least for now. If Alex Scarpello ends up being my brother, I'll make sure this guy eats a whole lot more than his Sicilian words.

The Zip driver never does tell me where we're going, but eventually we arrive. The street looks like a zombie apocalypse version of Alex Scarpello's classy neighbourhood. Same vintage of mansions, but most are boarded up and covered with graffiti. The rest have been made into rooming houses for the down-and-out, emphasis on the down. The house we pull up in front of looks like one of the latter — sagging porch, chipping lead-based paint. The surveillance cameras mounted on the roof are brand-spanking-new, though. One is trained on the front door, where I wait after being dropped off. The Zip took off as soon as I got out of the back seat. I don't blame him. I wouldn't want to park a car in this neighbourhood at night. Even Charlotte's shitbox would be stripped within the hour.

A looker of a woman answers the door, surprising me. My height, in six-inch heels, appears to startle her, as well.

"You are here for …?"

"The card game," I say. "I'm security."

"Oh," she says. She ushers me through the metal-reinforced door.

The inside is in way better shape than the outside but still gives off the feel of better days that got left behind with no one to do the dusting. The walls are papered in faded gold-and-cream felt, and striped satin couches with the sheen gone bare in places dot the large entrance hall. A wide staircase, with the steps worn down in the middle, is lit by murky wall lights. They have tattered orange shades with little balls fringed at the bottom.

"The gentlemen have not arrived yet," she says. "For the game of cards." This one is foreign, too, although I can't place the accent. She has on a flowing pant suit that I would have preferred to my Band-Aid of a dress, but it's virtually transparent through the misty green material. This woman has no trouble with people seeing her cooch.

"The game is upstairs," she says. But she doesn't take me up them.

Instead, I follow her through the main floor to the kitchen in the back. The appliances haven't been updated since stoves went electric. It smells of burned coffee and mould. She opens a wood-plank door next to a dingy white refrigerator. There are narrow stairs behind it leading up.

"Wow, I say. "Just like *Downton Abbey*." Alex Scarpello really must have studied that fucking BBC classic, taking notes to bar the help from using the main stairs. The woman smiles, like she's trained to, and starts her way up. I follow her as best I can. My red Mrs. Claus stilettos keep catching on the narrow steps. I've pulled the lifts off, and the sharp points keep sticking in the soft wood.

When we reach the first landing, there's a heavily padded door affixed with studs. I go for the handle, but she blocks my way.

"Not here," she says, smiling again. "The games are on the third floor." We continue our way up. The third floor has a door with a sliding-panel peephole like they used to have in speakeasies, back when the government was fucking insane enough to try to outlaw booze. She knocks, and a man slides the panel aside to get a look at us through Plexiglas. I suspect it's bulletproof, or else he wouldn't stick his face up so close to it. He sees me standing behind the woman in the see-through pantsuit and nods. The panel shifts back into place, and then the door opens. I don't hear any disengagement of locks. I guess the guy at the door, who is as wide as he is tall, serves as a human deadbolt.

I walk in and he pats me down, scooping my phone out of my leather jacket in the process. The broad in the pantsuit hightails it down the stairs.

"No phones. No weapons." He dumps my phone into a plastic tote full of other contraband. He points at the portable metal detector I'm supposed to walk through. It's framed with hard plastic lattice, like a cheap entryway into a butt-ugly garden.

"You better give me the shoes," he says, pointing at my red pumps, the metallic spiked heels flash in the fluorescent light.

"I've got to have something to walk in," I say.

He scratches his head at that. This guy really is a deadbolt.

"Why don't you hold them while I go through, and you can pass them to me on the other side?"

"Maybe I should ask the boss," he says, looking nervously around. I hear the murmur of voices in the other room, catch the faint whiff of cigar smoke. Shit, that's even worse than vaping. I've had enough of this bullshit. I stride right up and through the metal detector while the deadbolt still scratches his head. Sirens and lights go off like I just won the jackpot on a game show. But instead of a grand prize, two security guys rush from the other room and tackle me to the hardwood floor. They knock the wind out of me, but I recover enough to get one in a headlock. My dress rides up to my waist as I backwards head-butt the guy behind me. He falls back to the floor, holding his forehead like he's discovered he should have had a V8. At this point, Alex Scarpello shows up and leans over us sprawled in a tangle on the floor.

"Well, Candace," he says, peering down at me through the smoke curling up from his cigar. "It appears you have arrived."

After releasing the guy I had in a headlock at Alex's urging, I get up and take in my surroundings. The game room is a converted attic, with a sloping roof on both sides. A professional card table decked out in green felt with beige bumpers around the edges takes up most of the space. Black leather wingback armchairs surround it. Right now, they're all empty, the players yet to arrive. A woman in her sixties, wearing the sort of tweed suit favoured by the wives of Republican candidates and Miss Marple, is setting up at a desk stocked with blocks of blue-and-white striped poker chips.

My attention is soon drawn to the full-length bar that runs along the far wall, well stocked with top-shelf liquor that a Goon Tavern patron has only seen in their wet dreams. I bend myself almost double to duck under the sloping roof and make an aggressive beeline for it, taking care to avoid the guy with the goose egg on his dome that I put there. The other guy who tackled me has taken over for the numbnuts at the door who Alex banished to patrol outside in the cold for being such a screw-up. On a bar stool, the dealer for the evening sits idle, dressed not unlike the penguin from dinner last night. I pour myself a couple of shots of Johnnie Walker Platinum, offering him some, but he shakes his head, mouthing soundlessly, "No drinking on the job." I ignore this advice. It doesn't apply to me.

Soon the players for the card game begin to file in. Some wear Wall Street wannabe get-ups, the same as Alex's; others, loud velour track suits and gold chains, as if they're middle-aged white men in a rap-star entourage. They give each other a wide berth. Many are from warring factions of families or gangs, Alex explains when he joins me behind the bar. These men would shoot each other out in the street but keep it peaceful here for the sake of the game. High-stakes poker is a no man's land, where all bets other than those on the table are off. Alex continues to nurse the cigar he's been sucking on since I got here, taking infrequent but deep pulls into lungs I imagine to be as black as his soul.

Once all eight players have arrived, they line up for the buy-in. The woman issuing the chips sits behind her desk. She watches the screen on her laptop as the players place their phones one by one in front of an attached scanner before tossing them in the same bin that's holding mine. As she hands them their blue-and-white striped tokens, she speaks at times in Italian or Russian, occasionally Arabic, seemingly hired as an interpreter as well as cashier. Since the advent of Google Translate, these multilingual types have to take work where they can get it. When one player flashes his phone for the scanner, I catch a glimpse of a square on the screen that looks like a Rorschach inkblot for robots, what they call a QR code.

"Bitcoin?" I say to Alex, figuring they're using the underworld's cryptocurrency of choice to manage the cashless buy-in, the QR codes linked through an app to their accounts.

Alex gives a disdainful snort, like I've just asked him if he uses Rogaine to grow his short-cropped hair.

"Do you know how much is stolen from those exchanges through cyber fraud and hackers?" he says as he surveys the players taking their seats. "Over four billion just last year."

"That's a lot of coin," I say, making a mental note to ask Deep why he hasn't looked into this virtual bank bandit use of his skills.

"It is," he says, not taking his eyes off the room. "And I am not a man interested in exposing my assets to thieves."

Or to the FBI, I'm thinking. Those blockchain trans-actions are anonymous but still publicly accessible. The Feds only have to link your online trading persona to your real one to follow the dirty money. Easier said than done, but still possible. That's part of the reason they were able to nail the guy running the Silk Road drug market on the dark web a few years back. They figured out he was using the Dread Pirate Roberts as his handle, and you know no good can come from tarnishing the name of a movie as fucking flawless as *The Princess Bride*.

"So, how are you keeping track of the money?" I ask, partly because I'm interested and partly because I may be able to offer this information to Malone if there's something I need to trade for it. Crypto isn't the only kind of cashless currency.

"There is no money," he says, grinding the stogie out in a crystal ashtray on the bar. It smoulders there like the hellcat that ate the canary smile he wears on his face. That smile and the smoke make me just a little bit nauseous when he finally turns to look at me. "Now, let's put you to work, shall we?"

The guy I put in a headlock is named Bruno. He's the same guy who answered the door when I showed up for dinner. I've been sent with him to do a surveillance walk-through of the second floor. He grumbles to himself as we make our way single file down the back stairs. He's still pissed that I bested him in in my entrance kerfuffle.

"Listen, buddy, we're not going to have a problem here, are we?"

"Not if you do your fucking job," he says.

"I always do my fucking job."

"Yeah, I've heard that about you," he says with grudging respect. It appears that my street cred has preceded me. Which is good. It'll help us get past our little tussle on the floor.

He unlocks the studded door to the second floor. It opens onto a shadowy hallway lined with tightly closed doors. At the far end, I see an old-style front parlour. Table lamps draped with gypsy scarves hurl smears of washed-out colour around the room. Raunchy paintings of women either leaning back or bent over with ecstatic orgasm faces are hung at intervals on the wall. A nude sculpture of a Roman dude with a conspicuously large fig leaf stands in one corner on a pedestal. The furniture is an echo of what I saw in the foyer earlier, plush and overdone. The air smells like a mixture of cotton candy–flavoured lube and spent jism.

"I thought the Scarpellos didn't do prostitution?"

"Yeah," says Bruno. "Well, you thought wrong. Things changed when the old man got sick." He narrows his beady eyes at me. They look like raisins embedded in his bloated dough-boy face.

"Does Anya know that?" I ask.

"What the Russki doesn't know won't hurt her," he says. The threat in his stare implies that anyone who puts her in the know is going to lose more than a hand.

"Where are the girls?" I ask. Usually there are a few lounging in the common areas in a cat house like this, acting as window dressing. There is nothing but silence in the hallway. If they were engaged with clients behind those closed doors, you'd hear something — faked, over-the-top orgasm shrieks, the strangled cry of a john in a ball gag getting his rocks off.

"They're in their rooms. They've got the night off, on account of the game. At least until it's over."

I suppose with the high-ranking bosses on the third floor, they can't be too careful about who they let in the house. One guy posing as a middle-aged married man looking for some tail could take out half of Detroit's criminal elite if he wandered up the stairs to the third floor.

Bruno presses his finger to the tiny bud he has lodged in one cauliflower ear. He walks past me to the parlour and looks out the window, mumbling into the hidden body mic. They hadn't issued me one of these Secret Service knockoffs when I arrived. Maybe they didn't have enough, or maybe they didn't think I'd have anything important to say. After grunting a final reply, Bruno returns his attention to me.

"There's some movement on the edge of the property. Could be nothing, but I gotta cover Angus so he can go check it out. Wait here."

He disappears down the hall and through the parlour to use the proper stairs. Angus must be the deadbolt freezing his ass off outside. I didn't know they let Scots in the Italian Mafia, but they let that Irishman in, so what do I know? I lean against the wall to wait, slipping off one of my high heels to massage the instep of my foot. When I let out a sigh of relief, a tiny voice comes from behind one of the closed doors.

"Hello?"

I put my shoe back on and walk up to the where the voice came from.

"Yeah?"

"Can you open the door please? I need to use the toilet."

My first thought is that I don't have a key. But I see the bathroom-style lock in the door handle. I turn the snib and step back. A young girl with sad eyes and rich ebony skin emerges, dressed in a pink kimono-style robe. She can't be much older than Janet, although they may have her tarted up to look older. I can picture them pulling her tight extensions into pigtails on other occasions to reverse her age for the borderline pedos.

She scurries down the hallway into the washroom. I listen to her pee hitting the side of bowl. It goes on for a long time. She must have been holding it in.

After the flush, the bathroom door opens and she makes her way warily back down the hall, checking over her shoulder.

"Thank you," she says when she reaches me. "The other girls have toilets in their rooms, but I am new so I get the room without one."

"Doesn't seem fair," I say. Of course, nothing is fair about a girl being locked in a room, forced to piss in a wastebasket if I hadn't come along.

"Do not misunderstand me," she says, looking alarmed, her deep-brown eyes widen. "They are very good to us here," she insists. "Very good. They have doctors that take care of us. Give us shots to protect against disease." She lifts one side of her kimono, showing me a hip still faintly swollen from a recent injection.

"That looks fresh," I say.

"It takes some time for the skin to heal," she says. "It is a big needle." She drops the kimono back into place. We stand in the hallway together awkwardly.

"I am from Nigeria," she says. "Where did they bring you from?"

She's mistaken me for another working girl. Which I am, but of a different kind. I haven't been brought from anywhere exotic, though.

I'm about to set her straight when we both hear the heavy steps on the stairs. She darts around me and back into her room, closing the door with a quiet hush so

Bruno won't know she's been out. I leave it unlocked just in case she has to go to the can again.

I meet Bruno in the parlour.

"False alarm," he says, out of breath from the stairs. This guy is built for stamina, not for speed. "It was just a bum trying to set up camp behind the garden shed."

He checks the windows in the parlour, makes sure they're secure.

"We don't have to check the windows in the bedrooms," he says. "They're nailed shut. A couple of the skinnier girls managed to squeeze through the bars and jump. It was a fucking mess."

He knocks heavily on each locked door until he gets a response, ensuring the women inside are where they're supposed to be and not splattered on the pavement below.

"Come on," he says. "We're done here."

We return to the back stairs. He closes the studded door and starts making his way back up the steps.

"Aren't you going to lock it?" I say.

"Nah," he says without turning around. "Believe me, those girls aren't going fucking anywhere."

CHAPTER 16

THE REST OF THE NIGHT at the poker game is fairly uneventful. The players hardly speak, working at their hands like it's a dead-end job they're forced to show up for. Alex has left by the time Bruno and I come back, some more pressing deal forcing him to be elsewhere. Around two in the morning, the game breaks up and the men cash out, without using cash, scanning the QR codes from their phones after they've been returned to them from the bin. The woman who met me at the front door comes up to escort each one down the main stairs to the brothel. I slip out discreetly to lock the door on the Nigerian girl's room again before I leave. I don't want to get her in trouble.

I spend a fitful night's sleep at Alex Scarpello's after the driver returns me there with Bruno. They'd locked the fucking liquor cabinet, so I had nothing to lull me into my usual stupored slumber. When I wake up at dawn, Anya has already left for early morning Mass. I guess we all have our chosen opiates for the masses. Unfortunately, mine was locked up in the liquor cabinet last night.

When I went up to bed, Bruno and his partner were still working, standing guard next to Alex and Anya's bedroom doors. They must have been there the night before, too, after everyone went to bed. Can't be too careful when you've got a contract killer in the house, I suppose.

I make my way down to the main floor. The door is open on Alex's study. He waves me in.

"Did you enjoy the work last night, Candace?" he asks, sitting behind a banker's desk the size of a barn door. Some guys compensate with their cars, and others with their office furniture, I guess.

"Wasn't much work to do," I say.

"That's the whole point, Candace. You're there for intimidation more than anything else."

"I suppose so." I don't say anything about the brothel he's running. I'm sure it's not the only vice he keeps from his mother. He sent me down to the second floor on purpose, though, so I could see what was going on. He knows I know, but I sense it is not a topic for discussion, just another form of silent intimidation.

"We're having another get-together this evening. Some associates have arrived from out of town. Usually, we only meet once a week, but ours is a unique opportunity for men who enjoy a game of chance, and I would like to accommodate them."

"Okay." I'd wanted to meet with Deep and Janet today. To see if they had any more information that I could use as leverage for finding Angela, or for my own benefit. We'd planned on dinner at a greasy spoon, but I could meet them earlier for lunch, which would still leave me time to make the poker game gig. I'll have to call Deep soon and make arrangements. I'm hoping he's managed to hack those Russian birth records by now.

"I'm afraid I have some other matters to attend to," he says, getting up from the massive desk. "You'll have to amuse yourself here until your assignment this evening. But Bruno will keep you company, won't you Bruno?"

It is only then that I notice Bruno filling the doorway of the study with his bulky frame. Unlike last night, he's packing heat, not even trying to hide the shoulder holster under his suit jacket two sizes too small.

"So, I'm on fucking house arrest?"

"On the contrary, you may come and go as you please," he says. "As long as where you come and go pleases me. Bruno can arrange for a driver if there is anywhere you need to be."

There is no way I can let a driver take me to meet with Deep and Janet. I can't let the Scarpellos know about either of them. Besides, I hate that pervert of a driver with his metal-mouth teeth.

"I don't need to be babysat, Alex," I say.

"I'm sure you don't, Candace. You are certainly not my baby." He chuckles at this, and Bruno joins in. "But you are my asset. And I am protective of my assets, as I told you before." He steps out from behind the desk, places the smooth palm of his hand on my cheek. If Bruno weren't standing there with a .45 under his arm, I'd break it at the wrist in three places.

"You're family, Candace. And my mother seems fond of you. But if you work for me, I own you. Do you understand? Just like I own that girl you met last night." Shit, how did he find out about that?

He drops his hand, but I can still feel the slimy warmth of it on my face.

"There is breakfast in the dining room," he says. "Please help yourself. I want you to feel at home here." He motions to Bruno, who steps out of the doorway. This is my cue to leave. I'm being dismissed, politely, which is the worst way.

In the dining room, the gooey sweetness of maple syrup fills the air. Breakfast is set out buffet style, with coffee in a silver urn that looks like it should have somebody's ashes in it. Lifting the lid off a metal chafing dish, I find French toast and sausage kebabs skewered and sweating inside. The maid told me the bangers are vegetarian as she was putting on her coat to go run an errand. But I could have guessed. I usually have a keen eye for counterfeits.

I pile up my plate, hungry with the lack of booze in my belly, then sit down alone to eat. Suspicious of the fake meat, I go heavy on the maple syrup, but the veggie substitute ends up tasting close enough to the real thing. I can't figure out what it's made out of — probably tofu or some unpronounceable hippy grain. My dad worked at a butcher's when he was a kid. He told me you could pack a ground-up old boot into a casing and with the right spices, it'd still taste pretty good.

I'm licking the maple syrup off one of the metal skewers with the edge of my tongue when I hear the front door slam — must be Alex leaving for his more important matters. Bruno shows up on cue in the dining room to keep an eye on me, a sheepish look on his face. We'd developed a bit of a professional rapport last night, trading war stories as we watched the poker game. I told him about the time I beat a drug dealer unconscious with a toilet tank lid. He told me how he'd put a mall cop who'd welched on a bet in the hospital by running him over repeatedly with his own Segway.

"Where's your buddy?" I ask.

"What buddy?"

"Your partner," I say. "The one I butted heads with."

"He left with Mr. Scarpello."

"Hmm." I give the skewer one last luxurious lick.

"Did you narc on me about letting that girl out of her room?" I figure it must have been him. I thought he hadn't seen her when he'd come up the stairs, but I guess I was wrong.

"No," he says. "They saw it on the closed circuit." Damn. I thought the fig leaf on that Roman statue looked fucking suspicious.

I stand up from the table, wipe my sticky hands on a cloth napkin.

"I'm going to the can. You're not going to follow me in there, are you?"

"No, I'm not."

"Good."

In the upstairs washroom, I wave to the homeless guy lurking behind the low wall across the street, giving him the signal. Bruno thought he'd chased him away last night, but I discovered him hiding in an overgrown boxwood shrub when I did a final walk of the perimeter before the game broke up. I'd promised him a hundred bucks to help me out, and, like most guys with nothing to lose, he hasn't let me down.

Strolling around the curve of the stairs a few minutes later, I see Bruno run over to the front window, attracted there by the racket on the front lawn.

"What the fuck?"

I walk up and stand beside him at the window. The homeless dude is marching up and down in front of a forsythia bush by the driveway, smashing together two metal garbage can lids like they're cymbals and he's part of the band. He's hung a matted Christmas wreath around his skinny neck for a festive touch.

"Jesus," I say, taking in a maple syrup–infused breath. "You better check that out."

Bruno does his own marching to the front door. When he yells out of it, the homeless guy just bangs on his cymbals louder. He takes off down the front steps, but the guy is fast. Bruno, with his over-muscled frame, can't keep up with the smaller man's wiry amphetamine hustle. He chases him around the bush like a lumbering bear after a jacked-up mouse.

I slip the skewer from the breakfast kebabs out from inside my leather jacket and hightail it to Alex's study. It only takes a couple of jimmies of the lock on the door to get inside. Running over to the desk I try all the drawers, but only one of them is locked. I'm not sure what I'm looking for, but if there's something to be found, I figure that's where it'll be. I insert the skewer and with a few leveraged twists the lock pops as easily as the one on the door did. They really need to invest in mechanisms that can withstand something stronger than cutlery.

Inside the desk is a Glock 9mm, which I leave, because it'll be missed. But other than that, the drawer is stuffed with medication. Injectables, pills, the works. Most of them don't have any labels on them. I hadn't pegged Alex for an addict, but this has to be his stash. There's one bottle that's labelled. Ativan. It's three-quarters full, so I pour out a dozen or so in my hand and pocket them. You never know when a good solid tranquilizer might be of use. I rifle through the rest of the drawer for documents that might help me prove Alex Scarpello is not who everyone thinks he is, but there are none, only a bulk package of syringes shoved at the back.

A prolonged hoot sounds from the front yard, followed by some Sicilian swear words in response from Bruno. I glide the drawer closed again and press in the lock, leaving the way I came. The door is the kind that secures automatically when you close it, so I don't have to use my trusty skewer again.

Looking out the window, I can see that my hired distraction has climbed a tree at the end of the driveway. He's stripping off his clothes and throwing them down on Bruno, who shakes his fist when a grey sock that might once have been white hits him full-on in the face. He gestures at his gun, but I know he won't shoot the guy. It wouldn't go over well in this neighbourhood, picking off a half-naked vagrant in a cherry tree.

I ditch the skewer in the dining room, then slip out the sliding doors to the backyard. Hopping the fence, I can still hear Bruno shouting at the guy in the tree, who is now making monkey sounds. That boy's really earning the cash I promised him.

Skulking through the neighbours' backyards, I emerge on a parallel street and call Deep, arranging to meet him and Janet for lunch. They've got a place in mind. He'll text me the address.

"We'll see you there at noon," Deep says.

"Okay," I say. "And Deep?"

"Yeah?"

"If a homeless guy comes to the door, give him a hundred bucks."

I walk aimlessly for some time, although my subconscious GPS eventually locates a liquor store. I buy a mickey of Jack and find a park to drink it in. The browned-out green space borders on an old peeler bar called The Doll's House. Outside of it, a marquee with removable capital letters informs me that SANTA DROPS HIS LOAD HERE. It seems like the right neigbourhood to sit on a bench and drink from a paper bag, which I'm forced to do since I left my trusty hip flask back at the Scarpellos. I've got a couple of hours to kill before I have to meet Janet and Deep for lunch. Janet picked a spot in midtown that serves all-day breakfast poutine. Poutine is a Quebec version of fries and gravy that they totally ruin with cheese curds. The kid loves it, apparently. Must be a Canadian thing.

The first shot of Jack goes down harshly, mixing with the hearty breakfast still heavy in my stomach. But after a while, it warms me all over, improving my digestion of both the meal and my thoughts. It's strange being back in the game, working for Scarpello in a world I'd mostly left behind after that stretch I served in the pen. My dad was killed when I was in prison, and I didn't have the heart to continue with the family business without him. Or maybe I'd just had enough. It's hard to tell the difference sometimes between apathy and choice. When I'd followed in his assassin footsteps, I'd been travelling the path of least resistance. There was that brush I'd had with college, a plan for a different life, but a band of thugs who jumped me on campus put an end to that. They'd used me and left me for dead, driven by the sport of violating the daughter of a notorious killer. What you're born into can come back to haunt you worse than the dead can.

Maybe I won't go back to the Scarpellos. I could leave it all to Deep and his cyber surveillance. If we confirm Alex is my twin brother, then we can just do a remote blackmail and be done with it. I don't know if I'm even interested in a piece of the Scarpello power pie anymore. There's a lot of fucked-up shit going on in that organization, even by my standards. And let's face it, I've never been much of a team player. Janet will want me to stay close in case Angela comes back. But if she's in danger, she won't be returning any time soon to the Indian Village homestead. And if she's not in danger, then she's staying incognito for her own reasons. My sister will just have to accept that about our mother, like I did a long time ago.

I tell myself all of this, but part of me is still drawn in by the power, the money, as well as the commitment I've made to my sister. Taking another deep pull on the bottle, I decide to see it out, this road I'm on. Maybe it's too late to turn back, anyway.

I'm halfway through the plastic mickey in its brown paper bag when my phone vibrates up against me from my pocket. I take it out and check out the screen. It's Malone.

"You haven't been answering my calls," she says, all tight-assed and annoyed when I pick up.

"I had my phone turned off," I lie. "I keep getting calls from Peru telling me I'm wanted by the cops."

"You *are* wanted by the fucking cops. And the cop is me."

"Good morning to you, too, Malone."

"Don't you bloody 'good morning' me," she says. "What the hell are you doing in Detroit?"

Shit. Did she track me from my phone? But she'd need a warrant for a trace like that. The phone companies don't give up their customers that fucking easily. And I'm not dumb enough to subscribe to the Find My Phone app like my sister does.

"You've been spotted," Malone says. "You're hanging with the Scarpellos. How did you think that wouldn't get back to me?"

Wow, the department really does have their eyes on the family. Or maybe it's the Feds. The FBI co-operates with local law enforcement way more than you'd think. Another reality that doesn't match what you see on TV. I scout around the park. A girl with a butt hanging out of her pouty mouth pushes a snot-covered kid in a stroller. Whenever one of its wonky wheels gets caught in a pavement crack, she screams "Fuck." A junkie lies passed out in a dried-up fountain, bundled in a crumpled sleeping bag, while a couple of stone cherubs look on. Both cherubs are missing parts of their noses, as is the junkie. Cheap coke'll do that to you. An old guy drags a ladder over to the Doll's House marquee, holding a letter S under his arm. The one in Santa has blown off in the wind. I know undercover can go deep sometimes, but none of these have the whiff of the law about them.

"I'm looking for Angela," I tell her, figuring a half-truth will keep her bullshit radar from pinging. "This seemed like the best place to start."

"The best place to start if you want to end up missing like she is. I told you we'd handle it. And where the hell is Janet? You're supposed to be taking care of her."

"She went home with Aunt Stacey," I say, back to full-on lying again.

"That's bullshit." Ping.

"Blonde broad, heavy hand with the mascara. Short enough she could fit into my armpit?"

My accurate description of Stacey throws Malone, as I planned it would. She pauses, thinking, but then her instincts override my attempts at deception. That's why she's a good detective.

"I'm calling Social Services."

"Don't do that, Malone."

"You're leaving me no choice, Candace."

I need to hold her off somehow. If she checks things out, she'll find out Aunt Stacey crossed the border back into Canada alone yesterday, minutes after I threatened her in the alleyway. Windsor is only on the other side of the river from Detroit. That chick was so scared, she'd probably have swum across it to get away from me.

"What if I could help you out with this poker game thing?" I say, bartering with what I don't have. "Scarpello's got me running security on it."

"You're working for Alex Scarpello? Jesus, Candace. You could get busted for just associating with that bastard."

"Then why haven't I been busted?" Malone might owe me a favour and turn a blind eye. But she got this intel from others who don't have the same loyalties.

"They've got bigger fish to fry, Candace."

"So let me help fry them, Malone. I could be a big help to you, on the inside and all." I don't know if I'm up for informing on the Mob, but I've got to offer Malone something. "I worked the game last night. And I'm working it again tonight."

"Where are they holding it?"

"You don't need to know that, Malone." I can't have her raiding the place. Not until I figure a few things out. Or Deep does. "But I might be able to get a lead on how they're moving the money around for you."

"But what about Janet?"

"Janet is safe, Malone. I give you my word on that."

She mulls this over. Makes an executive decision. That's what I like about Malone. She's an independent agent, like me, when it comes to her work. She's not afraid to go out on a limb that could crack out from underneath her. Also, against all odds, she sort of trusts me. That happens when you save someone's life. But then again, she'd saved mine in return. A history like that doesn't make you even, as much as it joins your fates at the hip.

"You've got until tomorrow afternoon to come up with something and get out of town," she says. "If not, I'm calling Social Services about Janet and coming to Detroit personally to get you both. I told you, Candace, you're not safe there. Mob families are always a volatile place to be right after a transfer of power. And the dust hasn't settled yet. Alex Scarpello will be looking for ways to showcase his strength, to discourage other contenders. You don't want to get caught in the crosshairs of that."

"I'm touched by your concern, Malone."

"I'm serious. The dead woman in the freezer. Your mother's disappearance. They're all linked to you, Candace. And they all lead back to the Scarpellos. If even half the things they say about this new Don are true, he's not someone to mess with."

"I'm not someone to mess with, either, Malone," I remind her.

"I know. That's what scares me."

"Why?"

"Because, Candace. This time, you might have just met your match."

After a few more false assurances, I hang up the phone with Malone, and lean back on the bench. The old guy replacing the S on the marquee drops the ladder he was carrying with a clatter. It wakes the junkie in the fountain, who lifts his head and looks around. When he catches sight of my mickey in a bag, I can see his eyes light up, even from twenty feet away. I lift up one corner of my full mouth into a silent snarl. He crawls back into his sleeping bag, like a worm burying himself in dirt.

Alex Scarpello may be my twin, but I'd never thought of him as my equal. That kind of math tempts a betting girl's odds and cements my resolve to play things out. I know what I'm doing here in Detroit is a gamble, but the pot is too damn big to pass on. And I've never been one to fold my cards early.

CHAPTER 17

I GRAB A BUS TO MIDTOWN, where I've arranged to meet Deep and Janet for lunch at a place called the Brooklyn Street Local. Janet and Deep's food has already arrived when I get there. A rectangular platter in front of my sister holds a mountain of poutine topped with a fried egg that stares out like a yellow eye. Being the Brit that he is, Deep went for the fish and chips. I take a seat in the booth they've scored by the window. It looks out on a used car lot that promises approval to everyone no matter how shitty their credit.

"Did you find Mom, yet?" Janet asks, through a mouthful of fries and gravy. I don't even want to think about the cheese curds.

I warm my hands on the cup of java the waitress just poured.

"Jesus, Janet. You're like a broken record."

"That is what you're trying to do, right?"

"I'm trying to do a lot of things."

"Like shopping at Nordstrom?"

"For fuck's sake, I explained about that."

"And working for Alex Scarpello? I thought you said you didn't do criminal stuff anymore."

"I don't." Not entirely accurate, but close enough.

"Then why are you?" The logic of a thirteen-year-old girl is as black and white as the QR codes I saw flashed on the player's phones last night. I'm about to explain to her that I only took the job to help find Angela for her, a half-truth of the kind I used with Malone. But before I can, the waitress comes by and asks for my order. I haven't even had time to look at the menu. I'm still full from breakfast, but the half cup of maple syrup I'd ingested has tripped my sweet tooth rather than satisfying it. Sugar, like many powders that give you a rush, tends to leave the consumer always wanting more.

"What do you have for dessert?" I ask.

"We have a special today. It's a deconstructed pomegranate–lime curd tart."

"Deconstructed?"

"All the ingredients are laid out on the plate separately. Crumbled up graham crackers on one part, the lime curd on the other. And then a fresh pomegranate half in the centre. The cook made it fresh this morning."

"It sounds like the cook didn't make it at all." I want to ask about carrot cake, but I'm afraid they'll hand me a raw vegetable and some flour and expect me to bake it myself.

"I'll just have some more coffee," I tell her. After she pours me some, I take the sugar dispenser and add a generous helping of what a health-conscious female body builder I used to date referred to as "white death."

"What's he like?" Deep asks after the waitress is gone.

"Who?"

"Alex Scarpello."

"Let's just say that if we're twins, I'm not the evil one."

"Wow, that's saying a lot."

"It certainly fucking is," Janet mumbles, still mad at me about the shopping thing. She's wearing her big-ass specs again, and they magnify the accusation in her eyes.

Deep steps in, as he usually does, to change the subject and the trajectory of the conversation.

"I've made some headway on the Russian birth registration."

"And?"

"I found a birth certificate for Alex Scarpello. I'm sorry, Candace. But it confirms he was born in Russia."

"Could be a fake," I say. "The Russians don't exactly have a name for keeping accurate public records. Bribe a public official with a few rubles, and you could probably get them to issue a birth certificate for Mikhail Mouse."

"Maybe," Deep admits. He dips a piece of heavily battered fish into some creamy tartar sauce and takes a crunchy bite. His lips shine with the grease. It's strangely sexy, and I have to turn away until he wipes his mouth with a napkin from the silver canister on the table. "The registration date was over a year after the actual birth. That seemed a little dodgy to me. And it was issued in Moscow, a long way from where Anya was supposed to be staying with her family. The Smirnovs operate out of St. Petersburg."

"Smirnov, like the vodka?" Wow, a woman with a maiden name like that couldn't be all bad. No wonder I'd taken a bit of a shine to her.

"That's Smirnoff," he says, correcting me, but not in an arrogant way, so I allow it. "In any case, I'm still looking. Something else might surface. In the meantime, I have a mate in Pavlovsk I'll ring, ask him to see what he can find on his side."

I grab one of his fries and pop it into my mouth. It tastes like fish. "I've been doing some recon of my own," I tell him. "I broke into Alex's study today."

"That sounds unwise," Deep says, disapproval in his voice. But Janet beams at me. I'm finally doing something she considers more beneficial to the cause than buying evening wear.

"You told me to keep my eyes peeled for information around the house, Deep."

"I meant documents you might happen upon, not something that required a bloody break and enter."

"Yeah, like Scarpello's going to just leave his secrets lying around on the goddamn coffee table. Jesus, Deep." I steal another fishy fry. "Anyway, Alex wasn't there, and I kept the hired help busy while I did my thing. Got a guy to stage a distraction."

"Would that be the gent who came to our motel room asking for a hundred dollars and a pair of my socks?" Deep asks, raising an eyebrow.

"Yeah," I say. "That would be him." I'm glad to hear he made it out of the tree.

I tell them about the locked drawer and its contents, full of injectables and other unlabelled drugs.

"He's a drug addict?" Janet asks.

"He doesn't seem the type," I say, grimacing as I sip on the overly sweet coffee. "He's too smooth for that, too in control." *At least for a psychopath*, I think, but keep that observation to myself.

"That actually makes sense," Deep says. "I came across some information about Alex Scarpello's childhood. In his school records, there were a lot of absences for illness, even hospitalizations. The files are a little light on details, but his mother was so worried about him catching germs from the other students that she insisted on him having a separate toilet."

Deep shakes a generous helping of malt vinegar on his fries. The strong tangy smell puts a wrinkle in my nose. I was locked up once with a girl so desperate with the DTs she drank a whole bottle of that stuff, too dumb to know the malt part wasn't alcohol. It burned part of her esophagus, and she burped toxic gas for a week. I'm no stranger to the abundant abuse of alcohol, but at least I never got that fucking bad.

"So, you're thinking he might still be sick?" I say, going to steal another fry from Deep's plate, but I can't find one that doesn't have that damn vinegar on it.

"I'm thinking there are a lot of chronic illnesses that require people to inject medication," he says. "Diabetes, for one. Even cancer. My mom used to have shots for her rheumatoid arthritis."

"Alex Scarpello looked pretty damn healthy to me. But —"

Janet throws down her fork into her empty platter so hard, I figure she may have taken a chunk out of the white ceramic.

"I don't understand how this helps at all with finding Mom."

I don't appreciate tantrums, but I can see the kid's hurting. I'm not totally insensitive.

"We're just trying to find some information that might get us some leverage, Janet," I say, trying to reassure her. "So we can get the Scarpello's to give up where she is."

"But they told you where she is. She's at that retreat!"

"We don't know where that is, Janet."

I switch my attention to Deep, hoping to spread some of my kid sister's wrath his way. "Did you make any headway finding the location?"

Deep shakes his head. "That is proving harder to hack than the Russian Department of Vital Statistics."

"Why don't you just ask them?" Janet asks, her wrath still firmly focused on me.

"What?"

"You're so tight with the Scarpellos, living at their house, working at their stupid poker game. Why don't you just ask them where the retreat is that Mom's supposed to be at?"

"It's not that easy, Janet. We have to be cautious." I'm trying to keep with the reassurance shtick here, but this kid isn't making it easy. Like I said, patience isn't one of my virtues. "Besides. I think Angela is probably okay. Anya seems to actually care about her. My gut tells me they're expecting her to come back. I'll be there when she does."

"No, you won't! You'll be out shopping for dresses or getting Deep to find something on Alex so you can blackmail him for money. You don't give a damn about what happens to Mom. You don't even call her that. Just Angela, like she's not anything to you!"

She jumps up from the table and runs off toward the restrooms. Deep pushes his plate away, and he's not even finished his vinegar-laden fries.

"That went a bit pear-shaped," he says.

"You think?"

"It's been rough on her."

"It's been pretty fucking rough on me, too," I say, thinking about Alex putting his slimy butcher knife–swinging hand on my cheek this morning. I wipe at my face with a napkin before turning to Deep.

"Listen, I had a call from Malone this morning. She's wise to me being here in Detroit, and she's threatening to call Social Services about Janet."

Deep lets out a whistle from between his greased-up lips. "Shit, what did you say to her?"

"I offered to get her some information on the Scarpellos if she held off. They're betting some high stakes in this poker game they've got going, but the cops can't figure out how they're moving the money."

"You don't strike me as an informant, Candace."

"That's not informing, Deep. That's reducing collateral damage. If I can get her even a little bit of information, like maybe the online handles of some of the lowlifes at that poker game, I could buy us some time. Besides, I don't give a fuck about grassing on any friend of Alex Scarpello."

"You really don't like him."

"I don't like most people, Deep."

"You like me." He smiles, and it sets me off balance for a second. I do like him, goddamn it, but I'm not about to admit it out loud.

"The game is cashless. An old girl with a laptop is keeping track of it all. The players scan one of those QR codes to get into the game and to settle at the end of the night."

"Cryptocurrency?" Deep asks, making the same assumption I had.

"Maybe," I say. "But whatever way they're doing it, it's on that computer. If I got a hold of it, could you figure it out?" I have no idea how I might manage to lift the laptop and smuggle it out of the game. It's a lot bigger than a breakfast kebab skewer.

"I don't need the whole laptop," he says. "I could just give you a rubber ducky."

"What do I need with a bath toy, Deep?"

"A rubber ducky is a keystroke injection tool," he explains, using patience I could have used earlier. "It plugs into a computer just like a USB stick does. Virus checkers can't pick it up because they think it's just another keyboard. You can load it with thousands of lines of code, and it'll type it into the computer in seconds. Takes a bit of time to execute, but not that long. People use it to steal passwords, even create backdoors for remote access."

"Malware," I say. "I thought you only hacked for the greater good?"

"I have to keep up on the latest attack technology to protect my clients against it, Candace," he says, then gives a wry smile. "Plus, it's cool."

"So, you could remotely access this chick's laptop if I plug in this duck thing?"

"I can if she's connected to the internet. And most people leave their Wi-Fi turned on, no matter what they're doing on their computers."

"Why can't we just download the files onto a regular USB stick?"

"That takes time, Candace. Have you ever tried to back up a computer's hard drive?"

"I don't even back up my car if I can help it, Deep." The reverse has always been a bit sticky on Charlotte's car. Most of the time, I try to find two parking spaces nose to nose, so I can pull in through one to park in the other with the car facing frontwards.

"The point is, Candace, it would be hard to insert a stick and download all the files you need without being detected. It can take several minutes. Do they leave the laptop unattended for that long?"

"No." I can't remember the chip lady even leaving her post in front of the laptop for a pee last night. And even if she did, I'd have Bruno and the rest of security to think about. Something tells me I'd need more than a home-less guy banging garbage can lids together to get them all to clear out.

"With the duck, you'd need only seconds, a minute tops. Just pop it in, and watch the script execute on the screen. Once it's done, you can take it out and you're golden. If she links to the internet later, I can come through the backdoor and look at whatever she's got."

"So, breaking into Alex Scarpello's study was too much of a risk, but this is just fine and dandy?"

"I've learned by now that you're going to do what you want in the end, Candace. I might as well help you do it right."

The waitress comes and takes the empty poutine plate away. Janet's sketchbook had been tucked underneath it.

On the open page is a different sort of drawing from her usual ones, a close-up of a woman's face done in charcoal with smudges for depth and perspective. Deep must have bought her those new art supplies. The woman looks sort of like me and sort of like Janet, but older and with a sadness in her eyes that makes me turn away to study the blow-up Rudolph the Red-Nosed Reindeer across the street. He's fallen over onto his mutant nose and shudders in the wind at the entrance to the used car lot. It reminds me of Stacey, and that reminds me of Angela.

"Find out the address of that retreat, Deep. I'm not sure if that's where Angela is, but it won't hurt to check it out. And it'll keep the kid happy."

"Will do," Deep says, smiling, a man used to doing things that make others happy.

But for me, it's a new thing.

Back at the motel, it only takes Deep a minute to load the code to the duck he'd packed in his suitcase. He already had the malware script saved on his main laptop. For a guy who works only for the righteous, he sure has access to a lot of coder contraband.

The rubber duck looks just like a run-of-the mill USB stick, except for the black cover with the little neon-yellow bird on it. When you pull the cover back, it reveals a small grouping of black-and-silver metal chips and circuits, a miniature version of the disemboweled motherboard I'd seen in Deep's living room. I pocket it in my leather jacket before I leave the motel and start the long walk back to Indian Village. I need to clear my head, think hard on how I'm going to pull this caper off tonight. Finding an opportunity to plug the duck into the cashier's laptop with half of the Scarpello entourage and a roomful of gangsters watching is going to be next to impossible. But impossible and I have been neighbours in the past, and I usually find a way in the door to borrow a cup of flour.

I kick at a half-flattened beer can discarded on the sidewalk, send it skittering down an alleyway to join other abandoned things. Fucking Malone. I can't believe I'm doing something this risky just to keep my kid sister out of foster care. But then again, if Deep can get a look-see at how the funds are flowing in that card game, perhaps I could convince him to funnel some of the proceeds into our own bank accounts. I could even use some of the loot to help out those girls on the second floor, find them a way out from behind those locked doors. I haven't been able to get that Nigerian kid out of my head, so young and defenceless as she showed me the injection site on her skinny hip. I get that sex work is a legitimate gig and all, but something tells me that doesn't apply to women who'd jump out a second-floor window just to get away from their own profession.

I step around a pile of dog shit, frozen on the sidewalk, resisting the urge to kick it away like the can. I know Deep would never go in for stealing, from gangsters or from anyone else. I hate it when people have morals that get in the way of personal gain.

Especially when it's me.

CHAPTER 18

WHEN I GET BACK TO THE HOUSE in Indian Village, I'm almost as frozen as the dog crap on the sidewalk. Bruno gives me a fierce look when he opens the door.

"Where the fuck have you been?" he asks.

"Out to get some hooch," I tell him. "You locked up the good stuff."

I run up the stairs before he can interrogate me further, take a hot shower, and crash on the bed, still with the fluffy white towel wrapped around me. I hadn't intended to sleep, but I hadn't got much shuteye the night before, or perhaps the cold sapped my strength, because I doze off, wake up when the penguin knocks on the bedroom door calling me to dinner. I get up and force myself back into the little black dress for tonight's security detail. My phone's on the bedside table, and I leave it there to charge with the cord Deep gave me back at the motel. When I join Anya in the dining room, she's sitting alone, picking at a portobello mushroom stuffed with mashed potatoes.

"I am afraid Alex will not be joining us for dinner," she says, her tone clipped short as the chives sprinkled on top of her mash. "He said he will see you this evening at the gentlemen's card game."

I think about telling her how the gentlemen were practically tripping over each other's hard-ons to get to the second floor last night. But contrary to popular opinion, I do know when to keep my mouth shut sometimes.

"Thanks for the message," I say instead.

"He'd hoped to tell you himself, but you were not at home all day, I understand."

"I went to check out the cathedral. You know, where they're doing the beatification thing." I take a seat, tucking into my own dinner, already served up and still piping hot. The mashed potatoes burn the roof of my mouth, and I have to down a glass of ice water in a cut-glass tumbler to wash it down.

"You went to the Cathedral of the Most Blessed Sacrament?" she asks, an eyebrow raised.

"Yeah, that's the one." I hadn't actually gone there, but I'd looked it up online — initially confusing it with Solomon's Cathedral, which I discovered wasn't even Catholic and had little to do with that guy with the mine.

"Alex and I will be attending the ceremony tomorrow night there. The archbishop will lead the Mass celebrating Father Murphy and read the decree from the Pope. I would ask you to join us, but the Mass has been limited to ticketholders only. I don't believe you have a ticket?"

"I thought I'd just stand outside and watch it in on the jumbotron." I'm pleased with myself, remembering this tidbit of information provided by the lady behind the desk at the motel.

"The temperature is to drop even further this weekend, Candace." She tilts her head at me, forcing a tight smile. "I suggest you stay here and watch on the television." We both know this is not a suggestion and has fuck all to do with the weather report.

My absence today has aroused suspicion, something I can't afford until Deep strikes some pay dirt in his research into Alex's birth. Until then, the whole Scarpello clan will be closing ranks to keep a closer watch on me. I don't bear up well under scrutiny at the best of times. Even less when I've got a rubber ducky hidden in the inner pocket of my leather jacket, burning a hole there worse than the steaming hot potatoes in my mouth.

Bruno takes the place of the usual driver to bring me to the location of tonight's game. The Zip had to go for emergency root canal surgery. Couldn't have happened to a better guy, in my opinion. I hope he gets fucking lockjaw.

The game's being held in a different neighbourhood, but the house is much the same — a sprawling throwback mansion, piece of crap on the outside, shabby chic on the inside. This time, the girls are housed on the main floor, which has a front parlour done up in the dark red-and-yellow velvet wallpaper favoured by opium dens and old-school Chinese restaurants. There are servant stairs and there are regular ones. I don't even have to ask Bruno which ones we're meant to use as he leads me through a maze of murky rooms and corridors. The place is like a labyrinth. I keep expecting a minotaur to jump out from behind one of the credenzas.

The game room is on the second floor, set up in a converted porch off the back of the house. There's a couple of spot heaters running full blast to keep the chill out. Anya wasn't kidding when she said the weather was changing. Metal shutters that roll down like garage doors block the bank of windows that would normally look out over the flat roof of the garage. After handing Bruno my phone, I trip the metal detector when I stroll through it in my high heels.

"It's the shoes," I say to him, pointing at my shiny sharp stilettos. He pats me down just the same, but the duck is slim, and so am I. If he notices anything, he probably figures it's one of my pointy ribs. I've broken a few over the years, and those things never set properly after they've been busted.

When Alex arrives, he's too busy with his out-of-town players to give me more than a cursory glance. Tonight, the guests are all Micks from the Irish Mob, members of rival gangs run out of Boston. They're meeting here not only to play cards but to discuss a drug war looming between the two organizations. Alex is providing them with a neutral zone to get together and work out their differences over a few rounds of Texas Hold 'em. In exchange for this, he pockets a criminally large percentage of the night's winnings — but then again, he is a criminal. Bruno briefed me on all this on the way over in the car. He's stationed me in a corner by the shuttered windows with the guy I head-butted at the first game. I ask him his name, but he ignores me. I guess he still has a headache.

This time, the girls aren't in lockdown. Or at least a handful of them aren't. They file in from the service stairs that lead directly into the action. Four girls are soon working the room, chatting up the players one at a time, bringing them drinks. A couple are as young as the girl I ran into last night; others maybe just kissing their twenties. The youngest one by far wears a short baby-doll nightdress with matching peach stockings that cut high on her pale thighs. She has ice-blonde hair like Janet, but it's a dye job. From my height, I can see the dark brown strip of roots running along her middle part.

Most of the players keep their cool around the girls, but one asshole with a mop of ruddy red hair pulls the youngest one onto his lap and shoves a rough hand up the short skirt of her baby doll, laughing when she cries out. I've had some bad experiences with gingers in the past, at least one in particular. I go to stand behind him, using my own special brand of intimidation. He looks up at me, then releases the girl with a smirk. She runs behind the bar to fix him a Bloody Mary with shaking hands.

Once they all have their drinks, the men line up for the buy-in as they did the night before. The cashier issuing the chips wears the same conservative outfit. Her translation services aren't required this evening, so she just greets each player formally from behind her laptop, instructing them to scan their phones before confiscating them like a killjoy high-school teacher.

Alex walks right past me and whispers something to Bruno, who nods. Before leaving the room, he points to his eyes with V'd fingers and then aims those offending digits directly at me. Then he disappears down the hall that leads to the main staircase.

I cross the room to Bruno where he stands next to the metal detector.

"What the fuck was that about?"

"I think you know, Candace."

"Where's he going now?"

"Out," he says, sharply, staring straight ahead.

"Listen, Bruno, I know I gave you the slip this morning, but you don't have to be such an asshole about it." His head swivels on his thick neck to face me.

"Do you know how much shit I got into on account of you?"

"A girl has to have her freedom, Bruno."

"I don't like getting in shit," he says, bitching like a big baby. I can't believe this guy once picked pieces of mall cop out of the wheels of a Segway. He's such a whiner.

I'm trying to think of some way to smooth it over with Bruno. With all this suspicion brewing, I've got to work on distilling my allies. I'm about to compliment him on his physique, a ploy that usually works with guys heavier on the brawn than brain, when I see a flash of white in the hand of the asshole ginger. People who've been to prison like me have a sixth sense for the sharp and pointy. Shivs don't have to be made of metal. I once got jumped by a broad in the joint who'd made a hardened papier-mâché shank out of toilet paper and cornstarch glue. The ginger stumbles into the guy at the front of the line, making out like he's drunk.

"Knife!" I shout, but it's too late. The bone-white dagger vanishes between the shoulder blades of the man at the front of the line. He drops the phone in his hand and clutches at the centre of his chest, where the tip of the weapon sticks out after running his heart through. He falls forward onto the desk. The cashier screams and stumbles away when his cheekbone hits the scanner with a loud crack.

The ginger takes off down the hallway toward the main stairs. All hell breaks loose between the players. They trample some of the girls as they rush the back stairs to get out. The security guy I'd been stationed with earlier takes off after the assassin, as does Bruno, but not before he turns to me with a snarl.

"You stay here."

They really don't trust me. I'd be offended if it weren't for the fact that this lethal fiasco has effectively cleared the room. The chip lady has abandoned her post, leaving the laptop unattended. I can see blood splattered up the back of the screen. This is my chance.

I move toward the computer, fishing the duck out of my inner pocket as I go. But as I pass the card table, I hear a wet sniffle coming from beneath the green-felted card table. Bending down to look, I see the girl in the baby-doll nightdress, all curled up and sobbing into pale peach chiffon.

"Get out," I tell her roughly. I don't have the time to be gentle. She crawls out from underneath the table obediently, no stranger to barked commands.

"You need to get out of here," I say. But she shakes her head.

"I'm afraid," she says, through hitched sobs. "I want to stay here with you." I sympathize with her predicament, but I've got to get rid of her.

"I need you to go get some towels," I say. "To staunch the bleeding, okay?" I indicate the corpse slumped on the desk, who is long past the need of first aid. But she doesn't know that. "Get some hot water, too." I add this request so it'll take her longer before she comes back. It sounds like something off of *Call the Midwife*. Charlotte loves that fucking show.

When the kid still stands there trembling, I shout at her, "Now!"

That gets her moving. She runs off down the back stairs.

I step up to the laptop. One lifeless hand decked in fat rings blocks the USB port. When I knock it out of the way the dead guy slips off the desk and hits the wood-plank floor with a thud.

A crackle of gunfire sounds from below. They must have unlocked the gun safe where everyone, security included, had stored their weapons before the game. You might be surprised by that, but no self-respecting gangster is going to give up his piece at the door when Alex's goons are standing there packing. It's about trust, Alex told me earlier. More about distrust, I'd say.

I slip the duck into the USB port and immediately the laptop's screen explodes with dozens of windows filled with commands that scroll like the whole computer's messed up on crack. Deep told me not to take it out until the screen went clear again. I keep one eye on the laptop as I fish around in the confiscation bin for my phone, plucking it out and dropping it in my pocket in case I need it later. The laptop's screen is still pulsing with malicious intent when I hear the steps on the back stairs. That girl was fast. I'll have to head her off at the pass, send her back down to get some other useless thing I've learned from British television, at least until the malware finishes loading. But a scream that would freeze even the blood pooling beneath the dead guy on the floor rises up from below. Then silence.

I take off my fancy red shoes and tiptoe barefoot across the room, listening. There's the sound of hurried movement now. I crouch behind the wall by the entrance to the back stairs, clutching the high heels, one in each hand. The ginger bursts into the room, not noticing me in his mad bid to find a way out. What an amateur. Criminal 101's first lesson is never return to the scene of the crime. He must have got lost in the labyrinth.

Taking advantage of his breakneck momentum, I ram him full force from behind, flattening him spread eagle onto the far wall, where he stays, since I've nailed him there. A shiny red shoe sticks out from each of his impaled hands. When I removed the lifts from my six-inch stilettos earlier, I'd filed them to a deadly point. Like that broad from prison, I can also fashion a make-shift weapon out of what's on hand.

His own weapon clatters to the floor. It really was a bone, possibly from a forearm, also filed to a point. A clever way to beat the metal detector. I kick it across the room. Then I sink my fingers into his thick red hair and bounce his face off the wall until he hangs loose and unconscious from where I've crucified him into the drywall.

Snatching up the bone dagger, I step over the dead guy to get to the laptop. The screen has gone quiet. I pull the duck out of the USB port and pocket it, start making my way across to the stairwell where the scream came from. I'm halfway there when Bruno runs in huffing and puffing from the hallway. He stops dead when he sees the ginger hanging on the wall.

"Jesus Christ," he says. I'm not sure if this is an exclamation or a comment on the martyr motif.

I toss him the dagger. When he realizes what it is, he drops it to the floor in disgust. He really is such a baby.

"I heard a scream from down here before he came up," I tell him, indicating the narrow stairwell. "I'm going to check it out. I think it was one of the girls."

"Wait," he says, then starts talking into his radio headset, informing the rest of them of the situation. But I'm not waiting for the cavalry. I'm sick of being told what to do by these cowboys.

When I find the girl, she's crumpled on the bottom step, the towels still clutched in one hand. A battered kettle lies on its side next to her slippered feet. When I turn her over, I see the deep gash across her neck, a ruby-red choker that spills over to soak the front of her flimsy baby doll.

Bruno joins me. His bulk casts a shadow over her in the light from the game room above. I can hear the ginger up there, wailing as they pull him down from the wall. I guess he woke up.

"Unfortunate," a voice says from behind me. It's Alex. I can smell the stale smoke of his Cuban cigars. "But I hear you incapacitated the culprit, Candace. Good work."

He motions for me to move aside. The stairway is so narrow, I have to back down a few steps to let him pass. He pulls a knife from his pocket and leans over the body, working so quickly I don't have time to object. I can't see what he's doing from my vantage point below, but the girl is past caring. When he stands, he drops a gory package into a plastic baggie that Bruno holds out for him.

"Now get rid of her," Alex says. He steps on the girl's outstretched fingers as he makes his way around her and up to the game room to deal with the wailing that has now turned to whimpers. That ginger boy will be doing worse than that before the night is through. But I don't care about him.

I care about the kid in the baby-doll nightdress, now hiked up to her waist, revealing she wore no underwear. Her plump pink sex is waxed clean, making her look even more like the little girl that she was. A girl I sent on a useless fucking errand so I could get Deep's code loaded, and now she's dead because of it. But that's not what's making my stomach clench, threatening to bring up all those creamy mashed potatoes from dinner right there in the stairwell. There's a chunk of flesh missing off of the girl's pale round hip where Alex Scarpello cut into her.

"What kind of sick fuck does a thing like that?" I say, punching the wall. This one's old-style plaster instead of the more forgiving drywall upstairs. I might as well have punched a sheer rock face. It hurts like hell and feels good at the same time.

"Go home, Candace," Bruno says, putting the bloody baggie in the pocket of this suit jacket. "You've done enough for tonight."

I find my way out of the mansion, welcoming the cold night air of the abandoned streets. It clears the iron-rich stench of blood where it's curled up into my nostrils. I hail a cab and give him the address. When Deep opens the door, I walk in and drop the rubber ducky on the table.

"It's done," I tell him.

"Janet's gone to sleep," he says, and looking at his bare chest and plaid flannel lounge pants, I'm guessing he had, too. "Hey, I found the location of that clinical retreat. It's a rural property up near Lake Huron. I only got a hit on it late tonight. I told your sister we'd check it out tomorrow."

"It's already tomorrow," I point out to him.

"You know what I mean."

I stand still in the motel room, my feet rooted to the cheap carpet. I've heard that expression, not knowing if you're coming or going, but I've never really felt it like this. Deep looks down and notices I have no shoes on. I'd left the stilettos behind. I don't want them back.

"Candace," he says, stepping closer. "Are you okay?"

That's when I fall forward, like the guy pierced through the heart in the line for the buy-in. I collapse into Deep's arms, burying my face in his neck, trying to drink in the goodness that flows from him like some kind of compassionate radiation. I want that shit to burn me, to lay waste the cancer of the things I've done, the things I've seen. Not just tonight, but for the better part of my life. It is a moment of weakness, and I know it. But for once I don't care about letting my well-developed guard down. I run my hands through his long hair, snagging my fingertips in the waves. I press my lips against his, run my tongue along the inside of his generous mouth that tastes faintly of root beer and the salt of chips. He lays me down gently on the bed, pushing the escaped strands of hair out of the way that have fallen across my face so he can see me better.

"Are you sure about this?" he whispers, kissing the cusp of my upper lip in a way that makes my lower one tremble. I pull him in closer, guide his hand up my bare thigh and beneath the hem of my little black dress. He runs one finger along the edge of my lace panties, outlining them on my flesh like an erotic stencil, before he removes them slowly, kissing his way down to the sweet spot between my legs.

"Make me good, Deep," I moan softly as his tongue finds the mark. But he doesn't hear my hopeless plea for redemption. Which is probably for the best.

CHAPTER 19

WHEN I WAKE UP IN THE MORNING, the sun's already been up for a while. A thin line of bright light frames the blackout curtains. I reach over for Deep under the starched motel bedsheets, but he's not there. That's when I see the glow of the computer screen. Deep sits in front of it, his flowing hair backlit like a dark, wavy halo.

Deciding clothing is optional, I slip out of the bed fully naked and come up behind him in the chair. Pulling his hair aside, I begin giving him minute licks behind one ear. No reaction.

"You're going to want to see this, Candace."

I assume by his serious tone that he doesn't mean the throbbing erection I'd hoped for. I grab one of his dress shirts and pull it over my head without undoing the buttons, then join him in front of his computer. Strings of numbers and dollar amounts fill the screen, along with barcodes like you see on the back of a box of Corn Flakes, and pretty much anything else that's for sale.

"Is this what's on the laptop from the poker game?" I ask.

"It is. The duck did its job. I was able to access the desktop this morning when a user logged on to do some online shopping at Victoria's Secret." *Well, that naughty old broad*, I think to myself. I picture the chip-lady translator in her tweeds, combing the net for lingerie, completely unaware of Deep fondling her data undies.

"Watch this," Deep says. He clicks on one of the bar codes. A profile comes up, looking like something off Tinder, given the young hottie forcing a pouty face for the camera. Below her full-length photo is a map with a red beacon pulsing at an exact location.

"If you drill down further, there's financial records, a list of transactions for services rendered."

I'd told him about the brothel set-up. We both know what services get rendered by the woman in the picture.

"What's the map for?" I ask, mesmerized by the flashing red dot.

Deep clears his throat. "I believe it's her location."

"What?"

"I reckon they've got a GPS tracker on her."

"What the hell?" I look more closely at the screen. The red dot pulses like a heartbeat.

"They're normally used for people under house arrest, or for pets," Deep says. "Did you notice any of the women last night wearing a heavy ankle bracelet, or ..." he lowers his voice, embarrassed, "a collar?"

"No."

"Are you certain?"

"Those girls were wearing next to nothing, Deep. I think I would have noticed a big honking tagger on one of their ankles." *Or their necks*, I think, remembering the red gash on the dead girl's exposed throat.

"Well, there's another way," he says, removing his fingers from the keyboard.

"What's that?"

He swivels around in his chair to face me. "It's new. They're using it in some countries to keep track of dementia patients who wander off. It's a small RFID chip implanted under the skin. The battery for the GPS is charged using heat from the person's own body. They could be using one of those. You inject it with a large syringe."

I remember the excised flesh of the girl on the stairs, Alex dropping the bloody mess of it into Bruno's outstretched plastic baggie. He must have been retrieving the chip from the girl before they dumped her body, the only thing left of her he'd seen as valuable.

"I think that's what they're doing," I say quietly, not wanting to get into the details. No wonder Bruno said the girls weren't going anywhere. If they did, Scarpello would just find them using the GPS tracker. They wouldn't even know how they were getting caught. That Nigerian kid I'd met the first night thought she was being inoculated against STDs. Instead, they were injecting her with technology that would sing louder than that stolen magic harp in the Beanstalk story if she tried to run away.

I go over to the mini-bar, find it frustratingly empty. I'm about to accuse Deep of hiding the booze from me when I realize I got up around five this morning and drank it all.

"Okay," I say, slamming the door of the bar. "This is fucking messed up and all, but what the hell does it have to do with the poker game?"

Deep turns back to the computer, types in some commands to bring up something new on the screen. I lean over to see what he's looking at, but it's only that long list of numbers and figures again.

"It works a bit like a co-op," he says. "Each woman is a share owned by a unique ID. The owner's account is credited when she generates revenue, less a hefty admin fee taken off the top for the Scarpellos." Deep's speech is forced and wooden, like he's reciting poetry he can't stand. "Just like legitimate shares, they can be bought, sold, or in the case of the poker game, transferred in title without exchanging money at all."

I sit down hard on the bed.

"I'll be damned," I say, wishing to Christ I hadn't downed all the hooch early this morning. "They're betting fucking women."

"It appears so." Deep gets up from his computer, comes to sit beside me on the bed. "The QR codes you saw the players scanning represent the shares they're willing to wager. They're using the women as currency."

"Human trafficking meets bitcoin."

"I'd say so. There's no chance those women are there of their own free will, given the tracking device." Deep rubs at one temple, closes his eyes for a moment. This kind of sick shit is way too much for a guy like him. "I've downloaded all the records, taken some screenshots," he says. "You can send it to your friend, Malone."

"We do that, and the Feds will be on the Scarpellos faster than the speed of goddamn light."

"Wouldn't that be a good thing?"

I guess it would be, although it would be difficult to blackmail Alex Scarpello if he's in jail. I sense my cash cow being put out to pasture. But I'm starting not to care.

"I said, wouldn't that be a good thing, Candace?" Deep goes to put his arm around me. Despite what went on the night before, and what went on was damn fine, I pull away from him.

"I know it would be a good thing!" I shout, standing up. I expect my sister to come running into the room, wondering what the racket is. But it remains quiet on the other side of the adjoining door. She could be eavesdropping, but more likely she's choosing to ignore both of us, sitting with her earbuds in, sketching another nasty picture of me. I'm not her favourite person these days.

"I just have to think, okay Deep?" I pace the floor in my bare feet. Shit, even my boots are back in the guest bedroom of the Scarpellos.

"You heard from that guy in Russia yet, about the birth records?" I ask him.

"Not yet," Deep says, lying back on the bed.

"If we had proof of Alex's real identity, we could use it to force him to drop this fucking sick co-op, or whatever it is. That way, we could shut the whole thing down without ever involving the cops." That is if Alex Scarpello is who I think he is. But I'm rarely wrong when it comes to scams. I just know that egotistical prick is hiding something.

Deep doesn't respond, only sighs, looking up at the water-stained ceiling of the motel room. I think the adventure of all this is beginning to wear thin for him. Or he's disappointed in me. Hell, *I'm* disappointed in me. I want to get those women out of Scarpello's racket, but there's part of me that just can't be the harp that sings. A little bit of grassing to the cops can be useful quid pro quo, but this would be a fucking bumper crop's worth of snitching, a whole goddamn front-lawn of-the-White-House level of grass.

"You know I want to help those girls, Deep."

He rolls over on his side on the bed and props himself up with one arm. I tug down on the buttoned shirt I'm wearing in a futile attempt to cover up. I don't want to distract him, but he doesn't seem to notice.

"Then help them," he says.

I stop pacing and sit down next to him. He reaches out one strong arm and wraps it around me. This time, I let him.

"Okay, we'll send it all to Malone," I say, admitting defeat of a sort. At least the defeat of my honour among thieves. "But first I want to check out this retreat that Angela's supposed to be at before all the shit hits the fan. You said you found the address?"

"It's in a place called Carsonville, about an hour-and-a-half north of here. It was listed under the doctor's wife's name and zoned agricultural. That's why I had trouble finding it. They've got about twenty acres. I reckon it used to be farm."

I check my phone on the bedside table. It's already after eleven. "Okay, we'll get Janet some grub and then go. Be back in time to give Malone the goods before dinner." I start walking over to the adjoining door to roust Janet out of her hard work of ignoring me.

"You're not going to bring her to the retreat, are you?"

"Not a chance," I say. "I'm not sure if I'm even bringing you." I'm about to call out to Janet in the other room so she can let me in when a heavy knock sounds on the outside motel door. Deep gets up from the bed and starts making his way to answer it. I rush over and stop him before he can.

"Are you expecting someone?" I ask, keeping my voice low.

"No."

"Neither am I."

I can't risk peeking through the curtains to see who's behind the knock. I don't think I was followed last night, but the taxi I caught to get here wasn't that far from where the game took place. Someone might have seen me. I can't afford to take any chances.

"Where did you put my gun, Deep?"

"Honestly, Candace, do you really think —"

More heavy pounding on the door.

"Listen, Deep, that's not Avon calling. Now, where the fuck is my gun?"

His mouth forms a tight line before he opens it to speak. "I got rid of it."

"You what?"

"I told you I didn't want it, Candace. I couldn't stand having that bloody thing around. I tossed it."

"Where?"

"In a rubbish bin out back of the Brooklyn Street Local." The place where we went for lunch yesterday.

I picture my Ruger buried under greasy leftovers with deconstructed desserts stuck to the barrel. I don't care how good the sex was last night, I think I just might kill Deep for this.

Another loud rap at the door.

"Get back," I tell him. But he doesn't listen. Instead, he grabs a wireless keyboard and stands by the curtained window with it raised above his head. There's no time to argue with him, a key is turning in the lock. I press myself against the wall on the other side of the door just before it flings open. When the Korean lady from motel reception walks in, she barely escapes having the brunt of Deep's QWERTY keyboard come down on her black bobbed head.

"I bring your liquor," she says as she steps right past us and over to the mini-bar, plunking a box on the floor. She starts restocking the shelves with little bottles to replace the ones I depleted the night before.

Deep lowers the keyboard.

"Hi, Ink," he says.

Ink? Deep really is the Miss Congeniality of our little group. I'd crawled through the woman's living room and we still weren't on a first name basis.

Ink looks up from her task and beams at Deep. "Hello, Mr. Bains. How are you today?"

"Quite well," he replies, stepping over to the spare bed to drop the keyboard there and fetch a plaid robe to cover up his lounge pants and naked chest. I still stand there in nothing but the buttoned dress shirt that barely skirts my bush. "And you?"

"I am very good." She shuts the mini-bar and picks

up the box. "Thank you very much for your help with Skype yesterday. I talk with my cousins using it. All the faces on the screen, so wonderful to see people from so far away."

"Well, I'm glad we were able to get it sorted."

"How did you know we needed the mini-bar restocked?" I ask, still suspicious. I've stepped out from behind the door.

She turns to look at me, and her smile drops into a compact frown. "You call me at 5:30 in the morning. Say you need more liquor. I tell you to wait. I am not bartender."

I remember now, making that call. I was half-asleep, mumbling into the phone. I thought I was talking to her voice mail.

"You send the car for cleaning, Mr. Bains?" she asks, turning her attention back to Deep.

"No," he says. "Why do you ask?"

"It's not in the parking space I give you," she says, pointing through the open door.

Deep rushes over to take a look.

"Bloody hell," he says. "It's gone."

I stand beside him in the doorway, see the empty space where his Celica should be. I can't remember if it was there when the cab dropped me off. I usually have a keen eye for detail. But I suppose my mind was on other things.

"Do you have your keys?" I ask Deep. Ink has joined us at the doorway now, gripping her box of booze tightly with concern.

"I think so," Deep says, going to the closet to look through the pockets of his coat. When he doesn't find his keys there, he looks in his pants' pocket, and then the bedside table. Still no joy.

"Maybe I left them in Janet's room?" he says. "We were playing Risk in there last night."

I walk over to the adjoining door and knock. No answer. I knock again, this time harder. But there's still no response. I yell through the door so loudly that Ink chastises me with a sharp hiss.

"Stop making noise. You will disturb my guests," she says, dropping her booze box on the table. "I have key." She pulls a large ring from the inside of her blue motel reception blazer and goes to unlock the door.

After she opens it, Deep and I pile through the doorway like a couple of Keystone Cops. Janet's room is dark, and her bed hasn't been slept in.

I check the washroom, but she's not in it. Her big puffy parka is gone from the closet.

I turn on my bare heels to face Deep.

"Did you tell Janet the address of the doctor's retreat?" I ask him. Ink peeks through the doorway then retreats, knowing the start of a fight when she sees one. I bet that's why she left Korea.

Deep swallows hard before he answers.

"Yes."

I picture my thirteen-year-old sister jacking Deep's car in the dead of the night to go find our mother. That kid really does have a good dose of the family genes in her.

"Well, Deep," I say, sitting down on the empty bed. "You probably shouldn't have done that."

CHAPTER 20

DEEP AND I WASTE PRECIOUS HOURS looking for a replacement for my Ruger. They'd emptied the skip behind the Brooklyn Street Local, which was lucky for Deep, or else I'd have made him crawl around in the stink to look for it. Cruising the usual places and neighbourhoods for illegal trade, the best I can come up with is a guy who leads me to a trunk full of Prada purses.

"I said handgun, not handbag," I tell him. He still insists Deep and I fondle the knock-off leather before we go

We try a legit gun store, but Deep gets turned down because he isn't a resident of Michigan. We give up and start looking for a car to rent.

"I can't believe you threw my fucking piece in the garbage," I say once we're in the warmth of the Uber.

"I can't believe you tried to convince the bloke at the gun store that I'm Italian."

I reach down and pull at the tan Chelsea boots Deep gave me to wear. They're a half size too small, so I'm feeling the pinch of them. I wish Janet had inherited the family foot size along with her stubbornness and talent for theft. But when I tried to put on the polka-dot high tops she'd left behind in favour of her UGG boots, I couldn't even get them past my fucking instep.

The Uber pulls up in front of the address that Ink gave us. A friend of hers rents cars. She said she'd call ahead, and they'd give us a good deal.

"Are you sure this is the right place?" I ask the driver.

"Dave's Cars," he says, pointing at the small sign hanging crooked on the side of a rusted trailer. Late-model cars are strewn across the pocked asphalt in front of it, protected by a sagging chain-link fence. It looks like a place where vehicles go to die.

Deep and I get out of the Uber, walk up to the metal door of the trailer, and knock. A woman answers, her silver-blue hair sticking up at the back of her head. She's short and stout, like the infamous teapot.

"Are you Dave?" I ask.

She laughs, deep and throaty, then starts to cough, like she's going to hack up a lung right there on the steps of the trailer.

"Dave was my ex," she finally manages to say once her hacking has died down. "He took off with a bitch from the DMV years ago. But he left me this place. I figure between her and me, I got the better deal."

"We'd like to rent a car, please," Deep says. "Ink sent us."

"Oh, yeah, she's a terrific gal. Gave me some great herbal stuff for my emphysema. Although it was the herb that gave it to me, if you know what I mean."

"Do any of these cars even run?" I ask.

She laughs again. But this time manages to keep the hack to a minimum. "Oh, they all run all right. My son comes and tunes them up once a month."

"Would they run as far as Lake Huron?" Deep asks, looking doubtfully at a Ford F150 truck with its tailgate half falling off.

She doesn't laugh at that. "Oh, that is a fair ways. Most of my customers are just looking to toodle around town."

I look past the woman who is not Dave and see a clock on the wall inside the trailer. It's already almost two in the afternoon. We'd spent way too much time looking for a gun. But I'd really wanted to get a replacement for my Ruger. I hated the idea of going up to this retreat unarmed. My dad would be ashamed. He'd taught me how to stop a man's heart with just my hands and my wits. Reliance on a gun was just plain laziness in his opinion.

"C'mon, Deep," I say. "We'll just have to try somewhere else."

The car lady sees a potential customer falling through her arthritic hands and steps out of the doorway. "I could let you have the loan of my car," she says. "Seeing as you're a friend of Ink's and all. Cost a little bit more than my usual rate, though." I look at the cars on the lot, one of them has no roof, and it's not a convertible. I can't believe she has the balls to charge anyone for the use of these wrecks.

"We'd be very interested," Deep says, sensing the ticking clock as much as me.

"It's out the back." She locks the door of the trailer behind her. "Come with me."

The car behind the trailer is newer than the jalopies in the front yard, but so small you could park it in a bike rack. It makes Charlotte's hatchback look like an SUV.

"A Smart car," Deep says. But I don't see what's so smart about a car that only seems to consist of a front end.

"She can only go so fast on the interstate, but she'll get you where you want to go. Fifty bucks plus mileage if you return it by tomorrow. I'll take one of the rentals home tonight. What do you say?"

"We'll take it," Deep says. He gets out his wallet and hands her his credit card.

"That's the spirit, young man."

The car lady waddles away to run the card.

Deep walks up over to our new ride and kicks the tires, pronounces them safe. I feel the gap in the front of my jeans where the Ruger should be. This car might get us where we want to go, but I'm still worried about what we're going to find when we get there.

"You know, it might turn out just fine, Candace. Your mother could have been at the retreat all along just like Alex Scarpello said. We might get there and find both her and Janet with everything sorted." We've been driving for close to two hours. The fucking Smart car starts to whir like an overtaxed vacuum if we go over sixty.

"You think a guy who tags women like animals isn't above lying, Deep?"

"Yeah, but why would he lie?"

"Why does anyone lie?" But I try to hold out some hope for what Deep is saying. It would be a nice ending to the story. But most of the stories I've lived to tell don't end that well.

"It's more likely that Scarpello's been holding Angela there until he figures out what to do with her."

"You still reckon she was trying to blackmail him because he's her son?"

"Don't you?"

"I don't know, Candace. We found a Russian birth certificate for him. And so far, my contact in Pavlovsk hasn't found anything else to contradict that."

"We know Angela was making trouble for Alex, and that it had something to do with her son, Deep. There has to be some reason why that nurse who delivered my twin and me had to push up daisies in the deep freeze because of it."

He doesn't have an answer for that one. We drive silently for a while.

"Are you nervous?" he asks. "About seeing your mother again?"

"I'm nervous about a lot of things, Deep, but that's not one of them." I turn up the radio, the heavy bass starts the windows humming. Despite its economy size, the Smart car's sound system is epic. Top of the line Bose speakers fill up the space where a back seat should be.

The truth is, I'm not looking forward to the prospect of seeing my mother. What do you say to a woman who left you in the care of a contract killer when you were still sleeping with a night light? Although my dad did a bang-up job as far as I'm concerned. Even if the night light was a flashing red cherry he stole off the top of a cop car after too many beers.

Down a dirt road, hidden in the trees, we find the address of the retreat. There's no official sign, just one of those decorative flags with burnt-orange-and-yellow flowers hanging limp on a pole attached to the rural mailbox. I think it says *Welcome*, but you can only make out the *come* part without a breeze. A freshly painted white clapboard farmhouse sits at the end of the long driveway, with multiple peaked roofs and the trim they call gingerbread, after the story with the cannibal witch. Deep's Celica is parked next to a red barn with a rooster weathervane, also straight off of the fairy tale page.

"We better park on the road," I tell Deep.

He pulls the Smart car behind a cluster of sugar maples. There are buckets fastened to the trunks even though the sap has to be frozen. Probably a ploy to make it look more like a working farm, rather than a hideout for women whose hormones have run amok.

Deep and I find a path through the woods banking the house on one side. It's only 4:30 in the afternoon, but the sun's already beginning to set. December is a shitty month for light. But in this case, it's to our benefit. I don't want anyone knowing we're here until I'm ready. Deep carries a flashlight he found in the glove compartment of the Smart car. But I won't let him turn it on.

"What do we do now?" he asks as we crouch down at the edge of the tree line.

"We watch," I tell him, rubbing my hands together in the cold. Deep had offered me his gloves as well as his Canada Goose jacket, but I refused both. I'm still mad at him about the gun.

Half an hour passes, but there's no movement inside the farmhouse. No lights come on, even as the sun disappears behind the red barn.

"I'm going around the back," I say.

"Right. I'll come with you."

"No fucking way," I tell him.

"I'm not going to sit idly by while you storm the place, Candace. I'm not completely useless, you know."

He isn't, I realize. But his most useful asset is his non-threatening nature. It's a good yin to my yang.

"Okay, give me a minute, and then go knock on the front door. Pretend you're lost or something, or your car broke down and you need a phone. It'll distract them while I try to find a way in from the back."

"Nobody does that sort of thing since the advent of mobiles, Candace."

"Then tell them you want to buy some fucking maple syrup, I don't care. You got to improvise in these sorts of situations, Deep."

"Okay, but I still think we should be ringing the police."

"Janet will end up in Social Services for sure if you do that. She stole your car, remember, drove without a licence. Plus, we're here now, and I don't want to waste any more time. We'll just get her and get out.

"And if your mother is in there, as well?"

I look over at the dark farmhouse, wonder if the

mother I haven't seen in thirty years is behind one of those silent, white-framed windows.

"I don't know, Deep. Like I said, you gotta improvise."

The rear portion of the property slopes down into a ravine; flagstones mark trails through it, and there are handmade signposts I can't read in the failing light. They've built a modern, three-tiered, wood-plank deck off the back of the house. Stairs attached to it lead up to sliding doors. I keep down low as I make my way up them, then huddle behind some modular patio furniture, covered up for the winter. I grab a steel-wired brush from the gas barbecue pushed up against the railing. It's not a gun, but it'd rip the face off of a person if you got yourself close enough.

Soon I hear Deep's knock on the front door. It's met with silence. I peer around the stacked patio furniture to look through the sliding doors, make out the shadowy outlines of a country kitchen. No movement. Deep knocks again, more loudly this time. I'm starting to worry about putting him on the front line like this. Anything could happen. He's just a civilian. I'm about to come out of my hiding place when a light comes on inside. Flattened against a wicker settee, I hear the sliding doors move along the track. Deep comes out on the deck and shines his flashlight on me as I brandish the wire brush.

"The door was open," he says.

"Jesus, Deep." He removes the beam from my face and points it through the sliding doors.

It looks like nobody's home.

I find a filleting knife in a block on the kitchen counter. Long and slim with a deadly point, it's just as good for gutting people as fish. Deep takes up the barbecue brush, and we clear the main floor room by room but find no one, only low-slung couches and bay windows lined with embroidered cushions. I check out a curled-up schedule of daily activities tacked to a bulletin board on the wall. *Soul Collage. Yoga. Vision Boarding with Sue!* I wouldn't last a day in this place without stabbing someone in the sharing circle with a talking stick.

I make Deep walk single-file behind me as we mount the stairs to the second floor. The upstairs hallway runs the length of the house. We pass empty bedrooms on each side, the doors open, the beds made up with floral comforters and pastel afghans. All the heavy curtains have been pulled closed. Dust swirls in Deep's flashlight beam. It doesn't look like anyone's been staying in these rooms for a while.

The last bedroom at the end of the hallway is the only one with the door closed. I put my ear up flat to the door. I can't detect any sounds from within, just the usual creaks and settles of an old country place. Counting silently down from three with my fingers for Deep's benefit, I boot the door in with a basic stomp kick. I didn't have to do that, given the door was unlocked, but it provides an overall startle to an entrance that catches people off their guard. When Deep shines his flashlight on the two unmoving lumps in the canopy bed, it is apparent that they are well past being startled. They are also well past their best-before date. Deep pulls his plaid scarf up over his nose, but I'm used to the stench of death. I turn on the light switch and find the good doctor, not looking unlike his online picture, despite his face being contorted into a rigor mortis mask. The woman beside him doesn't have the luxury of a face. It's been blown off, leaving only hanks of bleached blonde hair sprouting around a bloody void. She lies naked on top of the covers, a victim of being in the wrong bed at a lethally wrong time. There's a jagged chunk of flesh missing from her hip.

All of this is disturbing, to say the least, but not as disturbing as the shattered pair of owl glasses that Deep picks up from the carpet in front of the bed. I guess my sister doesn't like to wear her contacts when she drives.

"Now, can we ring the police?" he asks, still holding the scarf up to his nose.

"Yeah," I admit. "Now might be a good time for that."

In the kitchen, I phone Malone, still holding the knife.

"Your time's up, Candace. You better be on the road back from Detroit."

"About that," I say. "I took a bit of a detour."

I tell her about the dead doctor, stinking up the room upstairs next to the blonde with no face.

"Razinski? The doctor on your birth registration?" Looks like she finally managed to pull the records.

"Yeah."

"Jesus, Candace. What the hell have you gotten yourself into?"

"I'm not sure, but it's got the Scapellos written all over it." Deep stares me down from across the kitchen island. I don't want to tell Malone the next part, but I can't think of a reasonable alternative to the truth in this case. "I think Janet may be mixed up in it," I finally admit to her.

"Why do you say that?"

"Because she was here, at the doc's place. And now she's missing."

"What was she doing there?"

"Looking for Angela."

Malone sucks in a breath that threatens to deplete my supply of oxygen right through the phone. She lets out a string of curse words on the outbreath that shows she's been hanging around me for too long.

"You were supposed to be taking care of her!"

"I was," I say. But I realize now that I wasn't. If I had been, we wouldn't be in this mess.

"You got to send the Feds to Alex Scarpello's, Malone. I know he has her."

"I can't just send the Feds in on your hunch, Candace. I need probable cause. The link between that doctor and the Scarpello's is tenuous at best. I'd never get a warrant."

"So, you're just going to sit there on your goddamn cop hands and do nothing?"

"Best I could do is send a couple of uniforms to Alex Scarpello's home, get them to talk to him."

"You can't do that, Malone! It'll drive him even deeper with Janet if he knows we're on to him. You can't go for Alex until you're ready to rush him."

"Then I'm going to need probable cause, Candace."

I think about those women tagged and reduced to numbers on a screen, traded like stocks on a pervert exchange. If that isn't probable cause, I don't know what is.

"What if I could get probable cause for you?" I ask. "It's not about this thing with the doc," I tell her, "But it should be enough to get you a warrant for something else."

"Okay, I'll bite then, what is it?"

"It's complicated," I tell her.

"I don't need complications, Candace. I need reasonable proof that a crime has been committed."

"I can send you proof. I just need a couple of hours." All the damning data on Scarpello is back at the motel room. Deep and I need to drive back and get it before I can send it to Malone.

"I still don't understand," she says. "Why are you so sure Alex Scarpello is behind Janet's disappearance and Doctor Razinski's murder?"

I could put her off on this question. But I'm getting tired of keeping this all from Malone. She needs to have the whole picture, so she can understand the seriousness of the situation with my sister. I tell her about Angela, and how I think she figured out that Alex was her son. About how Anya Scarpelllo needed a kid to validate her power marriage, and with the dead doctor's help, she'd used my twin brother to fill the cradle gap. I even admit to having thoughts about capitalizing on all of this, through blackmail or alliances. In short, I spill my guts. I think that confession with the priest earlier in the week has had an adverse effect on me.

"But Candace, that doesn't make any sense."

"I know it sounds crazy, Malone. But all the pieces fit."

"No, they don't, Candace."

"Why the hell not?" I don't appreciate Malone casting aspersions on my powers of deduction. I like to think I'm just as good at this detective stuff as she is. Maybe even better.

"Because we got more results on the DNA we lifted from the nurse in the freezer. The amniotic fluid from the other baby shows he had a faulty chromosome, a congenital birth defect."

"Then that only supports my theory, Malone. I found a fucking pharmacy of meds in Alex Scarpello's desk drawer."

"You don't understand," Malone says through the phone. "The birth defect was a fatal one. The baby would've been healthy on delivery, but the pathologist says he wouldn't have made it past his first birthday."

Deep jumps when I stab the knife into the butcher block kitchen counter.

"You're wrong, Malone."

"I'm sorry, Candace. I'm not. There's no possible way Alex Scarpello is your twin brother."

CHAPTER 21

"SO, YOU WERE WRONG."

Deep has been holding the accelerator flush to the floor of the Smart car for the entire trip. Despite this, we still don't seem to be moving much faster than a souped-up golf cart. I wish my sister had left the keys to Deep's Celica behind at the murder scene instead of her glasses.

"I was not wrong," I say. "All the people who were around when my mother popped out me and my twin have either been bumped off or gone MIA. Except for Anya. You saw that dead chick at the retreat. She'd had one of those trackers cut out of her hip. Alex Scarpello is the linchpin holding this whole fucked-up thing together."

"But he's not your brother."

"Maybe not," I still find it hard to let go of this theory, despite the evidence. "But he's got my sister. Both you and I know that."

Deep nods, not taking his focus off the road, or his foot off the gas pedal. He's worried. So am I. I don't like being wrong. But I hate being worried even more. Janet is the same age as many of the girls Scarpello's been trafficking. Every time I let my mind wander, I can see her big eyes tear up as they shoot one of those demented trackers under her light olive skin. It's all my fault. For taking her to Detroit. For focusing on getting dirt on Alex Scarpello instead of finding Angela. Janet had to take matters into her own hands because of me. I just may be the shittiest big sister ever. But that's going to change, right fucking now.

I look out the window, the flickering lights of Detroit are finally showing on the horizon. I turn to Deep. "Take me to Indian Village."

"Hold up, Candace. You said we were going back to the motel, to send Malone the information she needs for her warrant."

"You are. But I'm not. I'm going to get my sister back."

"I thought we were waiting for the police?"

"Janet may not have that kind of time, Deep."

The little car shivers and shakes as Deep guides it onto the exit for the city. I think he's going to argue with me about my new plan. But he doesn't.

When we pull up in front of Alex Scarpello's, Deep insists on hiding with me behind the stone wall across the street. He trips on a vine, and I have to catch him before he does a face plant into a garden gnome.

"I just want to see you get in okay," he says, righting himself. I'd tried to convince him to leave earlier, but he's being uncharacteristically stubborn. If I didn't need him to send that computer stuff to Malone so badly, I would have knocked him unconscious.

The beatification starts at eight. At 7:30, Alex and Anya Scarpello come out the front door of the house. He's got on a tux, made to slim order. She's wearing her three-quarter length fur coat, draped over a long flowing skirt. Bruno opens the door of a Lincoln Town Car for both of them, then gets in the driver's seat, acting as both chauffeur and bodyguard tonight. I guess the Caddy isn't fancy enough for saints.

That should leave Bruno's partner as the only one holding down the family fort tonight. Anya had told me they were giving the rest of the staff the night off for the event.

"There he is," I say to Deep, not long after the lights of the Town Car have vanished around the corner. I can see the lone patrol outside the house as he uses his surveillance of the perimeter as an excuse for a smoke break. The red-orange ember shifts in the darkness as he inspects the front lawn then disappears around the side as he goes to inspect the backyard.

"I'm going in."

Not giving Deep a chance to object, I run across the street, aiming for the side of the house opposite to where the patrol went. I flatten myself against the brick wall of the attached garage and wait. When the patrol comes around the corner after making his circuit, I'll have the element of surprise, not to mention the tricks of the trade my father taught me. I won't break his neck, although I know how. I don't like to kill people if I don't have to. I'll just put him in a sleeper hold, compressing both his carotid artery and the jugular vein so he'll drop like a sack of wet cement. It only takes ten to twenty seconds if you know how to do it right.

But the element of surprise belongs to the guy with the cigarette, because two minutes later he's got his nicotine stained fingers buried into my long shaggy mane, yanking me backwards by the roots. He'd come around the opposite way I'd expected, doubling back instead of going in a circle. I hadn't counted on that.

He wraps his arms around me from behind, pinning my arms in a crushing bear hug. I thrash and buck, but he's squeezing me so tight I can barely catch the breath needed for the effort. Using one of Deep's Chelsea boots, I come down on his right foot with all the force I can muster. It won't be enough to get him to release me, but it'll fucking hurt. Expecting the satisfying crack of metatarsal bones, I hear the crash of breaking pottery instead. The guy's arms drop, and so does he, falling to the ground with a thud. Deep stands above him with what's left of a shattered garden gnome in his hands.

"Like I said, I just wanted to make sure you got in okay."

I crawl over to the unconscious man who tried to squeeze me to death and shove the Ativan I stole from Alex's desk down his tobacco-reeking gullet. There's still a faint bump on his forehead from the head butt I gave him at the poker game, but it's nothing compared to the goose egg he'll have from Deep's handiwork. I'm glad I kept the pills in my jacket. Like I said, you never know when a good bedtime benzo is going to come in handy. I find his Uzi a few feet away. But after a quick inspection, I discover it's a replica. Alex wasn't kidding when he said it was all about appearances and intimidation.

"Well, it looks like I'm okay, Deep," I say, standing up and stretching, getting some of the kinks out of my body that the bastard on the ground put there. "Now it's time for you to go back to the motel and let me handle the rest."

This is the closest Deep's going to get to thanks from me, and he knows it. He drops what's left of the gnome on the grass and starts walking back to the car.

I grab a few zip ties from the garage and secure Sleeping Beauty with them. Then fashion a gag out of a greasy rag. The guy shouldn't wake up until New Year's with the amount of Ativan I've stuffed him with, but you can never be too sure. When I'm done, I pull him out of sight behind an azalea bush in the backyard.

He'd left the side door unlocked. I slip into the house and rush to Alex's study to get his gun out of the desk drawer. There shouldn't be anyone else here, but you never know. If I'm going to search the place for Janet or at least clues to where she might be, I need something to back me up in an emergency. The run-in with the bear-hugger has me spooked. I won't have Deep and his whimsical garden decor to save me if I let someone get the drop on me again.

But of course, the damn door is locked. It's solid oak, so I don't see myself breaking it down too easily. I run back down to the kitchen to find one of those metal skewers I used before. It takes me a while. I have to be quiet while I search, just in case there's someone else in the house. Although if there was, they probably would have shown themselves by now, having caught Deep and my antics with the patrol on the CCTV.

Who would have thought cooking could require so many goddamn specialized tools? One drawer seems to contain nothing but varying sizes of melon ballers, the other has a dozen different grades of cheese grater. I finally find the skewers in a drawer with a tofu press and a sushi bazooka, and I only know what those are because they've got labels on them. I grab a skewer and one of the nastier knives I came across during my search before I return to Alex's study. Deep should be back at the motel by this time, sending all the goods we found on Scarpello to Malone. I can't wait to see that son of a bitch do the perp walk. I don't even feel bad about ratting on him anymore.

It's tougher to spring the lock this second time around. Probably because I damaged it the first time I broke in, but eventually it gives. I race to the desk and am about to get to work jimmying the lock on the drawer with the gun when my phone goes off in my pocket. Deep had made me turn the sound back on when we drove back from the retreat, afraid we might miss a call from Janet if she was trying to reach us. I take the phone out of my jacket more to shut it up than to answer it, but then I see who it is.

"I'm just a little busy here, Deep," I say. Holding the phone with my shoulder as I attempt to spring the lock on the drawer with the skewer. I've dropped the knife on the desk blotter, so I can use both my hands.

"Candace, I'm at the motel."

"Have you sent the records to Malone yet?"

"I'm about to, but I got an email from my friend in Pavlovsk. He found a birth certificate for Alex. It didn't turn up initially because it was under Anya's maiden name. It's not what we thought, Candace."

"I don't care about that anymore, Deep." The drawer pops open, the syringes and other medication are there, but no gun.

"I've sent a copy of the birth certificate to you. Check your texts. You need to look at it. You need —" But Deep doesn't have time to tell me what I need. The phone's gone dead. I try calling him back, but it goes straight to voice mail. I bring up his text, open up the attachment, along with the translation of the Russian. Deep was right. It wasn't what we thought. Looking down at the contents of the drawer, I understand now what all those injections are for.

"Hello, Candace."

Alex Scarpello stands in the doorway of the study with the gun I'd hoped to find aimed straight at me. He walks up to the desk and whisks the knife away.

"Put down the phone, Candace."

I place my phone on the desk. What else am I going to do? Alex looks down at the birth certificate from Russia that fills the small screen. The record that proves that a child named Alex was born to Anya over thirty years ago. But it wasn't a son.

It was a daughter.

CHAPTER 22

"THIS IS ALL YOUR FUCKING FAULT," Alex shouts at his mother.

Anya stands beside a satin wingback chair, holding a pearl-handled Derringer to Janet's side. The gun looks more like a fashion accessory than a weapon. But unlike a Gucci bag, it's more than capable of blasting a hole in my little sister, or me for that matter.

"I'm sorry, Alex," Anya says, but she looks past him, and I wonder if her apology is meant partly for me.

He paces the floor like a mad animal, muttering to himself. Janet looks across the room at me, her cheeks streaked with tears. She could be one of those graphic horror faces she sketches with the shrieking open mouths, if hers weren't covered in duct tape. Her hands are zip-tied in front of her, and there's a bruise blooming around one of her big brown eyes. I am so going to fuck this guy up.

"Keep her around, you said! See if she leads us to Angela, you said!" Alex waves his Glock 9mm wildly around the room as he mimics his mother's Russian accent. Anya appears to shrink within her shimmering white silk blouse.

"What happened to Angela, Alex?" I ask him. And that stops him pacing. He trains the Glock on me, his face a twist of silent rage. The grandfather clock ticks loudly from the corner, possibly with the time I have left.

"You," he says finally, with a sneer. "You, are a pain in my fucking ass, cousin."

"You're not the first person to tell me that."

"When I couldn't reach security at the house, I knew it had to be your doing. I had Bruno turn the car around. I thought you might come for your sister. She's probably been screaming for you in the basement all this time. But you wouldn't have heard her. I keep it soundproofed down there for when I have business to conduct. I wouldn't want to disturb *my mother*." He smirks at Anya, then turns back to me. We all know he doesn't care who the fuck he disturbs.

"I know about your little sex trafficking scheme, Alex," I say, hoping to unnerve him. "And soon the Feds will, too. I have someone sending copies of all your fucked-up financial records to the cops right now."

"You mean your East Indian friend? I sent Bruno over to take care of him, Candace. You think I didn't have people watching you?"

I did, but I thought I'd been careful enough not to be traced back to the motel. Although last night, after the girl had her throat slashed on the stairs, I had not been myself. I'd let my guard down, and now I've let Deep down, as well.

"What is she talking about, Alex?"

"Yes, Alex, why don't you tell your mother about your little set-up, tagging and trading women like goddamn livestock. I think she'd like to know how you —"

Alex steps forward and pistol-whips me across the face. I remain standing but spit out two of my teeth onto the Persian rug lying on the varnished wood floor. If I ever get out of this, he'll pay for that. I'm going to have to get implants after this.

"You still didn't answer my question," I say, licking the blood from my lips. "What happened to Angela?"

"How the fuck do I know what happened to your crazy mother," he says. "That bitch was pushing for a paternity test. She actually thought I was the other brat twin she had alongside of you all those years ago. Can you imagine? Me, the product of that lunatic of a woman and some Polish nobody."

I ignore the jab. My dad was more of a somebody than this bastard will ever be.

"But you weren't Angela's son, so what did it matter?" I've got to keep him talking. There's still a chance Malone might have the Feds on their way.

"I wasn't anybody's son, Candace." He shakes the gun in his fist. "I couldn't take a fucking paternity test. Have everyone see a second X chromosome when they were expecting a Y. They'd never accept me as Don if they knew. Hell, in this organization, they'd probably tear me limb from limb.

"I had plans to get rid of Angela, but she must have gotten wind of it." He looks accusingly at Anya. "She disappeared. And then you showed up. We thought she might come back for you. But I guess your mother really doesn't give a damn about you, just like everybody says."

He thinks he can hurt me with this, but he can't. I got past that hurt a long time ago.

"Listen, Alex, I don't care about your goddamn chromosomes." And I don't. I couldn't care less how Alex Scarpello wants to live his life, or what gender he has on his birth certificate. I care what he's become, and that's a sick fuck who's getting ready to kill me.

"But don't you want to hear the whole sordid tale, Candace? After you've spent all this time and energy poking your nose into my private business, you'd think you'd want at least that." He gestures with his gun hand to Anya. "Tell her."

Anya doesn't say anything, just holds the Derringer shakily at my sister's side and looks down at the glossy arm of the wingback chair. Alex strides over and lifts her delicate chin with the barrel of his gun so she has to face him.

"I said, tell her what you fucking did." Each word is cold and calculated, like everything this guy does.

"I took the child," Anya blurts out. "But it was my father-in-law's decision to kill the nurse who'd helped with the birth of the twins. I never asked him to do that. I didn't know I was pregnant at the time, or I never would have taken Angela's baby. You must believe me, Candace."

"The doctor was too valuable an asset to the family to be eliminated," Alex continues the story, glancing over his shoulder at me. "Grandfather trusted him to keep quiet. And Razinski ended up being helpful to us in the end, didn't he, Mother? Getting me those shots I needed when I hit puberty. Old man Scarpello never knew about that part." He lowers the gun from beneath Anya's chin and steps away, a look of disgust on his face. "He's the one who told Angela they'd taken her baby, a deathbed confession that makes me wish the bastard were still alive so I could kill him myself. Angela must have phoned the police with the anonymous tip about the nurse in the freezer, to see if he was telling the truth."

"How did you know about that?" All these revelations are making my head spin, but I'd been right about the baby snatch. I'm looking forward to rubbing that in with Deep if Bruno hasn't killed him yet.

"I have my own contacts in the police department, Candace. That's how I knew they'd started digging into the birth records. It was only a matter of time before they contacted Dr. Razinski to follow up. I couldn't take the chance he'd remain silent on the real secret he'd helped my mother to conceal all these years. That your useless twin brother got sick and died, that soon afterward she gave birth to a child of her own, a girl, not a boy. My father was dead by then. She knew there was no chance for another child, so she ..."

"I was only trying to do what was best, Alex. I was only trying to —"

"Oh, for God's sake, Mother, save us your little sob story about how the world is run by men, especially in our family. About how you had no choice."

"But I didn't, Alex. I didn't." With every protest, she thrusts the gun farther into Janet's ribs, and I watch my sister silently wince from behind the duct tape.

"It was me who had no fucking choice," Alex roars at Anya. "You made sure of that."

"I did it for you," she says weakly.

"You did it for yourself."

He turns to me. "She knew that a girl child wouldn't be enough to solidify the alliance between her precious Russian family and the Scarpellos. When I was born, she had to make do with what she had. So she made me into a boy."

"Jesus," I say. "That's some fucked up shit, Alex." I don't know what I was expecting, but I wasn't expecting this.

"Oh, come now, Candace. Are you feeling sorry for me? You want to hear what it was like? How hard it was for me? How I cried when my mother cut my hair and forced me to wear boy's clothes, begging me to keep her secret? I'll spare you those violins. The hormone injections hurt like hell at first. But that's all water under the bridge now, isn't it, Mother?" He stares down Anya with a look that betrays how much that water still rages.

This is when it dawns on me. Alex is *not* a trans man. No matter what he appears to be, or who he portrays himself as now. Anya ramming a male identity down his throat from babyhood would be no different than ordering Majd's eight-year-old niece, Rima, to be the boy she was born as but knew she wasn't. In Alex's case, that cruel act of force-feeding had poisoned his mind. Gender can be a straightjacket if other people are allowed to wrestle you into the one they decide fits you. That's what that sicko conversion therapy is all about.

"You're not a kid anymore, Alex," I say. "You can be whoever you want to be."

He shakes his head. "What's done is done," he says. "I am who I am now. What I'm expected to be. The leader and the power behind the Scarpello crime family. That much my mother *did* do for me. And I'm not about to lose what I have because of the likes of you, Candace. I won't let you and your sister jeopardize that." He levels the gun at me again. Any sympathy I had for him evaporates under the heat of that lethal threat.

"You going to kill us right here?" I say, getting ready with a bluff. "I wouldn't recommend it. Deep told me on the phone that he'd already sent those records to the cops." He hadn't, but Alex doesn't know that. "They're probably already loading the SWAT team into the van to take you and your fucked-up prostitution ring down. You leave a couple of dead bodies lying around, and they'll know who's behind it."

"You think I didn't have a contingency plan, Candace? I'm not stupid." Alex pulls out a phone from his pocket, holds it up for me to see. "One text from me, and those women will be loaded into the next set of shipping containers headed for Mexico. The cartels will take over, use them in their own brothels, or sell their bodies for parts. I don't care. I'll get a fair price for my investors. I always do. Your evidence is just some numbers on a screen. Without the girls, it won't mean anything."

"What are you saying, Alex?" Anya asks him, her voice trembling as much as the hand that holds her petite gun. She takes a timid step toward Scarpello and away from my sister. "You told me you would never sell women. You promised, after what happened to my Karine —"

"Shut up, Mother!" Alex barks at her from across the room. "This is no concern of yours. Your sister was a whore who didn't know her place. She deserved what happened to her."

"How can you say this, how can you —"

"I am the one who gets to decide what happens to these women, to *anyone*," he shouts at Anya. "You, my dear mother, were the one to make sure I had the power to do that. You're the one who taught me how much a woman is worth."

Alex looks down at his phone, swipes the screen with his thumb, still holding his gun out with his other hand.

"I'm glad I let you live long enough to see this, Candace," he says, his eyes fixed on the phone. "It's your fault what will happen to these girls. If you thought they suffered being trafficked by me, that is nothing compared to what the cartels will subject them to. Your sister will be among them." He starts entering whatever code he needs to generate the fate of at least a hundred human beings. His own personal malware.

"No, Alex! You can't!" Anya lunges for the phone. When the gun goes off, I'd say nobody is as surprised as me. That is, with the exception of Anya, who drops to her knees, her mouth in a silent widening O. Anya moves one hand to the blood blossoming at the front of her white silk blouse, still clutching the tiny Derringer, before she collapses beside the two teeth I spit out on the rug. She lets out an interrupted gasp before she goes down, as if she had something left to say.

Alex hadn't meant to shoot her. You can take that as the gospel truth from this hitwoman prophet. He'd been focused on the phone, saw the movement out of the corner of his eye, and reacted. It happens. Sometimes in our business you don't have the luxury to make sure the target's the right one.

"Mother!" Alex screams, dropping the gun to his side. The phone slips from his hand and falls soundlessly onto the soft Persian rug. My sister stands frozen beside the wingback chair, her eyes wide, the duct tape smothering her own scream. I know that this will be my one opportunity, and I have to take it.

I rush at Alex and knock him to the ground. A burst of air erupts from his startled lungs, but he manages to hold on to the Glock. I've got him by both wrists, struggling for control. We roll across the room and hit an antique end table. A vase falls and smashes next to my head on the floor. Later, I'll find pale-blue porcelain scattered in my hair.

I've got to get him to drop the gun. I take his wrist in both hands and hammer it on the hardwood until the joint makes a sickening pop and the Glock skitters across the floor to rest next to a standing bookcase. The desired outcome, but I shouldn't have left his other hand free.

"You fucking bitch!" he yells from on top of me. He snatches a jagged dagger of broken vase up from the floor. It's got to be nine inches long, and sharp as a straight-back razor in search of a shave. Thick blood oozes through his fingers and runs down his wrist as he clutches it. I'm holding him back from plunging it into my throat but can't maintain my grip for long. My own fingers are sliding down his forearm in the slippery blood that spouts from his palm.

Lifting my shoulders off the floor, my cheek dangerously close to the makeshift blade, I ready myself for a Hail Mary head butt, mentally willing Janet to fetch the Glock and use it. My sister's hands had been tied in front of her, free enough that she could still pull a trigger. And I figure that's just what she's done, when I feel the swift breeze of the bullet speed past my neck to pierce Alex's right temple. The ceramic dagger clatters to the floor.

Damn, she's a good shot, I think as I slither out from underneath the dead weight of my cousin. If I'd known, I would have given my Ruger to Janet instead of Deep for safekeeping. But when I look up, my sister stands beside the wingback chair empty-handed. Alex's Glock remains where it landed by the bookcase. And it is Anya Scarpello who holds her Derringer weakly up from the floor, her eyes rolling up into the back of her head.

"Run," I shout out to Janet. But I have to go get her, have to drag my sister out of the living room, and down the hall to the foyer. I catch our fleeting reflections in the marred glass of the hall mirror before we burst out the front door together and Janet finally finds her feet.

I'll never know if Anya was aiming for me or for Alex with her Derringer. She and I won't get to have that conversation, or debate what she did to her own flesh and blood and to mine. But those Russian babes are notoriously good markswomen. Even if my sister isn't.

As Janet and I stumble down the front steps of Alex's mansion, I hear the sharp retort of a final gunshot ring out. Whatever her intentions or justifications, Anya Scarpello had saved her last parting shot for herself.

EPILOGUE

DEEP AND I ARE SITTING ON A PARK bench watching the little girl in the playground. Majd's niece, Rima, waves at us from the top turret of a wooden climber made to look like a castle. She's wearing a bright-pink snowsuit, which I appreciate because the neon colour makes it easier to keep track of her. Deep gives her a thumbs up, knocking over his crutches. He'd taken a bullet to the foot from Bruno's gun, and it's still healing.

"I still can't believe you managed to garrotte that guy with an HDMI cable," I say, helping him pick the crutches up from the pavement that's dusted with light snow.

"It was an ethernet cable. And I didn't garrotte him. I strangled him until he passed out."

"Still, I continue to be impressed."

"I told you I came from a long line of warriors."

"Was that the Brits or the Sikhs?"

"Both, I reckon."

I zip up the collar on the heavily lined leather jacket Deep bought me for Christmas. It makes me look a bit bulky, but it sure keeps the cold out. We'd exchanged presents early, since he'll be leaving next week for California. He got a job at Google, where I'm told they have slides for the employees much like the ones in this playground. I gave him a Black+Decker Dustbuster, to replace the one I shot to pieces with my Ruger.

After he'd subdued Bruno with the ethernet cable, Deep had managed to send the records we'd lifted from Scarpello's brothel bank to Malone. He'd also sent the details of the backdoor he'd created so the department's own hackers could enter it as they pleased. They'd gotten their warrant and raided all the locations where the girls were being held. That part was easy, she said, because of the GPS trackers. They put most of the women in halfway houses, although many have been deported now. It's a fucked-up world when you don't have enough room in your country for people who've been victimized by your own citizens. But I've never really understood politics.

"How's your sister doing?" Deep asks, handing me a thermos of hot chocolate. I take a swig and let it warm my insides. He'd made it from scratch on the hotplate at my place, using a battered pie plate and a bent spoon he found in a drawer. I've never been much for utensils.

"She sent me a text the other day," I tell him. "Said Manitoba was boring as hell, but her aunt and uncle are good people."

Malone had found relatives on Janet's father's side who were happy to take her in when they heard what happened. They hadn't even known Janet's dad had died. Families can lose touch like that. Even ones that aren't as screwed up as mine.

"She also sent me one of her sketches via snail mail." I pull the folded piece of textured paper from the pocket of my jacket, opening it before I pass it to Deep. It's a full-colour depiction of Janet and me standing on top of a mountain of poutine.

"I'm not sure what it means," I say.

"Maybe that's the point," Deep says, handing the paper back. I fold it up again carefully and slip it back into my pocket.

"Has she heard from your mother?"

"Not yet."

"Do you think she will?"

"It's hard to say. Alex put a price on Angela's head after she ratted to the cops about the body in the freezer. Roberto tells me that even with Alex gone, the hit's still active." The Mob doesn't take kindly to having their skeletons exposed, even when they're covered in frost. The case remains open according to Malone, as does the murder of the doctor and his bed buddy. But nobody's really pursuing either, having written both off to Mob violence. You lie down with organized crime, you wake up with a cap in your ass. Nobody expects much more than that or works too hard to find out why. They'd found Deep's car at the retreat, but Ink at the motel backed up his story about it being stolen. No one knows that Deep and I are linked. Or that he managed to delete my DNA profile from the department's database. Another early Christmas present.

"I heard a new Don took over for Alex Scarpello. Some bloke out of Sicily, but he was educated at Oxford."

"What did he take there?"

"International Business."

"That makes sense."

Unlike the other cases, the one concerning Anya and Alex is closed, as it was a clear murder-suicide. Malone managed to keep Janet and me out of the investigation. More to protect us from the Scarpellos than from the cops. As Alex had said, the family have their own sources in the department, and it wouldn't fly well if they were to learn of my sister and my involvement in the final shoot-out. I'm still hoping it never comes out that I blew the cyber-whistle on the Scarpello prostitution ring. Then I'd have a price tag affixed to my own forehead, with my sister thrown in as blowback. Bruno might have snitched on us, but he'd caught a shiv to the groin in the prison shower line-up before his trial. Word is he was looking for witness protection, which is something no one can protect you from.

"It must be tough on Janet," Deep says as I pass him the thermos back. When he takes a sip, it leaves a chocolate moustache on his upper lip. I don't tell him. I kind of like the way it looks.

"She's a tough kid. She can handle it," I tell him.

"Like you."

"Nothing like me."

"Oh, I don't know, Candace. I can see the similarities."

I tongue the two empty sockets in my mouth where the teeth were knocked out. I can't get them fixed until after the holidays.

"I'm more like Alex Scarpello than I'm like Janet, Deep."

"That's not true, and you know it."

I look at him, this nice guy who seems to have forgotten the slick individual he's talking to. "You know I've killed a lot of people, right?"

"Yes," he says, wiping the frothy moustache away. "But I don't know how much of that is down to what was expected of you."

"Because of who my dad was? I get tired of that comparison, Deep."

"Because of a lot of things, Candace."

"Alex Scarpello did what was expected of him," I remind him.

"He did," Deep says. "And I reckon that's what twisted him."

I look back at the playground. Locate Majd's niece as she makes her way across the monkey bars, grinning madly in her pink snowsuit. She tags another girl when she gets to the other side, and they run off together toward the swings, pigtails flying beneath their wool hats. Deep is right, I suppose. People are better off when they're allowed to define their own expectations.

"Maybe I'm twisted, too," I say.

"Maybe," he admits. "A tad. But there's more to you than that, Candace."

"If you say so."

My phone makes muffled music in the pocket of my new jacket. I take it out and answer without checking who's calling. This conversation of "what more I could be" has me looking for outs.

"Candace here."

"Did you get my package?" Charlotte asks, long distance from Newfoundland. That woman never lets up.

"It came on Monday. I haven't opened it yet." I already know what's in it. My Uncle Rod's mother used to knit me thick wool socks every year, and since her arthritis got bad, Charlotte's kept up the tradition. I must admit, they keep my feet warm at night when the aging radiator in my apartment above the E-Zee Market goes on the fritz.

"You can open it on Christmas," Charlotte says. "Although I wish you were coming here for the holidays. I could still get you a plane ticket. I've got Air Miles I haven't used."

"That's okay, Charlotte. You keep the points. I'll be okay on my own." I'm used to spending the holidays by myself, although I've thought about stopping by to see Roberto. They're serving turkey for Christmas dinner at the nursing home, deboned so nobody chokes.

"If you're sure, Candace."

"I am."

A wind stirs up frozen leaves in the playground when I hang up the phone. Deep slips his arm around my shoulder, pulls me in closer for the body heat. I'm going to miss him. But I don't tell him that. I'm afraid he might not go if I did. There's no future for two people with as different histories as we have. I'm used to people coming in and out of my life by now. Some have been family, some were something like it, some were neither of those things. People like that, they all leave their mark. If you're lucky, they also leave care packages, boxes you can open later full of woolly memories to keep you warm at night.

"What'll you do now?" Deep asks, tucking some of my hair into the toque he forced me to wear. It has a furry black ball at the top and matches the jacket he gave me.

"I don't know," I say. "But I got some cash from the old Don's will. Maybe I'll do something with that."

"Your great-grandfather left you money in his will?"

"Yeah, it shocked the shit out of me too when the lawyer called. Maybe he felt guilty about what he did to Angela. Anyway, it's not a lot. But it might be enough to set me up in a new line of work."

"And what would that be?" Deep asks, his eyes narrowing. I think he's concerned about expectations again.

I squirm a bit on the bench. I haven't told anyone about my pipe dream, too afraid that talking about it might cause the whole idea to go up in smoke. But Deep's the kind of guy you can confide in about hopeful things. Hope is a new concept for me. I've always pre-ferred the cold comfort of pessimism.

"I've been thinking about setting up my own PI firm," I say. "I can't get a licence on account of my record, but I figure I'm good enough at this detective stuff to land a few clients on the down low. Cheating spouses. Missing persons. Shit like that." I've thought a lot about this. I've spent a better part of my life learning to track people down. It may have been to kill them, but the basic skill set is the same.

Deep's face breaks out in a huge grin, and I'm half afraid he's going to laugh at me. Instead, he plants a kiss on the tip of my nose, right where a rogue snowflake has just fallen.

"I reckon you'd be good at that, Candace," he says.

I press my cheek against his to feel the warmth there, so I can remember it. I'll save it in a box marked with his name, for those cold winter nights.

I reckon I'd be good at it, too.

Snuggled into Deep on the bench, I don't hear the soft ping of the text in my pocket. Deep had helped me get rid of the whales. It's not until later when I'm alone again that I open the text message from Janet, back at my apartment above the E-Zee Market.

Slalom, it says.

I lie down on my bare mattress on the floor and listen to the radiator rattle. When I close my eyes, a box opens, marked with a memory that's not mine but could be. Within it, I savour the thrill of riding one ski down a snow-covered slope, laughing all the way.

ACKNOWLEDGEMENTS

I WOULD LIKE TO THANK MY EDITOR, Dominic Farrell, who knows how to give valuable creative advice that makes for a better novel. He also knows that the Good Humor ice cream man sells "fudge bars" rather than "fudgsicles" and how to use a prepositional verb. He is a multi-talented guy, and I would have been lost without him.

I'd also like to thank my family, who allowed for my frequent retreats to the writing shed in the backyard, and my husband in particular, who is building me something better than a shed.

To my friends, thank you for still being there, and supporting me as I go in and out of my creative funks. You are invited for a glass of wine when my new shed is built.

And finally, I'd like to thank Rima, a character in the novel, but also in my heart. She represents all the people who flourish when allowed to be who they are.

ABOUT THE AUTHOR

C.S. O'CINNEIDE is the author of *Petra's Ghost*, a Goodreads Choice Awards semi-finalist, as well as the hard-boiled Candace Starr crime series. As a blogger on her website, She Kills Lit, she features women writers of thriller and noir, along with the occasional nasty true crime story. O'Cinneide lives in Guelph, Ontario, with her Irish ex-pat husband, who remains her constant muse.